I0690348

SINGING FOR SPITFIRES

By
Jeremy D Rowe

Grosvenor House
Publishing Limited

This book is published by
Grosvenor House Publishing Ltd
Link House
140 The Broadway, Tolworth, Surrey, KT6 7HT
www.grosvenorhousepublishing.co.uk

This book is a work of fiction. Any resemblance to
people or events, past or present, is purely coincidental.

A CIP record for this book
is available from the British Library

ISBN 978-1-83975-138-7

DEDICATION AND PREFACE

I am pleased to dedicate Singing for Spitfires" to the memory of Mollie Wykes, who was a very special friend when I lived in Chipping Norton. In the story, she is the real-life character amongst a cast of fictional people, and I have tried to portray the generosity and dedication of this lovely, warm-hearted lady.

The story is also dedicated to the memory of Robert Evans, a very special friend, who was the historian who uncovered the story of the Chipping Norton plane crash, and was instrumental in getting the memorial placed in Church Street. I have used his name in the novel, but he wasn't a bank manager!

Stanley Wykes, Mollie's husband, was the headmaster of an East End School which was evacuated to Chipping Norton in 1939, but all other characters are fictional. Any resemblance to real people is co-incidental.

Part of the story is based upon the play "Home Fires Burning" which was written by myself and members of North Oxfordshire Music and Drama, and staged by us at The Theatre in Chipping Norton. For their contributions to the original play, I must thank Marjorie, Kipper, Robert, David, and Liz.

SINGING FOR SPITFIRES

CHAPTER ONE

Robert hesitated as he took hold of the brass handle of the bell. As the bank manager, he was well known in the town, but rarely did he visit his customers, and certainly never the formidable Marjorie Anderson-Grey. When she came to the bank, she would lean close to the brass grill as if she was about to accuse Robert of stealing her savings. Often she would bring her boisterous dog, which would jump up, putting its front paws on the counter and pant expectantly, grinning at Robert. How would the redoubtable lady react to the news he was bringing to her, in her own home?

It was a clear bright afternoon in early summer. Robert Evans had locked the bank at the end of business as usual, and then transformed into the ARP Warden for Chipping Norton. The golden stone of the town glowed in the sun, and all thoughts of war seemed very far away. It was hard to imagine that anything could disrupt the tranquillity of the small Cotswold town.

Robert smiled a little at his own timidity, and pulled hard on the bell-pull. In the house he heard the distant tinkle of the bell, followed immediately by the enthusiastic barking of the dog, and the sound of its paws

1

scratching at the door. There was a long pause, and then the grand door of the Manse opened. It was Mrs Anderson-Grey's sister.

"Oh, Mr Evans, we were not expecting anyone. I'm sorry you had to wait, but I was putting Buster in the kitchen so he wouldn't jump all over you. He's very friendly, but can be a bit alarming."

"Thank you, Miss Crawford," said Robert, struggling to avoid sounding nervous. "It's a very warm afternoon. I'm sorry to bother you, but may I come in? I wonder if your sister is at home? It's her I need to see."

"We're just having tea, Mr Evans. You can join us."

"Oh no, Miss Crawford, I'm sorry if I've called at an inconvenient moment."

A door opened, and Mrs Anderson-Grey was standing watching, looking puzzled.

"Mr Evans," she started imperiously, "how odd to see you out from behind your counter. You're not as tall as I expected you to be. I hope there is nothing ominous with this visit, nothing untoward with our bank accounts."

"Nothing untoward, Mrs Anderson-Grey. I'm not here on bank business."

"Then you must come and join us for tea. Rosemary, take Mr Evans's jacket. Heavens, it's much too warm to be dressed so formally. And Rosemary, go and fetch another plate and fork for Mr Evans. Sit, sit, we don't stand on ceremony here."

Perched on the edge of a large stuffed chair, Robert started to speak.

"I've come about something rather unexpected..."

"Take one of these strawberry cakes," instructed Mrs Anderson-Grey. "The strawberries are from our own garden, and Rosemary made the cakes only this morning."

"Thank you, Mrs Anderson-Grey. Now about this..."

"Rosemary, Mr Evans doesn't have a napkin. How do you take your tea, Mr Evans: milk or lemon?"

"Milk, please Mrs Anderson-Grey, and two sugars."

"Two sugars, Mr Evans? I think one is more than enough."

Stirring the tea, and desperate not to crumble the strawberry cake onto the carpet, Robert tried again. He spoke quickly before he could be interrupted.

"I expect you know that I have been appointed the Air Raid Precautions Warden for the town. Although we are not at war, and we pray that war does not come, we must have plans in place for evacuation of urban children. I am visiting all homes in the town to set up the evacuation plan, and I have come about including the Manse in those plans for billeting children who are evacuated. Part of my new responsibility is the task of organising the accommodations. My information tells me you have two spare bedrooms."

Marjorie Anderson-Grey put her teacup firmly into the saucer, rattling the spoon, and stared at Robert.

"Go on," she said.

"We have to be ready for large numbers of children to be evacuated, mainly from London, but possibly also from Birmingham and other big cities. We will need all the surplus space we can find. It could happen with very little warning. We have been instructed to have plans in place."

"Surplus space, Mr Evans?" said Mrs Anderson-Grey, severely. "Well I don't know where you get your information from, but we have no surplus space, as you call it."

"The file says you have two empty bedrooms, Mrs Anderson-Grey. We need them for evacuated children."

Marjorie Anderson-Grey's Brillo-pad hair vibrated slightly as her indignation rose. "Mr Evans, it is true that there are four bedrooms in this house. One is for myself and the Major when he is at home; another is for my sister here; and the other two are my sons' rooms, when they are on leave, although I do not think our bedroom arrangements in our own home are any concern of yours."

"With respect, Mrs Anderson-Grey, your sons are both fulltime professional soldiers. The authorities will not look kindly upon two rooms being reserved for two young men who are hardly ever here."

"Rosemary, do you hear what I am hearing? Are you suggesting that my sons' rooms could be used for evacuees?"

Rosemary looked from her sister to the embarrassed bank manager. "He is right, Marjorie. The boys are hardly ever here."

"I need to find as many beds as I can," continued Robert quickly. "I have told you that we must have evacuation plans in place: it's very urgent. We have no idea if there will be a war, or evacuation of schools, but we must be prepared. Can I put you down for four children, Mrs Anderson-Grey, two in each room?"

"No, you may not put me down for any number of children. I won't hear of it. I had enough trouble bringing up my own two boys, with my husband never here. I'll not start again, especially with urchins from the East End."

"I must ask you to think again, Mrs Anderson-Grey. The need is urgent. Many of the more humble cottages are taking three or four children. With one of the biggest houses in the town, surely you could take several."

"And have filthy urchins climbing over my furniture, and smashing my teacups? Not to think of what they may get up to in the bedrooms or bathroom. Bathroom? Why, some of them have probably never even seen a bathroom."

"That may be true, Mrs Anderson-Grey. We are likely to be looking after some severely deprived children."

"No, never. Should war come, and I believe it will, I will be making my own sacrifices: my husband, and both of my sons, will be drawn into the conflict, whenever it comes. That will be enough to bear, without a house full of dirty children."

There was a pause, and silence broken only by the barking of a very frustrated dog, and the loud ticking of the grandfather clock. Robert was unsure how to continue. Rosemary looked from one to the other: her sister red-faced and defiant; the bank manager nervous and timid. Suddenly she spoke.

"I've an idea, Mr Evans. We have heard talk that whole schools will be evacuated, not just the children, but their teachers with them." Robert nodded. "Then it may be that you must arrange accommodations for the teachers as well."

"Indeed, accommodations for teachers," Robert nodded again, seeing the way Rosemary was thinking.

"Perhaps we could offer a room for a teacher, a female teacher of course. Would that be a help?"

"It would," said Robert with relief. "What do you think Mrs Anderson-Grey?"

Marjorie glared at her sister, and frowned. "I not sure, but it would be preferable to marauding children. Just one teacher. Let me think about it. Rosemary go and release the hound: I can't stand that incessant barking."

Standing, Rosemary said, "I think it will be good to have a little more life in the house. It can get very dreary here."

Marjorie scowled, and spoke sharply to her sister, "I asked you to let the dog out of the kitchen."

Vicky Jones picked up the brown envelope from the doormat. It was undoubtedly her headmaster's hand-writing, but what could he possibly be doing writing to her in the summer holiday? Had she been given the sack? She opened the envelope and read.

"Dear Miss Jones,

"You may be aware that the government has requested that evacuation plans be put in place, for action should there be an outbreak of hostilities. Schools like Silvertown Junior, in the East End of London, are considered to be particularly vulnerable for aerial attack, as we are so near to the docks. If there is a war, the docks will be a prime target for bombing; and our school and the terraces of houses near it, are in an unusually exposed position. I am thus required to create an evacuation plan.

"At very short notice, the school will be required to move out of London. Special trains will be made

available, and the lady teachers will accompany the children to their destinations. No parents will be allowed to travel with the school, and the destination will not be revealed at the start of the journey. The two young men on the staff will stay behind for ARP duties, with the expectation that they will be called up to the forces. My deputy and myself, with my wife, will be travelling with the school.

"As one of the young ladies on my staff, I require you to pack a small suitcase in readiness for the journey. You should have your gas mask in its carton, ready with your suitcase. Just like Mr Chamberlain, I pray that war will be avoided, but we must be ready.

"A similar letter is being sent to all families, giving instructions for the very limited luggage that the children will be permitted to bring.

"Yours sincerely, Stanley Wykes, Headmaster."

"Bloody hell," said Vicky, out loud to no-one in particular. "It looks like there will be a war: so much for Mr Chamberlain's scrap of paper. Where the hell will they send us?"

Marjorie Anderson-Grey marched into the bank the following day. "Mr Evans," she spoke authoritatively, "My sister has persuaded me. With some reluctance, I am agreeing to taking a teacher if a school is evacuated to Chipping Norton; one female teacher, just one, no more; and of course, no children."

"Mrs Anderson-Grey," replied Robert, smiling, "I am very pleased. I am sure you will not regret your decision. Thank you very much. Now let us all hope that disaster can be averted at the last minute. Let us pray there will be no war."

"Amen to that," replied Mrs Anderson-Grey.

The dog, as usual, had jumped up, panting, with its paws on the counter. Robert was unable to tell its intentions, but it seemed to be smiling.

Vicky Jones and her landlady had been listening to the BBC news with growing horror. Nazi Germany had started to attack Poland. She had little appetite for breakfast, and was startled by a loud knocking at the front door. Her landlady opened it to find a very breathless telegram boy asking impatiently for Miss Jones. Vicky opened the telegram with shaking hands.

"Evacuation tomorrow – stop – report to school at six in the morning of 31st – stop – Wykes,"

Vicky nodded dumbly as her landlady put her arm around her. In recent years, Mrs M had been like a mother to Vicky, and it was certainly what she needed at that moment. "What day is it?" asked Vicky, pushing her mass of unruly dark hair back from her face.

"Wednesday, love," said Mrs M.

"The thirtieth?" said Vicky.

Rosemary and Marjorie were startled by the telephone ringing shrilly. Marjorie hurried to the hall. There was a pause as she nodded, and spoke with resolution. "Very well, Mr Evans, I will stand by my offer. But only one, mind you, only one."

"It will be war," Marjorie turned to Rosemary. "You will have guessed that was Mr Evans. They're evacuating London children tomorrow. Hitler won't retreat from Poland. It would be a blessing if there was a message from the Major, and some news of where the twins are. It can only be a few days now."

A little before dawn on Thursday morning, the last day of August, Vicky sat at the kitchen table with her land-lady, twisting a handkerchief in her hands, making small talk, and trying to hold back the tears. Her long black hair was pulled severely into a bun, a style she disliked, but used when stressed or anxious.

"That Mr Hitler," said the landlady. "I bet he don't care how many are crying today. All over the city, there's tears and red eyes. I remember the last one, supposed to be the war to end all wars."

"All over the city? All over the country, more like."

"All over the world."

"Dunno how long I'll be gone," said Vicky. "I'm only taking one little suitcase, that's all we're allowed. The rest of my stuff's in my room. Perhaps it will all be over by Christmas, and I'll be back."

"That's what they said the last time. Don't count on it, chicken. Now you've got to have a good breakfast, darlin'. Don't know when you'll get the next one. Oh, and I made you sandwiches. I had a tin of salmon – that'll be nice, won't it?"

Vicky smiled. "You're always spoiling me, Mrs M."

"Might be the last sandwiches I ever make for you," said the landlady, and burst into tears.

"I wish you hadn't said that," said Vicky, the tears welling up. "I'll be back, you'll see."

The sun rose early into a clear blue sky: it would be a beautiful day. At six o'clock, the staff of Silvertown Junior sat awkwardly in Mr Wykes's office. Stanley Wykes looked around the room at the apprehensive staff, strangely dressed in winter coats, despite the bright summer dawn, with their little suitcases and gas-mask boxes. He was struck by how young the three women were – not long out of college – and the horror of leaving Frank and Eric behind to face unknown challenges in the armed forces. He'd have his deputy head, Lawrence Powell to help him, but he was still conscious of the enormity of his role, not only to move almost two hundred children to an unknown destination in the country, but also to support his frightened staff. He looked grimly at his wife, sitting beside him.

"You OK, Molly?" he asked.

She nodded.

"Where's Lawrence?" said Vicky.

"He's meeting us later: he'll be at the station," said Stanley. "Let me explain. We've all been preparing for this moment. War has not been declared, but I am sure you've all been listening to the BBC." Looking to the two young men who would be left behind, he said, "I'm sorry you're not coming with us – we will miss you very much. Keep yourselves safe – when this is all over, I want you back on my staff. You are both fine teachers. I'm sure we'll all be back together after Christmas."

"Thank you, sir," said Frank. "We'll do our bit."

Eric gulped and blinked back tears.

Marjorie's telephone rang with a startling jangle. "Cursed thing," she said. "It always makes me jump." She marched to the hall to answer it. Rosemary followed.

"Marjie, old girl: you've heard about the evacuation, I suppose," came the Major's voice. "I just got through to tell you I'm working in Aldershot at the moment, and the boys are here with me. By lucky chance, they just got back from Wellington Barracks. You know they were on palace duty: looked excellent in their dress uniforms, two peas in a pod! It's not clear what will happen next. We're waiting orders, but no-one knows what will happen. If I can get any leave, I'll try to come home, but it's unpredictable. Don't get down-hearted; we'll find a way to beat this Hun; it will be alright in the end. Keep listening to the BBC."

"Can I talk to the boys?" said Marjorie, but the line had gone dead.

"God help us all," said Rosemary.

"The instructions are clear and simple," continued the headmaster. "We are to walk the children in a crocodile to Plaistow Station. Yes, I know it's a long walk, but that's what we have to do. Without Lawrence, who will meet us there, and our two young men, the children must be very well disciplined to walk properly with only you girls and myself to look after them. You all know my wife, Molly, who is coming with us – she will be an extra pair of hands and eyes when we cross roads, and on the train. The local police have been alerted to keep an eye out for us, and assist us."

Vicky spoke. "Can I ask, Mr Wykes, will the children walk in their class groups? What about brothers and sisters? They may be better if they stay together."

"Yes, I thought the same, although it will make it harder to be sure everyone is with us. You should take your registers, and register the children in their class groups in the playground, and then we'll sort out the crocodile allowing bigger children to take their brothers and sisters with them. I'll lead the line, and Mrs Wykes will come last to catch any stragglers."

Molly Wykes spoke for the first time. "We've got fine, tough East End kids in our school. I'm sure they will be OK to walk. We just have to make sure none has been given a very heavy suitcase!"

This brought a slight smile to the ashen faces. "Do you know where we are going?" asked Vicky.

"I understand that there will be an empty train waiting at Plaistow. That will take us to Paddington, where we shall be put onto a mainline train. At that stage, I think we will be told our destination."

"Bloody hell, it ain't going to be a picnic," said Vicky.

"Miss Jones," said Stanley, "I'd prefer you to control your language. We may be heading into a war, but we are still decent people."

"I'm sorry, sir, but it is bloody, I mean very, stressful. It would help of we knew the flippin' destination, God help us."

"Have faith, Miss Jones," said Stanley. "The ministry of education knows what it's doing. This evacuation has been very thoroughly planned. The tragedy is that the plans have to be put into operation."

"That was Mr Evans," said Marjorie, returning once more from the telephone beside the front door, "telling me that a school is on its way, being evacuated to our town. I am to go to the town hall at four o'clock, to meet our lodger."

"Things are moving very quickly," said Rosemary. "I'll check her bedroom, and make sure there's some room in the wardrobe for her clothes. If you're meeting her at four, I'll have the tea ready, and make a nice cake to welcome her."

"We're not waiting on this woman. It must be clear that she's only here under sufferance."

"I think she'll be very nice," said Rosemary.

"And she may not be," said Marjorie ominously. "I am sure many of these East London people are light-fingered. We must watch everything carefully. We should also check our supplies: you know the list the Major gave us: the candles and matches; the tinned meat and bottled water; gas masks and blankets and so on." Marjorie looked suddenly at her sister. "Goodness me, whatever's the matter?"

Rosemary was crying silently. "I don't know why I'm crying, the tears just started to come."

"I suppose it's the shock," said Marjorie, "even though we've been expecting it for a long time. Yes, it's the shock. We must finish breakfast, and you can make yourself a cup of sweet tea. You'll feel better then. Oh, and we must feed the dog, and tidy up the kitchen," said Marjorie.

"Are the Guards going to do palace duty with a war on?" said Rosemary.

"They must do," said Marjorie. "We can't have Hitler driving up the Mall and finding the palace without guards! The Major didn't say who'd be in London, but Bobby and Henry are both back in Aldershot; their tour of duty at Wellington Barracks finished last week. The timing is only co-incidental, but they're both with the Major."

"Awaiting orders, I suppose," said Rosemary. She looked out of the kitchen window at the summer garden. "It's a lovely day," she said. "Horrible to think that the Poles are getting slaughtered while we sit here talking. We must make the best of this weather. I'll do the lunch in the garden. Might be the last time we do it, for a while."

"Lunch for just the two of us, enjoying the peace of the garden before this teacher arrives; that's a most pleasant idea, Rosemary. Life will not be the same with a stranger in our midst. I'll take Buster over to the Castle Mound for a walk."

At half-past seven, the children started arriving. They were strangely calm, and some almost jolly at the idea of going on holiday. Most of the mothers were with them and even a few fathers, risking being late for work. Whilst the children seemed to be happy, several of the parents were distressed. The school staff checked each child in the register, and asked the same few questions:

"Have you got your gas mask? Have you got something to eat? Show me the label on your coat?"

Inevitably one or two children had huge bundles, which had to be prised away from them and returned to mothers – these were often the mothers showing the most distress; and some grasped big biscuit tins of sandwiches, enough for several days' travel.

Billy McCann was the only child without a parent in the school playground. Vicky was ready for him.

"Dad gone to work, Billy?" she said.

"Yea, always starts at six. Don't matter, m'case was packed ready, gas-mask in the box. I just got up like I always do. I've got m'key round m'neck, like always, but don't s'ppose I'll need it till we get back – if we ever come back, Miss."

"'Course we'll come back, Billy. It's only a short holiday."

"My dad says we're s'pposed to fank 'air'itler for the 'oliday. Be funny that, wouldn't it, if we never come back? I wouldn't mind."

"Your dad will miss you, Billy, even if you don't think he would. Now come over here with me, and help me get the class lined up. I'm supposed to be doing the register."

Molly Wykes was well known to the parents: she helped to run the local Girl Guides group, and often helped out as a volunteer at the school. Her husband had given her the difficult task of encouraging the mothers to stay at the school, and not follow the crocodile to the station. The two young male teachers, Frank and Eric, who were not being evacuated, hung around with her, making small talk with the despondent parents, but it was Molly who had the real influence.

"Just wave goodbye from here," she told them. "It will be easier, and save a lot of crying. Just be as jolly as you can, and that will help the kids on their way. We don't want any of them upset at this time of the morning. Tell them to have a lovely holiday."

Stanley Wykes checked with his teachers that most of the children were accounted for. Clearly a few parents had decided to keep their children at home, not sending them to the country as urged by the government posters, but Stanley had no choice but to go without these children. He had a strict timetable to adhere to. There was a little shuffling as older children gathered up their younger brothers and sisters, and then they were marching like soldiers out of the school gate and briskly up Prince Regent Lane.

Molly's judgement of the children was right: they were tough kids, used to life on the streets, and although the walk to Plaistow Station seemed long, the children marched along, and soon Stanley was leading the crocodile over the road bridge and in through the last, little used, door of the station. The children's feet clattered on the wooden stairs down to the platform, and just as expected, an empty District Line train stood waiting, with "Silvertown Junior School" stickers on the windows. The driver was waiting with Lawrence Powell on the platform and waved to the headmaster.

Stanley led the crocodile along the platform, and watched to see when Molly came down the stairs. She waved to him, confirming that everyone was present and correct, and he gave the signal to board the train. The driver in turn waved to Stanley, went into his little cab, and closed the doors.

It was a tube journey quite unlike any of them had ever had, as the train sped non-stop through station after station. Without the usual stop and change of trains at Earl's Court, they were quickly at Paddington. Stanley had already told the staff how they would leave the train, using all doors, and soon the entire crocodile was reassembled on the platform. Once more Stanley took the lead, and marched his school up the stairs to the mainline station.

What a sight met their eyes! Paddington was always dirty and noisy, with steam trains and crowds of people; but today the strange hum of hundreds of children, and many fraught teachers created a new kind of chaos. Seeing the school emerging from the District Line stairs, a young policeman hurried over to Stanley Wykes.

"What school are you, sir?"

"Silvertown Juniors," replied Stanley. "I hope we are here at the right time."

The policeman checked his clipboard. "Platform Nine," he said, "in forty minutes. You're early. You'll have to keep the kids here on the concourse for half an hour. You're sharing the train with a school from just round the corner here in Paddington. It says here, Paddington Basin Junior, front of train; Silvertown Junior, middle, another school in the rear. They'll be stickers on the windows. Try and keep the children together while you wait."

Stanley Wykes got the children to sit down, despite the grubbiness of the floor. With the children seated, they were much easier to keep an eye on. Vicky and the other Silvertown staff looked around. There were countless schools, mostly sitting in lines like their own school: some were boisterous, as if leaving for a jolly holiday – one school even waving little Union Jacks; others were subdued, with small knots of children sobbing; and most were sitting still, shocked at the unfolding events of the day. Looking at her own children, Vicky could see that many were struggling to avoid being upset, and most were clearly overwhelmed by the situation.

Lawrence Powell walked over to her. "All OK at school this morning?" he asked.

"Yes," replied Vicky. "Molly stayed 'til last and managed to keep most parents back. The mums were more upset than the children."

"They just look bemused, as if they don't know what's happening," said Lawrence.

"They don't," said Vicky. "Don't forget, most of them have never been up West, never seen a station like this filthy great place. Their world was very small until this morning, just the few Dockyard streets around the school and their homes. Suddenly they're here, with all this going on." She looked at Lawrence's luggage. "What have got there? I thought it was just one little suitcase each. You've got a big bundle as well. Brought your own bedclothes?"

"No, it's a Tommy gun!" smiled Lawrence.

"Bloody hell, really?"

Lawrence shook his head: "No."

"Well what is it?" said Vicky.

Lawrence leaned close to Vicky. "My spare wooden leg," he said.

Vicky's eyes went very round. "Oh," she said, "sorry I asked."

"Don't want to be caught on the hop!" said Lawrence.

"Christ, that's a bad joke," said Vicky, but despite the dismal surroundings, she found herself smiling for the first time that day.

Robert pulled the Manse bell with a great deal more confidence than before, and although Marjorie looked daggers at him when she opened the door, her dog was jumping enthusiastically behind her.

"Only one," she said quickly, before Robert could open his mouth.

Robert smiled. "No, I've not come to ask for more beds," he replied, "but to ask a favour of your sister."

"Me?" said Rosemary, grabbing the dog by its collar, and appearing behind Marjorie.

"I've got to go down to the station to meet the train," said Robert. "There will be a big crowd at the Town Hall waiting to meet the school. Can you come to the station with me at four o'clock, just to be available if they're late, or I need to send messages to anyone. I know it's a bit last minute, but I suddenly realised I'll be on my own. It would be reassuring to have a friendly face with me."

"Of course I'll come," replied Rosemary. "My sister will be meeting our teacher at the Town Hall, I'm sure she'll organise everyone there. I'll leave the tea things all ready and join you. It's quite a jolly lark, isn't it?"

"I'm not sure about that," said Robert, "but we must all put on a good front to avoid the children being upset."

"I'm looking forward to it," said Rosemary.

Marjorie simply looked at her sister in amazement.

The transport police seemed to know what was happening, and after a long and tedious wait, one of them came to Mr Wykes. "Platform Nine," he said. "The other school's at the front of the train, you're in the middle, there's another one behind you. You can only use carriages with your school name on the window."

The children stood and stretched like greyhounds after a morning in bed, and Stanley led them to Platform Nine. Sure enough, ahead of them another school was embarking at the front of the train, and looking back, he saw another crocodile of children following.

A railway worker was waiting beside the train. "Cotswolds Express!" he said to Stanley.

"Is that where we're going?"

"Yes: now listen careful: the train will be non-stop to Moreton-in-Marsh, where that school behind you will get off. Make sure you stay put. Then the train will go on to Chipping Norton, which is your stop. The platform is short, so the front and back of the train won't be beside the platform, but that won't matter – your two carriages will be at the platform."

"And the school at the front?" said Stanley.

"They're going to a village called Bloxham. Never heard of it myself, didn't even know there was a station of that name. Apparently it's near Banbury, but that's not your worry, you'll be in Chipping Norton, but for God's sake, don't leave any kids behind on the train, else they'll be taken to the next stop."

The teachers found the carriages with "Silvertown" labels stuck on the windows, and got the children on board. There was some excitement at seeing their school name on the windows, and a great deal of struggling as small children tried to heave their suitcases onto luggage racks which were much too high for them. At last everyone was settled. Stanley had previously instructed the staff to spread out amongst the children, not sit together in a huddle, and finally everyone was seated.

"Chipping Norton," thought Stanley. "Sounds a bit different from Silvertown. I wonder what we're in for?"

As always, the stream train made a huge fuss about starting out. Grinding and spluttering, screaming and whistling, the train prepared to move, and with a snort and lurch, which made the children shriek, the train started. It gathered speed through the suburbs and soon was out into the countryside. At first the children looked out of the windows, and were particularly puzzled by the wide expanses of field. "Where's the 'ouses, Miss?" was a regular comment. There was huge excitement when a field of cows was spotted.

Vicky was struggling not to sleep, when a commotion brought her wide awake. One of the girls was crying loudly, and when Vicky looked over, she wasn't surprised to see Billy McCann standing over the howling girl and laughing.

"Billy McCann," called Vicky, "come over here at once, and bring your stuff with you. You can sit with me."

"I ain't done nuthin', Miss," said Billy.

"That's just what it looks like," said Vicky, "so get yourself over here a bit quick."

Billy made a grand performance of moving, dropping his gas mask, falling over feet and generally causing a nuisance, but at last he was installed in a narrow space between Vicky and the window. No sooner had he sat down, than he turned to his teacher. "Can we have our sandwiches?"

"What were you doing just now?" said Vicky.

"Nuthin' Miss. Just looking."

Vicky smiled. "Look out of the window. It's interesting."

"And our sandwiches, Miss?"

"Yes you can. What have you got?"

Billy proudly pulled a brown paper bag from his pocket. "Made 'em meself, s'morning. Got the crusts from both ends of the loaf, and nearly finished up the dripping bowl."

"Have you got anything else?"

"No Miss, there wasn't nuffin else in the pantry."

"You need a drink, Billy."

"Bloody hell, Miss, I could murder a cuppa tea."

Vicky smiled. "You mustn't swear, Billy," she said. "But you're right. So could I."

"There's lots of fields, isn't there, Miss? They sort of go on and on."

"That's the countryside, Billy. I expect it will be like that in Chipping Norton."

"S'funny name, innit Miss?"

"They'll probably think Silvertown's a funny name."

"They better not. I'll hit anyone who thinks that."

"No you won't Billy."

Billy smiled. "I might."

The town clerk arrived to unlock the town hall at three o'clock. There was already a queue of women standing there, and they were pleased to get into the cool of the hall after the oppressive heat of the afternoon.

"I'll get the kettle on," said one of the earliest.

Trestle tables had been set out by the town clerk, and the women set to work with a couple of old sheets, washed and starched for the occasion, to lay them on the tables. Trays of sticky buns were brought from the Co-operative Bakery, and soon the large collection of chipped white cups and saucers was being noisily set out. There was an air of forced jollity, as the women prepared a welcoming party, smiling despite knowing that war was imminent.

Marjorie Anderson-Grey strode into the room, and there was a slight hush in the working women.

"No, this will never do," she pronounced, marching forward to the table. "It needs to be at the other end. These city urchins will simply demolish the whole lot if they rush in and the first thing they see is that pile of buns. They will probably knock the table flying; and, anyway, who thought of giving them these buns? Their sticky fingers will be everywhere. You will have to wash the whole town hall after they've left. And you'll have sticky fingers everywhere at home when they get there."

The women rolled their eyes, but reluctantly could see that Mrs Anderson-Grey was correct as usual: they sighed, and set about moving the tea things.

Rosemary, meanwhile, had met Robert Evans at the station.

"It's very quiet," said Rosemary.

"The calm before the storm," said Robert.

"The storm of the children arriving, or the storm of war?"

Robert sighed. "Both, I suppose."

They sat on a station bench, and listened for the train.

On the train, many of the children were dozing: most had had little sleep the night before, and been up very early in the morning, so the rhythmic movement in the carriages was rocking them to sleep. Stanley Wykes walked though the carriage, speaking quietly to each teacher.

"All OK? No problems?" Stanley was looking at Vicky, but it was Billy who replied.

"'Allo, Sir. Exciting, innit?"

"Yes Billy, it is. Keep quiet now, lots of the others have gone to sleep."

"Do we have to change trains, Mr Wykes?" said Vicky. "Perhaps at Oxford?"

"Apparently not. All regular services have been suspended for several days, so that all the evacuation trains can go straight through to their destinations. Don't forget, we must get off at the second stop."

The station master walked leisurely along the platform to Robert and Rosemary. "It's just left Moreton," he said. "Be here in ten minutes."

Vicky had restrained Billy from getting off at Moreton-in-Marsh. Once she'd told him that the stop was for a different school, he grinned.

"That would have given them a bleedin' shock, if I'd turned up with them, wouldn't it?"

"I suppose it would," smiled Vicky, "but it would have been a big shock for you as well, on your own in a little country town."

"Are we nearly there?" asked one of the girls for the umpteenth time.

"Mr Wykes said that we go through a tunnel, and then we're there," said Vicky.

"Listen," said Robert. "I hear it; it's in the tunnel."

With a sudden whoosh of steam and smoke, the train emerged from the tunnel, its brakes squealing as it slowed to the platform.

"This is it," said Robert, and once more Rosemary had to suppress her inappropriate excitement.

As the train came to a halt, every door from the two "Silvertown" carriages opened, and Stanley Wykes's whole school was suddenly decanted onto the normally sleepy platform. Stanley looked around. What would happen next? He was not accustomed to being unsure of what to do. Robert had worried that he'd not know who to talk to, but Stanley was unusually tall, and stood out, head and shoulders above not only the children, but his staff. Struggling through the complex mess of children and their luggage, Robert caught up with Stanley.

"Mr Wykes? I'm Robert Evans, ARP Warden and evacuation officer for Chipping Norton. Welcome to our town. I hope the journey was not too stressful?"

"Mr Evans, good afternoon. Oh my God, I'm so sorry."

Stanley's gaze had turned to the flower beds along the platform. Large numbers of little boys were urinating into the flowers.

"Miss Jones, did you say they could do this?"

"No, sir," said Miss Jones, "but it's not surprising. Billy said he's been bursting ever since Oxford."

Rosemary looked from the horrified face of the headmaster to the astonished face of the evacuation officer, and then to the amused face of the teacher. "I think that's the funniest thing I've seen in a long time," she said quietly to Robert. "I think we're going to enjoy this school."

"That's not what the station master is thinking," said Robert. "And heaven help us all if your sister hears about it."

"She will," said Rosemary. "She gets to hear about everything."

"Get these children out of my station," spluttered the station master. "I've never seen anything like it."

With some difficulty, the teachers persuaded the children back into a crocodile, just like they'd started the day, so many hours before. Rosemary marched ahead to alert the women at the Town Hall, and with Robert to guide Stanley, they walked up Station Approach, and onto the pavement of New Street. Molly Wykes looked around the empty platform: there was a lone suitcase. "Billy McCann's," she thought to herself, "sure to be." It seemed that everyone was in the crocodile, so she hurried to bring up the rear.

Suddenly there was a screech, as Billy came running back down the platform. "My case!" he shouted.

"It's OK," said Molly. "I've got it for you. Now hold my hand and let's catch up with the others."

"It's not far," said Robert to Stanley as they marched up the hill. "The ladies are waiting at the Town Hall.

One of our local bobbies is waiting at the top, to cross us over the road."

Anxious faces peered from the Town Hall windows, as the crocodile crossed the road and walked round to the grand portico and the main doors, which stood open. Far from the stampede anticipated by Marjorie, the tired children walked in and sat exhausted on the floor.

"Welcome to Chipping Norton," Robert cleared his voice. "We hope you will have a nice time here. We all know that you are here because there may be a war. Let us hope and pray that it will not come to that."

"We don't need a speech, Mr Evans," said Marjorie. "Give these teachers a cup of tea, give out the wretched buns, and let's get this business over with."

"Most of the girls need the toilet," said Vicky. "Where is it?"

"Downstairs," said Rosemary. "I'll show you."

Almost every girl jumped up and formed a long queue down the narrow staircase. The boys attacked the buns.

Vicky was grateful for the cup of tea, but Billy spotted it as soon as she'd taken a sip.

"What about a cuppa for us?" he said. "I'm proper gaspin!"

"There's water for children," said Marjorie. "Over there, and with tin cups. I'm afraid they will have to share the cups, but that should not be a problem for this kind of child."

"You're proper posh, aren't you?" said Billy. "It's going to be good here, innit?"

Marjorie gave him one of her well-practised looks, and even Billy cowered and slunk away, muttering, "Oh Gawd....."

It took some time for the situation to settle down, but eventually Robert decided he should start allocating the children. Slowly children were matched to mothers, and gradually dispersed. Molly gave Billy his suitcase, he joined two of his friends, and was marched away like everyone else. He looked back at Miss Jones, and she mouthed "Be good," to him. He grinned, and hurried to keep up with the others.

At last the hall was almost empty. Stanley Wykes was in earnest conversation with the headmaster of Chipping Norton Junior School, St Mary's. Edward Harding had been head of the little town school for some years, and he and his wife would be providing temporary lodgings for Molly and Stanley. The two headmasters had to work out how they would share the classrooms, whilst their wives would have to share domestic arrangements.

Vicky looked around, reassured that all the children of her class had been claimed and taken to their lodgings. Robert was now going to each adult in turn, introducing them to their host.

"And you are?" he asked.

"Victoria Jones, but call me Vicky."

"This is Mrs Anderson-Grey. You will be staying with her for the duration."

Marjorie Anderson-Grey looked down upon Vicky with slightly narrowed eyes. "Miss Jones," she said. "I hope you will be very comfortable at the Manse. I think you may have already met my sister. This whole tedious process has taken far longer than I expected, so let us make tracks." She turned on her heel, and marched down the Town Hall steps. Vicky grabbed her suitcase, and with Rosemary at her side, hurried after her.

They could hardly exchange a word as Marjorie marched ahead. "Sorry," gasped Rosemary. "My sister can be a bit abrupt."

"Don't worry," panted Vicky. "I'll survive."

Rushing down the steep hill of Church Street, Vicky gasped when they turned into the broad sweep of the drive of The Manse. She had not expected to be staying in such grandeur. Stopping in the porch, Marjorie, hardly out of breath despite the rapid walking, turned to the other two who were panting.

"Welcome to The Manse," she stated, without any feeling of welcome in her voice, and turned, opened the door, and marched inside. There was an immediate burst of frenzied barking.

"I wasn't expecting anything like this," said Vicky. "I thought in the country, everyone lived in little cottages with thatched roofs and roses round the door."

"Come in and shut the door," said Marjorie. "Rosemary, would you mind taking Miss Jones to her room? And then put the kettle on. Afternoon tea is waiting in the parlour, although heaven knows, it's very late for tea."

Buster continued his frantic barking. Opening the kitchen door, Rosemary said, "I'll just put the kettle on, then take you upstairs. Hope you like dogs."

Buster came flying out of the kitchen, delighted to find a new person to leap at. Vicky was alarmed at this huge bundle of red hair, bouncing all around her, trying to nibble her hand. "He's not like the cat my landlady had in Limehouse," she said. "He's a bit big, isn't he?"

"Wouldn't hurt a fly," said Marjorie. "I'll put him out in the garden. Buster, this way boy!" Eagerly the dog bounced down the hall and out through the garden door.

"Where's the rest of your luggage?" asked Rosemary.

"This is all there is," said Vicky. "We were only allowed one small suitcase."

"Jones?" said Marjorie. "Are you Welsh? All that jet black hair looks Welsh to me."

"No, I'm what you call, 'salt-of-the-earth' East End. I had a Welsh granddad, who went to London to escape going down the pit, but I never knew him. My hair is the only Welsh thing about me."

With the kettle on the Aga, Rosemary led the way up the broad staircase, and stopped at one of the many doors on the landing. "This is your room. I'm next door, and Marjorie is down the hall. That smaller door at the end is the bathroom. I've made some space in the wardrobe for you. This is usually Bobby's room, but he's away at the army. Come down when you're ready."

Vicky walked into the room and sat on the hard bed for a moment. She looked around, and jumped up to explore the space. The room was almost as large as her classroom in Silvertown, and very much a boy's room. A dark Turkish carpet was surrounded by large pieces of dark, heavy furniture: a dressing table with brushes and a comb; a huge wardrobe with brass handles; and a tall chest of drawers upon which perched a large moth-eaten teddy bear. Thick net curtains made the room rather gloomy, and pulling the curtain to one side, Vicky could see a wide lawn and some very large trees. There was a cricket bat in one corner, with multiple autographs on it, and around the room various flags and pennants pinned to the wall. Extraordinarily, in one corner a pair of oars was propped up, wedged against the high ceiling. Quickly she could see that the occupant had been to Radley College, and she assumed he was an enthusiastic rower.

Incongruously, a clear glass vase with a bunch of tall sweet peas on the dressing table, brought a feminine fragrance to the room, and Vicky leant across and sniffed. She smiled.

She opened the wardrobe and found a cavernous space big enough for a dozen winter coats. She took hers off, and hung it up, embarrassed at its pathetic appearance in such a grand space.

Opening the door quietly, she tiptoed down the hall and opened the door which she hoped would be the bathroom. A mass of chromium fittings and black and white tiles met her eyes. "Crikey!" she said out loud. The bathroom was bigger than her bedroom in Silvertown. When she flushed the toilet, she was horrified at the great gushing she unleashed, realising that the whole house would know every time she pulled the chain. She returned to her room, and sat on the bed again. She pulled out the grips, and shook her hair out from the bondage of the bun.

"OK, girl," she said to herself. "You might have landed on your feet, I hope so. Now let's meet these two old birds properly."

CHAPTER TWO

Vicky Jones took a deep breath, stood and walked reso-
lutely out of the bedroom and down the stairs. She
could hear voices beyond a door which was slightly ajar,
so she pushed it open and went in. Marjorie was sitting
up very straight, holding a delicate china tea cup and
saucer.

"I think it would be polite to knock before entering,"
said Marjorie.

"Sorry Mrs Anderson-Grey, I thought I was invited
to tea."

"Well since you've come in, you may as well stay.
Perhaps you'd like to sit down."

Vicky perched on the edge of a big stuffed chair.

"Not there, that's the Major's. It would be better for
you to sit over there," said Marjorie, indicating a
wooden dining chair.

"This is a very big house," said Vicky. "How many
people live here?"

"Just the two of us," said Rosemary.

"And the Major and the boys, when they are at home," said Marjorie.

There was a silence, broken only by the ticking of a grandfather clock and the distant barking of Buster. Looking at the newcomer, Rosemary was struck that she looked very like a film star she'd seen in magazines, with her mass of black curls and serious face. Who was it who had such luxuriant dark hair?

"Have a slice of cake," said Rosemary, "and then we can all introduce ourselves."

Vicky picked up a plate and put a slice of the cake on it.

"It's seed cake," explained Rosemary, "made with caraway seeds. I made it this morning."

"Brilliant!" said Vicky, "One of my favourites." She picked up the cake and took a bite.

"The cake forks and the napkins are on the table," said Marjorie. "We have standards, you know, even if a war is imminent."

"Forks and napkins!" exclaimed Vicky. "I haven't got enough hands for all that. I hope the kids aren't being given forks and napkins, they won't know what to do. I'm not sure myself."

"I expect many of them are going to bed already," said Rosemary, trying to change the subject. "They all looked very tired up at the Town Hall."

"Now," said Marjorie, pausing for effect to ensure Vicky was listening, "I'm Marjorie Anderson-Grey. My husband is Major Anderson-Grey, and my sons are Bobby and Henry Anderson-Grey. They are all three in the army, in the Guards. They visit occasionally, although their visits are rare. Currently, they are in Aldershot, awaiting orders."

"Oh, it must be a worry, Marjie, with three away," said Vicky. "I feel sorry for you."

"There's nothing to feel sorry about," said Marjorie. "They all know their duty to the King and country. I don't feel sorry: I feel proud. And I must say I prefer you to call me Mrs Anderson-Grey. I think that at all times we will maintain standards."

"I'm Rosemary Crawford," said Rosemary, hurriedly. "I'm Marjorie's younger sister. Most people call me Rosemary, but if we are to live together and be friends, you can call me Rosie."

"And I'm Victoria Jones," said Vicky, "but no-one calls me Victoria, except when I was a kid and my mum caught me being naughty! Please call me Vicky."

"I think 'Miss Jones' will be more suitable for the time being," said Marjorie.

There was another silence. The grandfather clock continued to tick loudly.

"Miss Jones, was that the headmaster of your school, I saw at the Town Hall?" said Marjorie.

"Stan? Yes, he's here with his wife, Molly."

"Stan? You call the headmaster, Stan?"

"No, not to his face: he's Mr Wykes; but behind his back we all call him Stan."

"I wasn't introduced," said Marjorie. "I really must speak to Mr Evans about the way to do things properly."

"He and his wife are staying with Mr and Mrs Harding," said Rosemary.

"It's been a remarkable day," said Marjorie, ignoring her sister. "I don't remember when we had tea this late before. Why, it's already dark. I think, Miss Jones, that it's time for you to go to your room. Perhaps you would be good enough to use the bathroom quickly, and then the rest of us can go to bed." With Vicky dismissed, she turned to her sister. "Rosemary, I'm rather tired, so I wonder if you would be good enough to see to the dog. I'm going up to my room."

She rose and left the room. For a moment Vicky wondered if she should have stood up, as if it was the Queen who had risen to leave, but instead she bit into the seed cake again.

"Have another piece," said Rosemary, "you'll not get anything else until breakfast."

Later, sitting on Bobby's bed, after a quick 'flick' in the bathroom, Vicky reflected on the extraordinary day.

It seemed ages since she'd been sitting with her landlady in Silvertown, with an early morning cup of tea. The train journey had been almost surreal, and it was odd to think that nearly two hundred Silvertown children were dispersed amongst the cottages of this little rural town.

She looked around the room once more. It was a very big house, and she was intrigued to explore; but in the morning she had to go to a staff meeting, and see how two schools would fit into one school building. Outside, she could hear the dog barking, and Rosemary calling it into the house. Sleepily, she got into bed. The strange silence of the countryside was broken only by a pair of owls hooting. Vicky was quickly asleep.

It seemed that it was only a few minutes later, that there was a knock on the door.

"Good morning," said Rosemary. "I brought you a cup of tea, but don't tell Marjorie, she doesn't approve of tea in bed."

"Is it morning already?" asked Vicky. "I only just fell asleep. What's the time?"

"Six-thirty. Marjorie will be up soon, and I've already let the dog out. Come and find us in the kitchen: we always have breakfast in there."

Vicky drank the tea. It was strangely weak and without milk or sugar, but she was grateful for it. She found a huge and heavy dressing gown in the wardrobe and put it on. It dragged along the floor behind her. "Crikey," she thought, "this Bobby must be very tall."

Putting her head out of the bedroom door, she could hear that someone was in the bathroom, presumably Marjorie. "How's this going to work?" she wondered. "We need a rota!"

In the kitchen she found Rosemary stirring a pot of porridge. "There is a toilet downstairs if you can't get into the bathroom," she said. "We have porridge every day: it's the Major's favourite, and we have it even though he's not here."

Vicky eyed the dishful she was given, with some alarm. "Can I have some sugar?" she asked, "or milk, or honey?"

Marjorie had appeared in the kitchen doorway. "Of course not: we take a little salt, but nothing else. What would the Major say if he caught us putting milk onto porridge?"

Molly and Stanley were sitting down to breakfast with the Hardings.

"I've been thinking," started Edward Harding. "The Chippy children will be arriving as usual for school on Monday – first day back after the summer holiday. We'll have school assembly with our children when they come at nine, and tell them what's going on and about the new timetable for sharing the classrooms: Chippy children nine-to-one, Silvertown children one-to-five. You can have the hall at twelve thirty to talk to yours."

"We've no resources, we've brought nothing," said Stanley. "We're very dependent on you."

"We'll survive," smiled Edward. "We'll put your first-years in our first-year classroom and so on, so they can share the books, and in fact share everything, the crayons and pencils, the pens and ink, everything. We just have to find some extra paper."

"I'll walk with you," said Rosemary, "and bring the dog, but you'll get the hang of the town quickly. It's small and easy, and soon you'll know where everything is. Everything is always up-hill or down-hill."

Vicky pulled Bobby's dressing gown protectively around herself. "Thank you," she said. "Oddly, there's no hurry, as we're not meeting until ten o'clock. We'll find out how we're going to share the school building. It's going to be a bloody challenge."

Marjorie frowned. "We don't swear, Miss Jones," she spoke coolly, "and I'd prefer you to wear your own clothes, Miss Jones, not my son's."

"Sorry, Mrs Anderson-Grey, but I've nothing else. One small suitcase was the limit."

Later, as they walked up the hill of Church Street, Rosemary said, "Don't worry about clothes, Vicky. I'm a bit taller than you, but we're similar size round the waist. I've lots of things I never wear, and you can borrow. It will work out."

Vicky stopped and looked around. "Thanks for that Rosie," she said. "It's really lovely here, isn't it? Fancy looking straight past the church and only seeing green hills and trees. We don't have many trees in Silvertown, and no hills. This is a very pretty row of cottages."

"The almshouses" said Rosemary. "Hundreds of years old. Mind you, not as comfortable as they look, especially in winter when it snows. Later on, I'll show you round the town."

Stanley Wykes paused, and looked around his depleted staff. He had not expected the loss of the two young men to be so noticeable, and he was worried about their fate, if war was imminent. Here he was in a strange school, in a strange town, with just three young women and one disabled man, expected to educate nearly two hundred children, all abruptly torn from their familiar homes, and dumped with little warning into alien families.

"So, that's how it will work. We collect the children from the playground and bring them into the assembly hall at twelve-thirty, and then take them to their class-rooms. It's going to seem odd working through to five o'clock, but I suppose we'll get used to it. Just keep very calm for the first few days, and we'll solve each problem as it arrives. Mrs Wykes will be available to help out when a problem arises."

"And I'll bring you a cup of tea halfway through the afternoon," said Molly, "to keep you happy! Try and have a restful weekend everyone: perhaps explore this little town, and get some extra sleep: next week will be busy and demanding."

"Sharing the school premises seems very challenging," said Marjorie. "Chipping Norton children in the morning, your children in the afternoon? I suppose you know what you're doing. What will the children do when they are not in school? They will be marauding round the town, and no good will come of it. Mark my words!"

"It's difficult to keep up with everything what's happening," said Vicky. "It's still less than twenty-four hours since I arrived. I don't really know you yet, and my mind's a whirlwind. Do you mind if I have a little lie-down? I don't usually, but I seem to need to?"

"I'll get the tea whilst you snooze," said Rosemary, "and after tea I'll take you on a tour of the estate. Why you've not even met the chickens!"

"Sleeping on a Friday afternoon!" exclaimed Marjorie after Vicky had left the room. "I thought these East Enders were tougher types."

"I think she's pretty tough, Marjorie, but she's had a stressful couple of days. Let her sleep."

"It's not looking good," said Edward Harding, over tea at the headmaster's house. "I put the wireless on as soon as I came home. It seems we're not at war, but it feels as if we are. The BBC is repeatedly telling everyone to keep listening, and there are constant programme changes, and music being played."

"I've been listening to the wireless whilst you were asleep," said Marjorie over tea. "It's not looking good."

"I expect that's what everyone's saying," said Rosemary, "everyone in the town."

"Everyone in the country," said Vicky.

"The whole world," said Marjorie. "I was a teenage gal in the Great War, and the Major fought in it towards the end. I remember all the talk of a war to end all wars. The talk on the wireless makes me shudder: we are sliding towards another war – may the Lord help us if it's as bad as the last time."

"Perhaps Herr Hitler will change his mind, and retreat from Poland," said Rosemary.

"And pigs might fly," said Vicky. "The government wouldn't have sent me here, evacuated all these kids, if they didn't think a war was coming. It's bloody depressing, innit? And look, the sun's shining, there's a blue sky, it's a lovely afternoon, and we're sitting 'ere talking of war. Hell's bells and buckets of fire."

Marjorie looked at Vicky and made the strange "Hrumph" noise which she would come to recognise as Marjorie's way of showing her disapproval.

"Finish your tea, and we'll walk round the garden," said Rosemary. "I'll put the lead on Buster, and then we can take you down to the chickens."

Mr and Mrs Harding lived in a modern house on The Leys, and after tea they took Stanley and Molly out into the garden. The view across the valley was quite unlike anything in East London, and the two Londoners sat on garden chairs admiring the distant hills.

"It's very peaceful," said Molly. "Fancy living here. You can't imagine how different it is from where we live."

"It seems a long way away," said Stanley.

"And what's this interesting building down below us?" said Molly.

"The Bliss Mill," replied Lizzie Harding.

"Bliss...." said Molly. "What an interesting name. If only we were sitting here enjoying this view, expecting nothing but, let me think, ... blissfulness, instead of war."

They sat silently contemplating the elegant mill building, with its single chimney rising from the dome.

With Rosemary and the dog leading the way, Vicky stepped out of the kitchen door into the garden of the Manse. Marjorie was soon into 'Lord of the Manor' mode, as she described her domain.

"This was the Victorian vicarage for the town, built at a time when the vicar was a significant person, and his house had symbolic importance. Not long ago, it was decided that this place was far too big and expensive for a vicar, and he was moved into a much smaller house, just across the road. I wanted to keep a link to the religious use of the building, which is why the Major and I gave it the name of 'The Manse'".

They were standing on a wide lawn, mowed with stripes. Vicky was amazed.

"This is what a park looks like where I live, a park! I've never thought of anyone living with a garden like this, part of their own home. Who mows all this grass?"

"I do actually," said Rosemary. "We have a petrol mower, with a seat. Although we have a gardener, I love to sit on the mower and buzz up and down."

"I wouldn't mind having a go at that!" exclaimed Vicky. "It is just like 'aving your own park."

"I like to imagine Victorian vicarage teas on this lawn," said Marjorie, "and once a year we have a charity tea. You've missed it, I'm afraid, it was in June. We do it each year to support the British Legion."

Buster was jumping impatiently on the end of his lead.

"He's used to being off lead here," said Marjorie. "He can't escape from this part of the garden, so can have a good run. You must always make sure all the gates are closed. He's keen to show you the rest. Onward to the kitchen garden, Rosemary."

To one side of the lawn, Rosemary opened a gate and they went through to the kitchen garden. Rows of vegetables stood in military formation; and of weeds there was no sign. Tall canes of beans alternated with low lying rows of leaves that Vicky could not identify.

"Bloody hell, you don't do all this, do you?" spluttered Vicky.

"Of course we do," said Marjorie. "And if you're staying here for a while, we'll soon get you out here. Build up a bit of stamina, you won't need an afternoon siesta. Of course we have a man a couple of times a week, to do the heavy digging, and hedges, but I like to keep everything ship-shape."

"Crikey Moses, I don't know what half of these things are," said Vicky.

As they walked along the path, Rosemary recited the names of the crops.

"Runner beans, ready for picking now, lettuces nearly finished, beetroot ready to pull, French beans, peas, carrots, parsnips won't be ready till Christmas and need a frost to make them taste good, potatoes."

"Isn't everything all muddy when you dig it up?" said Vicky. "The veg we get from our greengrocer's is always quite clean."

"Of course sometimes it's muddy," replied Marjorie impatiently, "but that's how everything grows. I've never in my life bought anything from a greengrocer's. When I was a child we had a bigger garden than this, and a gardener, although I helped in the garden then, and still enjoy coming out and having a good dig."

"I've never done digging," said Vicky. "I should think you get quite dirty."

"We've a small orchard as well, and we'll soon be picking apples and pears. The plums are finished. I think you will be very useful when it comes to harvesting the apples."

"'Arvesting?" laughed Vicky, "I never did any such thing. I don't know about climbing trees. 'Ere look at them red stalks – what kind of veggies have red stalks like that?"

"Beetroot, of course," snapped Marjorie. "You must know what colour they are."

"Oh yes, but the beetroot in our market is boiling in a big pan at the back. It's a nice smell, fills the place with the smell."

They stopped at the end of a tall row of flowers, delicate colours amongst the rows of vegetables. The perfume filled the evening air.

"These are the flowers in my bedroom," said Vicky. "I didn't imagine you'd grown them. Flowers in Silvertown are jolly rare, and they come from shops, mainly for funerals, but not like these. These is quite lovely."

Marjorie turned aside to Rosemary. "Did you put flowers in her room? I don't want to make her too comfortable."

Buster was pulling impatiently towards another gate at the end of the path. "Remember, all gates must be shut at all times," said Marjorie, walking through to the chicken run, "and it's especially true here. If a fox got into the chickens, they'd be all hell let loose."

"Chickens?" said Vicky. "For eggs?"

"Of course," said Marjorie. "And for the table."

"You eat them?" said Vicky. "That means you have to kill them."

"If the Major's not here, or one of the boys, I do it," said Marjorie. "You can have a go if you like."

Vicky shuddered. "I'm not sure about that."

"We taught both boys to wring a chicken's neck," said Marjorie. "I don't think you should eat anything you'd be uncomfortable to kill, or see killed."

"I hope we don't have beef for Sunday lunch," said Vicky. "I'd hate to see you kill a cow."

"Now you are just being silly, Miss Jones."

"Where are the chickens?" said Vicky.

"In the coop, they're roosting, it's evening. I came down and shut them in whilst you were having your siesta. We shut them in every evening to make sure the fox can't get them. Look, I'll show you," said Rosemary.

Lifting the lid, Vicky could see the chickens snoozing in the coop.

"Stroke one," said Rosemary. "They quite like being touched."

Gingerly, Vicky put her hand into the coop. "Will it peck me?"

"Of course not. Stroke it, go on."

"So smooth, and warm," exclaimed Vicky. "I've never stroked a chicken before. Amazing."

"I'll bring you down in the morning," said Rosemary, "when I let Buster out, and you can collect the eggs for breakfast."

"I think it's time for supper," said Marjorie. "We usually have supper in the kitchen. Welsh Rarebit tonight, I think, Rosemary."

"Oh lovely," said Vicky. "I love cheese on toast."

"Welsh Rarebit is not cheese on toast." Marjorie stared at Vicky. "She's a school teacher," she thought, "and yet she knows nothing."

Saturday 2nd September 1939 was a very strange day. Nothing happened, and yet everything was happening. Lizzie Harding took Molly for a long walk all around the town. On every street they met children, Chipping Norton children playing with Silvertown children, and excitedly they would come up to the two women with stories to tell and little keepsakes to show.

Molly was unprepared for the panoramas of the surrounding countryside which the hilly town afforded. At each turn, it seemed, she glimpsed new views of distant fields and farms; and perhaps her greatest pleasure came from breathing the clean Cotswold air, so different from the smoky fug of the East End.

In the churchyard they met Rosemary and Vicky, taking a similar hike around the town, and Molly was suitably impressed by The Manse when Vicky pointed it out to her.

The four women stood in the churchyard, with nothing to say, and yet everything to say. This strange day of limbo was unsettling to all the adults, whilst the children filled the town with shouts of glee, enjoying the glorious summer weather, and the thrill of the great outdoors.

The women parted with the inevitable agreement to go home and once more listen to the wireless, impatient for, and yet dreading, the news.

Later that day, there was little comfort from the BBC. The German army was in Poland, and making deadly progress across the country. The two headmasters had spent the morning completing an elaborate timetable, dovetailing their two schools into the small primary building, and when their wives returned, and a rather glum lunch was finished, they sat together in the garden, with the glorious view before them, and the depressing voice of the BBC coming from the wireless behind them.

Marjorie had made an elaborate salad for lunch, with multi-coloured leaves from the kitchen garden, as well as cucumber and tomatoes from the greenhouse, and cold chicken.

"Are we eating one of your chickens?" asked Vicky.

"Of course," said Marjorie.

"It's very nice," said Vicky, "although I'm still not sure about the killing. Mind you, it's nice with this posh salad cream."

"Mayonnaise, Miss Jones, made with our own eggs; we don't have salad cream."

Marjorie frowned at her sister, and 'hrumphed' as if to indicate how odd she considered this working-class woman to be.

After lunch, they sat on the edge of The Manse lawn, the picture-postcard view of the church and the Castle Mound before them, and the drone of the increasingly pessimistic voice of the BBC close behind.

As the afternoon drew to a close and a glorious sunset filled the sky, reflecting golden hues in the windows of the town cottages, even the children felt the sense of impending doom, and crept quietly indoors, country children and city children, sitting together at the feet of the adults, listening to the solemn music and sober announcements, as dusk fell upon the town.

"Well," declared Marjorie, speaking, as it were, for the entire nation, "nothing's going to happen tonight. We must get some sleep. God knows what we shall wake up to in the morning."

Sunday 3rd September started with yet another glorious late-summer dawn. Restless adults, and their confused children, were awake early, and wireless sets were brought to life even before breakfasts had been eaten.

Vicky had gone with Rosemary to the hen house and bravely put her hand into the straw under the chickens. She brought back a basket of eggs; Marjorie unexpectedly produced a small package of smoked salmon; and Rosemary made toast.

"What's that fishy stuff?" said Vicky.

Marjorie rolled her eyes. "It's a special treat. Smoked salmon. Goes very well with scrambled egg."

"I've heard of that," said Vicky. "It's dead expensive, isn't it?

"It comes from a smokehouse in London," said Marjorie. "Might be near Silvertown for all I know."

"Yes, but it's for the posh 'otels up west, innit? Not for us."

"Make the most of the treat," said Marjorie. "I don't think you know how lucky you are. When the war comes, and come it will, treats like this will be a thing of the past."

Lizzie Harding was frying bacon, with the wireless turned up loud to hear the BBC over the sizzle, when she heard the warning to stand by for an important announcement. She turned and looked at the others sitting at the kitchen table. Military music filled the room. "I feel a bit sick," she said, "but we must have some breakfast."

"We all feel sick," said Molly. "I think we'll feel better once the announcement is made, whatever it is."

A large black car sped down Whitehall, and into Downing Street. With almost no ceremony, George VI stepped from the car, and was greeted briefly by Neville Chamberlain. For the few who glimpsed the scene, both men were looking strained and ill. The door of number ten closed quickly behind the King and his Prime Minister.

Marjorie, Rosemary and Vicky sat silently in the parlour, forgotten cups of tea getting cold beside them; the two headmasters and their wives sat at the kitchen table, the breakfast things not cleared away, congealing on the draining board; throughout the town, and throughout the nation, families sat and listened; evacuees sat beside their new-found friends; lonely parents, their children whisked away to the countryside, sat in awkward silence; the nation held its breath.

A little after eleven in the morning, the BBC's Alvar Lidell introduced the Prime Minister, speaking from 10, Downing Street.

"This morning the British Ambassador in Berlin handed the German Government a final note stating that, unless we heard from them by 11 o'clock that they were prepared at once to withdraw their troops from Poland, a state of war would exist between us.

"I have to tell you now that no such undertaking has been received, and that consequently this country is at war with Germany."

Chamberlain spoke at length about his regret for making such an announcement, and his belief that Hitler could only be stopped by force, but the nation, reeling from the initial statement, did not remember much of the rest of the speech. Chamberlain concluded, *"Now may God bless you all. May he defend the right. It is the evil things that we shall be fighting against – brute force, bad faith, injustice, oppression and persecution – and against them I am certain that the right will prevail."*

"So now we know," said Marjorie. "There's a sense of relief now that war has been declared."

Hardly had she spoken, than the town's air-raid siren started its awful wail.

"Shit!" exclaimed Vicky. "That was a bit quick."

"Oh, no," said Rosemary. "I didn't expect that. What do we do?"

"We do what we practised," said Marjorie, calmly, "down to the cellar. Bring the dog."

Vicky looked dazed from one to the other women, and felt herself shaking. "Go where?" she said.

"To the cellar of course, come on, get a move on."

Opening a door under the main staircase, Marjorie revealed a steep ladder-like stair down to the cellar. The women climbed down and Buster made a kind of uncontrolled leap from top to bottom. The dog set to work to sniff every dark corner of the cellar, thoroughly enjoying the distractions of the unfamiliar spaces.

There were a few old chairs, and they sat down. A single bulb hung from a nail, giving a dim light. Vicky looked around. "It's a bit spooky down here, innit?"

"Did you bring your gas mask?" said Marjorie.

"Crickey, no," said Vicky. "I'd better go and get it."

"No you won't," said Marjorie. "We just have to hope it's not needed."

"We're planning on getting an Anderson shelter," said Edward Harding, "but I've done nothing about getting ready for it. I didn't expect the siren to sound so soon after the announcement."

"Nobody did," said Stanley. "Perhaps they're just trying out the system."

"I'm afraid we've nothing to do but sit here in the kitchen," said Edward.

"No," said Molly, "in London, we were told to go and sit under the stairs."

"Well we can do, if you think that's what we should do, but I'm not sure what we'll achieve," said Lizzie.

Sitting on four kitchen chairs in the little alcove under the stairs, the four felt slightly ridiculous.

"I feel such a mixture of emotions," said Molly. "I'm upset, and frightened, and near to tears, and yet I have a strange feeling that I might giggle. Look at us."

"It is bizarre," said Lizzie. "Out here, in the Cotswolds, miles from London, we're four grown adults sitting like garden gnomes under the stairs," and she gave a little nervous laugh.

"I'm going outside," said Stanley, "to see if there is any danger."

All around the town, people were thinking the same, and emerging from their homes to look at a clear blue sky, bright sunshine, and a lovely September day. It was inconceivable that there could be any danger.

"Blimey!" exclaimed Billy, "we had that 'orrible noise at 'ome. I didn't know you had them sirens in the country. We 'ad practises, when we 'ad to pretend Jerry was coming and we'd all get bombed. We never even knew the school had got a cellar – it was an adventure going down there the first time, but it was hot and stinky, so we never wanted to stay long."

"How long do we have to stay down here?" said Rosemary.

"Until they sound the all-clear, of course," said Marjorie.

"Will we hear it down here?" asked Vicky.

"I hope so," said Rosemary, "or else we'll be down here a very long time."

CHAPTER THREE

Stanley came back into the house. "Actually you do look rather comical sitting like that, under the stairs," he said. "I don't see any need to be sheltering. Surely if there was a danger of any sort, we'd hear it coming."

"Is there anything to worry about here in the country?" asked Molly. "I thought we'd been evacuated here to get away from any bombing. We were told the docklands would be a prime target for Hitler's bombers, that was logical enough, but surely we're safe here?"

The four of them carried the chairs back to the kitchen, and went outside. They stood on the lawn with its peaceful view of the rolling Cotswolds.

"Before that terrible announcement, I was going to start to make lunch," said Lizzie. "We may not have much appetite, but I just as well get on with it. After all, it's your first Sunday roast since coming from London – we should try to enjoy it."

"There's a good joint of beef in the oven," said Marjorie. "I'm damned if Hitler's going to let it get ruined. Miss

Jones, Victoria, I'll check the roast, and then ask you to come with me to the garden. You just as well make yourself useful, and get the potatoes and vegetables for us. Rosemary go across and apologise to the vicar that we didn't go to church this morning. Buster, come on, we're going back up."

The dog looked at the steep stairs. He'd tumbled down them easily, but he'd no idea how to get back up. He did a funny dance. Marjorie looked at him, and picked him up. "You're a bit heavy, boy," she said, as she half-carried, half- threw the dog up the ladder.

"Sunday lunch has always been Marjorie's prerogative," said Rosemary to Vicky as they climbed out of the cellar. "I do most of the cooking, but she's thinks she's got a superior touch when it comes to roast beef, and Yorkshire pudding of course."

"What's this?" said Billy McCann, eyeing the plate of food warily.

"Roast beef, darling," said Mike's mum. "Haven't you had it before?"

Billy was finding it hard to get used to Mike's mum, and he found everything about Mrs Thomas's home to be very alien. For a start, there was a bathroom, and it seemed he was expected to wash his face every day, and his hands before each meal. Sharing a bedroom with Mike was alright, but Mike didn't seem to know anything about how a boy should behave. When sent to bed, he just went to sleep, and stayed asleep – this was very puzzling to Billy who was used to getting up and exploring at night.

"Roast beef?" asked Billy, "and there's a big bun on the plate with it!"

"Yorkshire pudding," said Mrs Thomas, raising her eyebrows and looking at her taciturn husband.

"Best dinner of the week," said Mr Thomas. "Eat up lad."

"D'you reckon we're gonna get that bloody 'orrible noise every day?" said Billy. "We 'eard it in London, but that was just trying it out. Stan said it was just practising. We was pleased we got out of lessons, even better than an old fire drill. But 'ere? Was that a practise or are we gonna get bombed?

"I don't know, darling," said Mrs Thomas, "but don't worry your little head about it. Eat your dinner."

Billy attacked the food on his plate with both hands, to the horror of Mr and Mrs Thomas.

"Please use your knife and fork, Billy."

Billy grunted with his mouth full, picked up a potato on his fork and ate it lollipop-style.

"S'nice," he spluttered.

Marjorie led Vicky to the vegetable garden and handed her a fork. "Just dig one potato plant, it should be more than enough," she said.

Vicky looked from the fork to the plants, and hesitated.

"Oh, come on, young lady, you'll have to learn quickly. Look, that's a potato plant, just push the fork in gently below it, and tip it over, like this. The soil's quite dry at the moment, so it will be easy to pick the potatoes."

Marjorie turned the plant over revealing a beautiful crop of small potatoes.

"Pick them up, and don't leave any behind,"

Vicky gingerly put her hands into the warm earth, which was drier than she expected. The potatoes were surprisingly clean, and soon the basket Marjorie had brought out was filled.

"They're lovely," she said, "slightly warm, and very smooth."

"Earliest crop of Jersey Royals," said Marjorie. "Now we'll go for carrots, and runner beans."

Reaching the tall column of beans, Marjorie continued to give instructions. "Now pick only middle-sized beans," she said. "The biggest we leave to form next year's seeds, and the smallest can grow on for another week or two."

The Hardings and the Wykes sat down to lunch. None of them was hungry, all felt confused, and yet they felt they had to continue some kind of ordinariness despite the desperate situation. Stanley summed it up for them all.

"I feel as though we should be doing or saying something significant," he said, "but we're just sitting here ..... being normal,"

"Not really normal," said Molly. "Normal would be Sunday lunch at home in Silvertown, hearing ships' sirens, not air raid sirens, just the two of us. Here we are miles from home, with two very nice new friends, eating a lovely lunch, in the knowledge that our country is at war. We must thank you, Edward and Lizzie, for bringing us into your home, and looking after us so well."

"We don't know what the future holds," said Edward, "so we must make the most of the present. Perhaps, Lizzie, we can get washed up and then have a cup of tea in the garden. Let's cling to the best of today – the sunshine and the green hills of home."

"Don't get maudlin'," said Lizzie. "You men get out of the way. Perhaps Molly will help me, and we'll soon be tidied up. We'll bring a pot of tea out in a minute."

After a bowl of brown soup, the roast beef, with blister-ing mustard, Yorkshire pudding and vegetables, and an apple pie, Vicky sat back, pleased that she had survived a rather formal meal, with more cutlery than usual, and starched napkins. She had to admit that Marjorie did indeed know how to make an excellent Sunday roast.

"Phew!" she exclaimed. "That was bloody brilliant. Best roast lunch I've ever had. Mrs M, my landlady, is a pretty good cook, but nothing as good as that. I'm proper blown-out!"

"I hope you still have enough energy to help Rosemary wash up," said Marjorie. "After all the stress of the morning, I'm going to put my feet up in the parlour. Rosemary will bring me a cup of tea in a minute, won't you dear?"

"Can I go out and play?" said Billy, scrambling down from the table.

"Haven't you forgotten something?" said Mr Thomas.

"Oh – yes – can I have a cuppa tea?"

"That's not what I was thinking," said Mr Thomas. "I was thinking that you should thank Mrs Thomas for a very nice lunch."

"Oh – thanks Miss Thomas. Now can I have a cuppa?"

"Mike will have a nice drink of milk, won't you dear? I'll get milk for you as well," said Mrs Thomas.

"Yuck," said Billy. "I 'ate milk. I need a proper cuppa tea."

"School tomorrow," said Vicky. "Not sure how it will work out. Bet there's gonna be a lot of mothers round the school gates, 'changing stories about our kids."

"School tomorrow," said Stanley. "Better get there early, ready to meet the children."

"Ready to field the complaints about the children," said Edward.

"Complaints about my children," sighed Stanley. "They are lovely, really, just takes a while to see the beauty in rough diamonds."

"School tomorrow," said Mrs Thomas. "Bath-night tonight, and scrubbed faces and clean clothes in the morning."

"I ain't got no other clothes," said Billy.

"But you've been playing the street in those clothes, and climbing trees," said Mrs Thomas.

"So?"

"You can't go to school like that. What else was in that suitcase of yours?"

"Nuffin much. I brought my lucky stone with a hole in it. No clothes ... and Golly, I couldn't leave Golly behind. He's in bed."

"Golly?"

"Yes, my Golliwog. D'you want to see him? I'll get him."

Billy ran upstairs, and was back down, jumping the stairs three at a time.

"Here he is. D'you want to hold him?"

Billy held out a large stuffed doll. With its black face and staring eyes, mass of curly hair and brightly coloured clothes, it was a cheerful toy, a beacon of brightness in the grubby life of the little boy.

"My mum gave him me, when she was dying. I don't remember her really, but when I hold onto Golly, I'm holding onto her. That's why Golly sleeps with me. I nearly left him at the station, but Miss Wykes had him in the case."

"He's lovely," said Mrs Thomas, giving the doll back to Billy. "You look after him. Don't worry about clothes, I'll sort out some of Mike's things, good job he's bigger than you and I've got some cast-offs. I'll have a word with your teacher in the morning about getting you some more stuff."

Billy clutched Golly, and walked to the foot of the stairs. Turning he said, "Don't tell anyone about Golly. I kept him in the suitcase on the train, so the girls with their sissy dollies wouldn't laugh at him. I've told Mikey, he's a secret."

"Your secret is safe, Billy. Now go on upstairs and have a bath."

Later that evening, with both boys bathed and in bed, Mrs Thomas spoke quietly to her husband. "His mum died just after he was born. His dad is a stevedore in the London docks. He's had a rough life, we can't be too hard on him. Fancy, he didn't know what a good Sunday lunch was. Poor little bugger."

Monday morning saw Vicky up early, and she hurried to the kitchen for her bowl of porridge. Rushing in, still wearing Bobby's dressing gown, she was surprised to find an unknown woman making the porridge.

She stood at the door. "Oh, I'm sorry, I thought Marjorie or Rosemary would be here."

"You must be the London teacher," said the woman. "Mrs Anderson-Grey told me you would be here. I'm Mary Wheeler. I come Monday, Wednesday and Friday: Mondays for washing, Wednesday for ironing, Thursday cleaning. Just missed you last week."

"Pleased to meet you Mary," said Vicky.

"Got any washing?" said Mary. "I'll be doing it straight after breakfast."

"Not really," said Vicky. "We was only allowed one little suitcase, so I'm really short of clothes. Only my smalls, and I've never had anyone do them for me before. I was going to rinse them out in the bathroom this evening."

"I wouldn't do that. Mrs Anderson-Grey would never approve. Get them after breakfast and bring them to me. I'll see to them. It's going to be a good drying day, so I want to get everything on the line as soon as I can."

Anticipating the confusing and challenging day, the two headmasters were at the school early, and their two staffs joined them. Hasty introductions were made, although Vicky was unsure if she'd remember the names of her new colleagues.

The children also started to arrive early, coming into the playground, Chippy children and Silver kids coming muddled together. Most normal mornings, there were very few mothers coming to the gate, as most children walked to school unaccompanied; this morning was different, and a considerable crowd had gathered. The chatter was a mix of reactions to the announcement of war and the antics of the rough East End children.

Edward Harding had posted a note at the gate, telling the parents that the Chipping Norton children could be collected from one o'clock, but that the Silvertown children would not finish until five. There was a great deal of gossip amongst the mothers about how they'd cope with children coming and going at varying times.

Edward rang the handbell, and the Chipping Norton children ran into lines. The Silvertown children watched with some admiration at the smartness of the country children, and Stanley, with Lawrence at his side, gathered their children at one side of the yard. As Edward led his children to their classes, Stanley raised his voice to tell his children that they must play in the playground for the morning. Turning to Lawrence, he said, "I'll leave you with Miss Jones to keep an eye on things. You could have a go at teaching them to line up like the others. Apparently it's OK for them to climb the trees, but they mustn't go outside the playground. I'll get the other staff to come and relieve you after a while. Mr Harding has given us some footballs. Let's hope they don't get too bored and start fighting."

"What's your digs like?" asked Vicky.

"Very nice," said Lawrence, "except for the steepest twisting staircase you ever did see. You know that house down the hill to the station, the one with a room on an archway? I'm there, and I've got the big room over the arch. It's normally the sitting room of the house even though it's upstairs. I have to be a bit careful and slow going up and down the stairs."

"Not posh, though?" said Vicky.

"No, not posh. Just really nice. It's an elderly couple, got a grown-up son who works on a farm somewhere near here, but not living at home. They said they were too old to take on any of our kids, but they're happy to have me – very generous. And you?"

"You wouldn't believe where I am. You remember there was a dead posh woman at the Town Hall on Thursday, the tall one?"

Lawrence nodded.

"It's her I'm with. Dead posh. Great big house, loads of space. I learned how to dig up potatoes yesterday, and we have chickens to get eggs.... Billy McCann, don't do that! ....We went down into the cellar when they sounded the air-raid. Great big cellar under the house."

"But what's the woman like, this Anderson-Grey?"

"She's as tall as Molly," said Vicky, "but there the similarity stops. Where Molly is curves and soft edges, Mrs Anderson-Grey is sharp angles and brittle. Where Molly smiles and finds the good in everyone, especially the children, Marjorie looks down her nose, and seeks out faults. It seems I have rather a lot, faults that is, not just with things like table manners, but with my knowing nothing about life in the country. We never had a window box where I grew up, much as ever a dirty great garden with flowers and vegetables and chickens, and God knows what else."

Lawrence looked across the playground. "Billy McCann, you heard what Miss Jones said. Don't do that! ....So what did you think about Chamberlain's speech?"

"Marjorie, that's her name, Mrs Anderson-Grey, said it was a relief to know where we stand."

"She's right. How strange, an announcement of war being a relief," said Lawrence. "It's because it's been a long time coming."

"We must be thankful that the woman has to go to the school every day. The house will be a bit quieter during the day," said Marjorie.

"I like Vicky," said Rosemary. "I'm sure she'll be a help in the garden at the weekend."

"She will have to learn quickly; there's so much she doesn't seem to know. I'd hesitate to let her do weeding – she's sure to pull up the wrong plants."

"She's a teacher, so we have to hope she's a quick learner," said Rosemary. "Now, I'm going to mince the beef and make a cottage pie for us, and we can save her some to warm up when she gets back from the school this evening."

The day was surprisingly uneventful at the school. The Chippy children enjoyed their unexpected long afternoon on the playground; and the Silvertown children made the most of playing in the morning and going to their new classrooms in the afternoon. Everyone was a little wary of one another, and went out of their way to be careful and polite.

Later, Stanley and Edward congratulated one another on such a smoothly run day. "Let's hope that was not just beginner's luck, and tomorrow when everyone relaxes, we don't have unexpected challenges."

Vicky was delighted to come home to Rosemary's excellent cottage pie, and when her plate was almost licked clean, she turned to the two sisters.

"So what do we do round here in the evening?" she asked.

"We listen to the wireless, and we catch up with knitting. With these light summer evenings, one of us may take the dog for a walk."

"That would be fun, and we could call in for a pint. I walked past the Fox on the way home from school: looks nice."

"I have never been in a public house in my life," said Marjorie.

"You don't know what you're missing. Nothing like a booze-up. Better on Fridays of course, might not be such a good idea on a Monday."

"I'd like to take Buster out this evening," said Rosemary, "and perhaps we might go and see what the Fox is like."

"Rosemary," said Marjorie severely, "I don't want you to start getting common habits, just because this young woman is staying with us. We do not frequent public houses."

"Sorry, I'm sure," said Vicky. "I just thought it would be nice to do."

"In the last war, my mother kitted a large number of socks and scarves. I'm sure there will be similar needs this time, so I suggest you organise yourself. Rosemary, can you find some needles and wool for Miss Jones, and get her started on a scarf."

"I think I'd like to go out for a walk," said Vicky, through gritted teeth. "The knitting will have to wait."

"Don't be late, Miss Jones. I don't expect to hear you come in after nine o'clock. Oh – and don't ring the front door bell, come round to the kitchen door. It won't be locked, unless you are very late, in which case you'll be locked out."

Vicky walked up the hill to the marketplace, struggling to calm down and not allow Marjorie to get her upset. She went around the Town Hall and into the Fox. She was instantly relaxed by the welcoming atmosphere of the old pub, and delighted to find Lawrence sitting with two elderly people. She plonked down into a stick-back chair beside them, and Lawrence introduced the old couple as his landlady and her husband.

"I need a drink," said Vicky. "It's been a long day."

"And you've got Marjorie Anderson-Grey to contend with," said the old lady.

"She's hard work," said Vicky.

"I expect that's what she says about you," smiled the old lady, "but if you think she's a bit posh, wait until you meet the Major."

Lawrence smiled at Vicky, and said, "Have a glass of this," holding up his beer glass. "It's made near here, and it's called 'Hookey' – I don't know why – but it's excellent."

Vicky enjoyed the Hookey, and vowed to come to the Fox as her 'regular', but at five-to-nine, she suddenly jumped up. "I must run," she said. "See you at school." With that she was gone, sprinting across the market place, and accelerating down the hill. She slipped into the kitchen at the Manse just as the grandfather clock was striking nine.

The next day, and the following days, saw the town settle into its new routine. The expected animosity between the city children and the country children was rarely seen: mostly they played together well. Chippy children had lots to teach the Silver kids: the names of plants in nearby fields, and which were edible; the trees which were good to climb; the unexpected alleyways leading to stables where they could stroke horses, or smack coarse-haired pigs, which grunted as they gobbled the smelly brew boiled for them in giant cauldrons. The Silver kids loved exploring the town, and encouraged their country cousins to be bolder in climbing to the tops of walls and racing along the top, arms waving like miniature aircraft.

The two headmasters could hardly believe that everything was so peaceful and easy, and were jittery that the calm wouldn't last. Mike's mother visited the school one morning, about a week after their evacuees had arrived.

"Can I talk to you about Billy McCann?" she asked.

Stanley sighed. "Of course you can. I just knew he'd be the first to get into trouble."

"No, he's not in trouble," replied Mrs Thomas. "It's just that he's got nothing with him. His little suitcase was almost empty. I've a few of Mikey's old clothes for him, but I'm struggling to keep him clean and decent. He gets fearfully dirty every day, and he needs a few more clothes."

Stanley smiled. "It's nice to know he's not in trouble. Lots of our children are from very impoverished homes. Billy's one of the worst, but he's not the only one. Perhaps we need a jumble sale to get clothes for several of the children."

Edward had been listening. "There's just as much poverty in the country," he said. "Lots of children are coming to school in hand-me-downs. I think you're right: the answer will be to have a jumble sale, but we'll say it's for children's clothes only."

"I'd be pleased to help," said Mrs Thomas, "but we've got to sell everything very cheap – just a penny or two for each thing."

Stanley smiled again. "An excellent suggestion. Can we hold it in the school?"

"We could," said Edward, "but the town hall will be better. Then we can have tea, like the day you arrived, and make a good 'do' of it. I'm sure my wife will be more than pleased to help."

"And Molly, my wife," Stanley explained to Mrs Thomas, "will be very keen to join in. She's organised many jumble sales in Silvertown."

"A jumble sale!" exclaimed Marjorie. "Terrible piles of old clothes. I really don't think we can help with that."

"It's for the kids," said Vicky. "Some of them have got next to nothing to wear. They didn't have much at home anyway, and they brought even less when they were evacuated. It's an easy way of helping out."

"But everything will be alive," Marjorie shuddered dramatically. "Fleas and goodness knows what else live in old clothes. The town hall will need fumigating."

"We have jumble sales at school in Silvertown," said Vicky. "They're not smelly, and lots of people appreciate it. Why, if some old grandmother kicks the bucket, she'll probably leave a good winter coat, and a cardy or two, and who knows what else?"

"You sell dead people's clothes?" said Marjorie, becoming increasingly horrified. "And people buy them and wear them?"

Vicky turned to Marjorie and spoke fiercely. "Most of the East End is walking around in second-hand clothes. Of course there's grand department stores up West, but it's worlds away from ordinary life in Silvertown. East-enders don't go up West except to look in the windows. They buy from jumble sales and second-hand markets. You should go down Brick Lane of a Sunday morning. It would be an education for toffs like you, with your posh schools and big houses. I'm from a very poor 'ome, and was I bleedin' lucky to get to train as a teacher, and I said I'd always go back and work with these poor kids and give them a bit better start in life. It's bloody 'ard work, and the kids is tough, and yes some of their mums and dads wear dead people's clothes. Hardly any of the kids get anything new, their clothes start as second-hand, and then become hand-me-downs. You know some of our kids take their shoes off when they go out into the yard to play, so's not to wear them out? You live in this big house, and have no idea what the rest of the world is like."

There was a silence. Rosemary started to say, "I'm sorry. We don't really know..." but her voice trailed away.

"I'm going out for a walk," said Marjorie. "I'll take the dog with me."

As Marjorie sailed out of the room, Vicky burst into tears. Rosemary put her arm round her. "Please don't cry," she said. "She's had it coming to her."

"But I've only been here a week, and it is a lovely house. I didn't mean to get cross, but something snapped."

"It's the tension and stress of the war," said Rosemary. "We're all on edge."

Marjorie calmed down, and at Rosemary's suggestion, turned out a big bundle of children's clothes which she had kept from her own sons. She'd rather vaguely been keeping the little shirts and shorts for grandchildren. "There's lots of wear left in these things," she said to Rosemary, "but I suppose we should help those poor little things from London. After all, charity does begin at home. When the boys get married and have children, I don't suppose they'll want hand-me-down garments. However, I'd rather not go to the jumble sale myself. Rosemary would you take the things up to the Town Hall?"

The jumble sale was a great success, and astonishingly made a small profit of a little over three pounds. Stanley agreed that the profit would be put into a fund to pay for a good Christmas party for all the children, Chippy and Silvertown. "If we're still here," he said, "but nothing seems to be happening. It's so odd. We're apparently at war, and yet nothing...."

Molly was resolved to go back to her home in Silvertown to collect some more of her own clothes, and things for Stanley. She offered to take Vicky with her. They were able to take a train on a Saturday morning, hoping to return on Sunday afternoon. Vicky was not able to get a message to Mrs M, and looked forward to surprising her when she got there.

The journey was tedious, as the passenger train was regularly shunted off the mainline to allow troop trains to pass. Eventually they pulled into Paddington, as dirty as ever, and full of snorting steam engines. The District line trains were running as usual, and there was little sign that the country was at war.

"It's very strange," said Vicky. "I expected everything to look different somehow, but it doesn't. In fact, it's as if we've never been away. It's still crowded everywhere, just like any other Saturday."

"But no children. It's more than strange, it's really weird. A whole city without children," said Molly. "All evacuated."

"And yet no sign of danger. Perhaps we can all come back, and get the school re-opened."

"I don't think that will happen," said Molly. "The evacuation programme was enormous, with hundreds of children, thousands. The government would never have done it without good reason. They're scared of something."

Vicky left Molly at Plaistow Station, and almost broke into a run to get to Mrs M's. She knocked at the front door, then fished her key out of her purse, and let herself in.

"Who is it?" came Mrs M's voice.

"It's me, Vicky, come to surprise you."

Mrs M emerged from the scullery, drying her hands. "Oh darling," she said, "how lovely to see you. I've just washed up; I'd have made you some lunch if I'd known you were coming."

"A cup of tea would be good, Mrs M," said Vicky. "I had a sandwich on the train, made with eggs from the chickens in the garden where I'm staying. I've got such a lot to tell you. It's been quite an adventure."

"Are you going back tonight?"

"No, I'm stopping overnight, but I've got to get back to Paddington early tomorrow. There's not many trains."

"Sit you down in the front room, and I'll get that tea, then you can tell me all about it." Mrs M hurried back to the scullery to poke the range and get the water boiling.

Vicky sat in the slightly unfamiliar front parlour, and looked around. There was no sign that the country was at war, except that there were no noises outside. There were no children playing in the street.

Mrs M brought in a tray with the tea things.

"We never used to sit in here," said Vicky. "The back room was where we used to sit and natter."

"Those were them days. Mrs Taylor, my friend over the road, said 'If we're going to get bombed, I'm not going to let Hitler have my best sofa without sitting on it a few times', and she's right. She's even played her piano once or twice."

"We were evacuated to escape bombing," said Vicky, "but there's not been any has there? There's quite a few talking about coming home already. We might have to think about opening the school."

"That would be a big mistake," said Mrs M. "When the bombing comes, and it will come, Silvertown will be in the firing line. There won't be any warning. One night, the sirens will sound, and if you've brought our kids back from the country, you'll regret it for the rest of your life – if you survive, that is."

Vicky shuddered. "You make it seem very real. It doesn't seem real in Chipping Norton, like the war's just an abstract idea. Nothing's happening."

"Don't be fooled, darling," said Mrs M taking Vicky by the hand. "Listen: with a threat of war, it was bad enough; but now that war has been declared, we must expect the worst. I don't mean be down-hearted, we must try to stay cheerful, but we must expect the worst. I lost my husband in the Silvertown explosion. It was 1917, he was thirty-two, one of the managers at the factory. I was here, at home, getting his tea. About seven o'clock it was. Biggest noise I ever heard. All the front windows blew in, so much glass everywhere, good job I was in the scullery. I went out to the street: all the wives were out there; they said the factory had gone up. Tommy never stood a chance, probably in his office in the factory – blown to smithereens. Never found a body."

"Oh Mrs M, I never knew," said Vicky. "You've never mentioned it before."

"In the end, you put these things out of your mind. We were all so busy getting cleaned up – it took ages – that there wasn't time to be upset. And of course at that time, everyone was losing someone in the war. But it just goes to show. You never know what's round the next corner. They should never have put a munitions factory so close to ordinary people's houses, probably a decision by some toffs in Whitehall, couldn't care less about ordinary people."

"Funny you said 'toffs'. I'm lodging with a right toff. It's not easy. She's no idea how the other half live."

"Make the most of it while you can," smiled Mrs M. "And don't you dare think of coming back home, or bringing any of those kiddies home. I feel it in my bones. That bloody Hitler is looking at a map of London, and he's putting his Kraut finger on Silvertown. 'Those docks,' he's saying, 'vee shall blown zem up first!' Mark my words, when it comes, it will come here."

Vicky laughed. "You are a caution Mrs M. Now what I need to do, is to go upstairs and pack a couple of suitcases, ready for tomorrow, then this evening, I'll take you out for fish and chips."

"It's Saturday night," said Mrs M. "There'll be a sing song down the Pig later on."

"Oh, I do miss Silvertown," said Vicky.

Paddington Station was quiet on Sunday morning, and Vicky met Molly as arranged.

"We've our got tickets, but no train yet," said Molly. "Apparently it's mostly troop trains they're running, but there's no sign of them here. We just have to wait."

The station buffet slowly filled up with hopeful travellers, who sat quietly sipping cracked mugs of railway tea. Molly produced a big packet of Rich Tea biscuits, and another woman pulled a pack of Garibaldi from her bag. After an hour or so, the strangulated voice on the loudspeaker in the corner made an indistinct announcement.

"Did she say Oxford?" said Molly to the Garibaldi lady.

"I'm not sure, but I think we should go and see," said the woman.

As if rehearsed, the entire crowd in the buffet stood and processed to the platform.

"Slow train to Worcester," said a guard. "Reading, Oxford, most stations in between to Worcester, and might even go on to Hereford."

The travellers soon filled the train and sat to wait for it to leave. Eventually, after a great deal of noise from the steam whistle, the engine chugged into life and pulled the creaking coaches out of the station.

"What's going to happen at Oxford?" asked Vicky when the ticket inspector came to clip their tickets.

"No idea," said the man. "Might be a Banbury train, or if not you'll have to see if there's a bus."

"Won't they have a timetable of trains to Banbury?" said Molly.

"There is a war on, you know," came the tart reply.

"They were calling it 'the phoney war' down the pub last night," said Vicky.

"What does that mean?" said Rosemary over camomile tea on Sunday evening.

"War's been declared, but there's nothing happening," said Marjorie. "I'm sure the Major would know what's going on, although he wouldn't be allowed to tell us. Miss Jones, did you say you went to a pub last night?"

"Yes, it was Saturday night, a sing-song down the Pig."

"The Pig?"

"The Pig and Whistle."

"You people," said Marjorie, "working so hard to fulfil the stereotype. It's like all Scotch being mean, or all Irish being stupid: all you East-enders have to go down to your public house and sing old songs. You don't have to do that you know. You could try and rise above it."

"We enjoy a singsong at the Pig," said Vicky firmly. "I struggled to get out of the gutter and train to be a teacher: it wasn't easy, but I did it. But I didn't do it to rise above it, as you put it. I'm proud of my background and I work hard to help other kids, like I was, to get on at school and learn to read and try to understand the world, but never forget where they came from. Us common people have proper values in life, we look out for one another. We did it in the last war and we'll do it in this one if we have to. I expect you remember that famous explosion at the factory in Silvertown?"

Marjorie nodded, taken aback by Vicky's tirade. "I was a young woman."

"Well my landlady lost her husband in that explosion. He was a manager at the factory. She told me all about it, and how everyone rallied round and helped and looked after the injured, and helped repair all the damage, and comforted people who'd lost people."

"It was very tragic," said Rosemary.

"And it shouldn't have happened," went on Vicky. "That factory was in the middle of 'undreds of ordinary houses, working peoples' houses. The toffs in Whitehall didn't care about the workers, the canon-fodder. They'd never put a factory like that in among, I don't know, a load of posh houses."

"But it was only workers who died, wasn't it?" said Marjorie. "No-one of any importance."

Vicky turned to Majorie and spoke very slowly and quietly. "You really don't understand, do you? With all your swanky education and elegant living, you really don't get it. We're all people, we all count. That's why I'm here, bringing these kids, these poor kids from their grubby homes with no bathrooms, and no gardens, to save their lives if bloody Hitler bombs Silvertown. And every life is worth saving, every one. Now I've had a long tiring journey, I'm dirty from the train, and I'm worn out. I'll put my suitcases upstairs, and if you don't mind, I'm going to have a bath. I appreciate the luxury of having a bathroom indoors, and not going down the public bath house, and I thank you for letting me come here."

With that, Vicky stood and left the room.

Marjorie turned to Rosemary. "Well," she said, "What do you make of all that?"

CHAPTER FOUR

Whilst Vicky struggled to remain calm around Marjorie, Marjorie seemed to have no problem sailing on as if nothing untoward had happened. Over supper the following day, which Vicky had been dreading, Marjorie announced that she'd inspected the orchard during the previous weekend, and that she had decided that the following Saturday and Sunday would be devoted to harvesting the fruit. There was no discussion about this decision – Marjorie had decided.

Saturday dawned bright and warm, and breakfast was devoted to Marjorie giving instructions not only to Rosemary and Vicky, but also to the gardener and Mary who had both been drafted in for the harvest. When they went outside, Vicky discovered that the gardener had produced two tall ladders, and Mary had already assembled numerous baskets and boxes.

Marjorie marched ahead, and they formed a strange little procession with the ladders and baskets, across the lawn, through the kitchen garden, passing the chicken coop, and through another gate into the orchard. Vicky had never been there before, and gasped at the many varieties of trees, laden with fruit.

"Rosemary and I will start on pears," said Marjorie, "as they require a somewhat delicate touch. Vicky, you will work with Mary on Bramleys, and Mr Harper will fetch and carry for us as we get baskets filled."

Vicky looked blankly at the many trees filling the orchard, but Mary rescued her, and with Mr Harper's help, they erected a large ladder at the nearest Bramley tree. "Up you go, Miss Jones; I'll stay here to steady the ladder."

"Please call me Vicky," said Vicky. "We're a lot like one another, you and me, and I hope I can call you Mary."

"Of course, Vicky," said Mary. "Just drop the apples down and I'll put them in the basket."

Vicky clambered up, and grabbed the first huge apple. The Bramleys were enormous, bigger than any she'd seen in Silvertown market, and she tugged hard on the first one. The tree shook, and the ladder wobbled, but the apple remained firmly attached to its branch. Vicky tugged again, then heard Marjorie's ringing voice coming from the other end of the orchard. "Twist and pull, twist and pull; doesn't that girl know anything?" There was a pause, then she said loudly, "And don't drop them; we don't want anything bruised."

Vicky raised her eyebrows and looked down to Mary, who nodded. As usual, of course, Marjorie was right. Vicky grabbed the same apple, twisted it, and pulled.

Sure enough it came away in her hand, and she dropped it to Mary.

"One!" she said under her breath.

The fruit picking went on all day: and Vicky was exhausted by the end of it. At one stage, Mary went to the kitchen and made ham sandwiches for them all, which they ate in the orchard. Mr Harper toiled back and forth to the kitchen door with boxes and baskets. Once she had got over her fear of the wobbly ladders, Vicky found herself quite enjoying the task. As the sun started to set, she wandered with Mary back to the kitchen door. "Did we pick all those?" she asked in amazement at the many containers brimming with fruit, piled around the kitchen door.

"Toast with lashings of butter and sardines," announced a jubilant Marjorie, "then an early night, and soft fruits tomorrow."

"Lashings of butter," thought Vicky: "has she forgotten there's a war on?"

Vicky had no idea that picking the fruit would herald the beginning of a frenzy of peeling and boiling, culminating in bottling, and filling all shapes and sizes of glass jars. When she got home from school on the Monday, the fruit factory was in full swing. "Ah," said Marjorie, "just in time to fetch another box of Kilners from the pantry."

Standing vaguely at the pantry door, Vicky hoped that a "box of Kilners" would identify itself by jumping out at her feet – but no such luck. Mary, noticing her confusion, once more came to her rescue, and pointed to a very big box on the floor.

"Don't you dare drop them," came Marjorie's voice. "We'll need everyone we've got of that size."

The rituals of bottling gave way to packing beans in salt, and then pickling and jam-making. Despite Marjorie's constant admonishments, Vicky enjoyed learning all these new rural skills, and wished Marjorie could relax and deal with her constant ignorance. Vicky was inadequate because she'd never encountered this business of preserving fruit before; but Marjorie continued to consider Vicky's shortcomings as typical of her class.

There was, however, a small chink in Marjorie's middle-class armoury: she discovered that Vicky had exceptionally beautiful handwriting, and decided that she should write the labels for all the jars of preserves. Rosemary produced an exquisite fountain pen, filled with distinctive green ink, and Vicky set to work writing the labels in an elegant copperplate hand.

"You're good at that," said Rosemary.

"I should be," replied Vicky, "as I teach calligraphy to the kids."

After many evenings of bottling and labelling, the pantry was a magnificent reflection of the kitchen garden and orchard, and Vicky got a lot of satisfaction from the sight of all the preserves lined up like glass soldiers, with their green ink labels.

Whilst Marjorie failed to understand Vicky, and made few allowances for her, it was a constant struggle for Vicky to cope with Marjorie. The challenge for the young teacher was to become considerably greater a few weeks later, with the arrival of the Major and his two sons.

Marjorie was excited. "My husband, the Major, has arranged to escape for a day, and is coming for lunch. Not only that, but he's bringing the boys. He's got a staff car to bring him up. Sometimes, it really is a boon having a telephone. It was awfully nice to speak to him at last. Now we'll find out what's really happening with this phoney war. I'll get Mary to work for the day, to help with the lunch. She won't mind working on a Saturday. I expect the driver will want feeding, and he can have something in the kitchen."

"Are they staying overnight?" asked Rosemary.

"No: it will be a flying visit." She turned to Vicky. "We won't have to turn you out of your room, Miss Jones. I told the Major all about you, and he says he's looking forward to meeting you. He says you are to have lunch with us."

"Perhaps I should have something in the kitchen with the driver," said Vicky.

"I did think that," said Marjorie seriously, "but the Major says you are to join the family."

When the three women were in the house, the space seemed cavernous and empty; but when the Major and his sons arrived, the house was suddenly very full with three confident men. Not only were the father and sons larger than life, but the dog took on a new level of boisterousness, contributing to the feeling that the house could somehow burst.

The three were driven to The Manse in a staff car. Marjorie had been waiting nervously in the hall watching for the car, and opened the front door just as the Major's driver opened the car door for him, and saluted. Bobby and Henry unfolded their long limbs from the back seat and stood stiffly behind their father. Rosemary released the hound, who leapt and bounded at his master.

"Marjorie, old stick, sorry it's been so long. Been a bit busy y'know," said the Major. "Buster, calm down." The dog grovelled on the gravel, but continued to wag his tail violently. "Rosie, good to see you; and I expect this must be your Miss Jones." He held out a leather-gloved hand and shook Vicky's hand vigorously. Vicky was struck by this man's quiet presence; he did not have a loud voice as she expected, but was quietly commanding. He walked forward into the house with Marjorie, Rosemary and the dog all fawning about him. Vicky watched them into the house, and then turned to the two enormous soldiers who were standing grinning at her.

"You're so tall," was her immediate observation; and the two young men broke into laughter.

"Are we?" said one. "We hadn't noticed. I'm Bobby."

"And I'm Henry."

"No, I'm Henry," said the first, with greater laughter.

"And so am I," said the second.

Vicky found herself blushing. Most soldiers look similar in their uniforms, but these identical twins were completely indistinguishable. Looking up into their sparkling eyes, Vicky felt very small and insignificant. Whilst their father had a voice of quiet authority, his sons had booming voices which echoed around The Manse driveway.

"Come on," said Bobby, (or was it Henry?), "let's get washed up and then we can have some lunch. I hope Mary's in – she does a great deal better than the mess grub."

The boys rushed past Vicky and could be heard all the way down the hall, calling to Buster, and telling their Aunt Rosemary how good it was to see her. Vicky was left dumfounded at the door. She turned and saw the driver, still standing by the car, looking rather dazed.

"Wotcha, mate," she grinned, "you're getting something in the kitchen. I'll show you where to go."

"Thanks miss," said the squaddie, relaxing. "I'm a bit punch-drunk with those two shouting their heads off in the back of the car. I don't know how the Major stands for it. Everyone else at the barracks is scared of him. I suppose that's what public school and Sandhurst does to you."

Mary had made sure she had a good lunch for the driver, and soon he was sitting at the end of the kitchen table with a large shepherd's pie, complete with a bottle of brown sauce. "'Ere, this is brilliant," said the squaddie. "Thanks ma'am."

Mary smiled. "My boy's in the army too, probably about your age. He's always pleased with my cooking when he comes on leave, not that I've seen him for ages."

Stanley and Molly were about to sit down to lunch with the Hardings. Sharing the domestic routine had worked well, and Molly had made this meal. Lizzie Harding enjoyed giving her kitchen over to her new friend, and often worked in the vegetable garden on days that Molly cooked.

"Half-term," said Stanley. "I'm wondering about going home. It's been lovely here, but very strange. All the rush of evacuation, and then nothing."

"I hear that some children are being sent for," said Lizzie.

"Yes," said Molly. "Their parents miss them and worry about them, and with it all quiet at home, they come and get them. We always have a half-term holiday at the beginning of November, and it seems to be a cue to get the children back to London."

"I think they'll regret it," said Edward. "This phoney war won't last much longer, I'm sure, and when the bombing starts...."

"It will start in Silvertown," said Stan, finishing Edward's sentence.

The dining table was laid formally, as Marjorie had done for Sunday lunch, and again Vicky was presented with more cutlery than she thought necessary. Seated between the two boys she felt like a child squashed between two large uncles, although she realised that she was older than the twins.

Despite the intimidating circumstances, Vicky had survived the new experience of devilled eggs, which Mary had produced on a kind of mammoth bird's nest made of macaroni.

Mary brought in a big platter with two roasted chicken, which she placed in front of the Major. "No, no," he said, "you carve on the sideboard, Mrs Wheeler, and I think our Miss Jones can serve."

Mary put down the birds and said, "I'll get the vegetables first, if that's alright," and rushed to the kitchen to start bringing in the steaming tureens. Vicky hovered near the roasts, unsure what to do.

"Miss Jones," said the Major with his quiet voice, "why don't you start carving the meat before it gets cold?"

"I'm a leg man," yelled Bobby (or Henry).

"And me," yelled Henry (or Bobby). "Can't stand breast."

Vicky took a deep breath and looked around the room. She had a choice: either to stand up to this family, or to burst into tears. She took a second breath, picked up the formidable carving knife, and sliced into the breast of one of the chicken.

"I think I should serve Mrs Anderson-Grey first," she said. "Ladies first."

In a crass attempt at a Cockney accent, one of the boys called out sarcastically, "Oh, Mrs Anderson-Grey! Mother: your Miss Jones knows her manners, don't she?"

And the other joined in with, "Nice bit of breast for Aunt Rosie, too, if you please Miss Jones!"

The Major looked askance at his sons. "OK, boys, enough of your fun. I think we should treat Miss Jones with a little respect. She is our guest after all."

The boys went quiet, but smirked at one another. "Later...." mouthed Henry to Bobby (or it may have been Bobby to Henry).

Mary arrived to relieve Vicky at the sideboard, and soon everyone was served.

"Now, Miss Jones," said the Major. "Tell us about yourself."

"I don't know what to say; there's not much to say really. I was born in Plaistow, went to the local school. I had this great teacher, Mr Perry he was called. He used to read to us every day. I remember "Swallows and Amazons"....."

"I read that," said Rosemary, "by Arthur Ransome."

"Don't interrupt," said the Major. "Go on, Miss Jones."

"Mr Perry's reading opened up a whole new world. Life was pretty drab and grey in Plaistow, and I decided that I'd become a teacher and try to do what Mr Perry was doing for me." She paused. The room was quiet as everyone looked at her.

"It was a struggle, but I got a place at West Ham College. I worked in the cafe, washing up, to pay for the course, and I qualified as a teacher in 1935. I could have applied for a job in some leafy suburb, but I knew all along that I wanted to work with East End kids. So I do, and that's about all there is to tell. Of course, I mainly teach the little ones, so they're not old enough for 'Swallows and Amazons', but I read them lots of little stories by Enid Blyton."

"We didn't have Enid Blyton at Radley," said Bobby.

"Actually, nobody read to us at any school we went to, not even at prep," said Henry. "I think it would be quite nice to be read to."

For a moment, Vicky could see that these two big soldiers, with all their noisy banter, were young boys at heart, and had missed just as much in their early lives as the East End kids, despite being born into a wealthy family.

"Pity you're not stopping," she said, "as we could have started 'Swallows and Amazons'."

After queen of puddings, one of Mary's specialities, and a big piece of Cheddar cheese served with salty butter and cream crackers, the meal was almost over. The Major asked Rosemary to take the boys to the parlour for coffee, whilst he asked his wife to remain behind.

"And you too, Miss Jones, please wait for a moment."

With everyone else gone, the Major got up and shut the door. Returning to his seat, he said, "Marjorie, I need to talk very seriously to you; and from what I've seen, it would be good to for you to listen too, Miss Jones. I can say only very little, as most of what I know is top secret. However, I can tell you that this so-called 'phoney-war' is nearly over. Hitler has been preparing, and so have we, although obviously I can't tell you what we've been doing. I know that all this evacuation business has not been easy for either of you, but I'm pleased you've taken Miss Jones in, Marjorie, and I'm pleased to have met you Miss Jones."

"I can tell you a little of the planning that's been happening. Some of it will be obvious to you, like the expansion of Rissington Aerodrome. There will be quite a few RAF squadrons based in the area, and you'll see more airmen in the town. There are also plans to house prisoners of war in the Cotswolds."

Marjorie frowned, "Prisoners of war?"

"Yes, we must expect them. Once a man is captured, he must be detained. We can't have any enemy chaps trying to get back home. If the last war is anything to go by, most of them will be very happy to sit out the war, away from the dangers and fighting."

"I can tell you, in the strictest confidence, that next week all three of us will be in France. This is very secret, and you must not speak of it anyone. I am taking a risk sharing such information with you, Miss Jones, as I hardly know you; but I judge that I can trust you."

"And one last thing, Miss Jones. I said the 'phoney-war' is nearly over. I mean what I say. We are expecting aerial bombardment, and your part of London, dear girl, is going to get it first. Keep the kiddies here, don't let the mothers take them back. I'm sorry to say it, but you will soon have proof of how important this is."

There was a silence, and Marjorie and Vicky looked grimly at one another.

"Soon have proof," whispered Vicky.

"Now," said the Major, rising, "let's join the others for coffee and relax for an hour or so before I have to go."

Vicky survived the rest of the day without further incident, but felt that the two young soldiers were constantly laughing at her conspiratorially. Late afternoon, it was time to retrieve the driver, gossiping with Mary in the kitchen, and for the three Anderson-Grey men to depart.

"It has been a pleasure meeting you, Miss Jones," said the Major, as he was getting into the car.

"A great pleasure," said Bobby, sarcastically.

"A very great pleasure," said his brother, with a smirk.

Vicky was certain that the two boys were laughing in the back of the car as the doors were slammed shut. The car accelerated quickly up Church Street, and the women retreated to the parlour.

"Their visits are so few and far between," said Rosemary.

"We must be thankful for seeing them," said Marjorie. "Who knows when they will be here again? God knows what will happen when they go abroad. Who knows if they'll even be able to stay together?"

"Tell me," said Vicky, "if they are in the Grenadier Guards, does that mean they wear busbies, and guard Buckingham Palace?"

Drawing herself up to her full height, Marjorie picked up framed photographs, and smiled proudly as she showed the pictures and replied. "They're called 'bearskins', not busbies, but yes, all three of them. The Major has been in the Guards for some years, and taken part in the Changing of the Guard countless times, as well as three times in the Trooping the Colour. The boys have just finished their first tour in Wellington Barracks, and their first assignment at the Palace. It is good to see them continuing the family tradition."

Vicky nodded. "The only men I've ever known in the army were squaddies, and not in the Guards."

"Yes, they would be," smiled Marjorie. "The Major and I are very lucky to have such wonderful boys."

Vicky smiled to herself. It was typical of Marjorie to think of these two immature and rather rude young men as wonderful, but she said nothing. She held the secret of their deployment to France to herself, and realised that they were being sent into unknown dangers. Perhaps she should not judge them too harshly.

Later, when Rosemary was getting ready for bed, she was alarmed by some shrill shrieking from Vicky's room. She hurried next door.

"Look," stuttered Vicky. "There's a strange creature in my bed."

She had pulled back the covers to reveal a kind of green hedgehog.

"A bunch of sweet chestnuts," laughed Rosemary, "but I can see why you were alarmed. She gathered the green prickly fruits in her hands, and told Vicky to get into bed. Vicky tried to, but could not put her feet and legs into the sheets.

"There's something stopping me," she gasped. "Whatever's happened?"

Rosemary pulled back the eiderdown. "Apple pie bed," she said. "Typical boys prank. I'll help you sort it out. I usually get the tricks and jibes, but they've transferred their jokes to you now. I wouldn't drink the water in your glass if I was you."

Vicky eyed the glass of water by the bed. It had a strange yellow hue. "They wouldn't...." she said.

"They might," nodded Rosemary, "although Marjorie would never believe us if we told her."

Mid-December, and the town began preparations for Christmas. Mr Harper, the gardener, arrived with a surprisingly big tree which was erected in the hall of The Manse, and Rosemary found the box of glass decorations to go on it. The three women worked together to decorate the tree. Vicky was nervous of the fragility of the baubles, but managed to hang them without incident, and without Marjorie giving her too many instructions. Rosemary found the little candles with their twisted wax and clips, but Marjorie warned them that, "the candles would not be lit, of course, for fear of burning down the Manse."

A few days later, Vicky found two parcels under the tree: a long narrow box for herself and a little square one for Rosemary; clearly put there by Marjorie. She realised that she had been bought a Christmas gift. In the following days, more gifts appeared – labelled for the Major, one each for Bobby and Henry, one addressed to Mary, one addressed to Mr Harper, even one addressed to the postman. It seemed that Christmas melted Marjorie's heart a little, but she spoilt that idea by telling the others, "It's all a waste of money of course, and rather childish, but the Major and I started the habit when the boys were little, and we can't seem to stop."

Vicky decided she would be charitable and find something nice for Marjorie, although she was challenged to decide what would be suitable. Rosemary was far easier, as Vicky had been with her when she had admired a scarf in the window of one of the shops in the town.

Stanley was struggling to keep the Silvertown children in Chipping Norton. Although the public were aware of fighting in Europe, it hadn't reached England, and many urban parents were very anxious to have their children back. The government was in a dilemma: if they left the teachers in the evacuation centres, many children would be at home with no school to go to; but if they brought the teachers home, that would be a signal to end all evacuation, and all the children would be back into the target areas for bombing.

Vicky took the Major's warning very seriously, and spoke at length to her headmaster and his wife. Both Stanley and Molly agreed that it would be best if they all remained in Chipping Norton; and Stanley resolved to go back to Silvertown to try to persuade the parents to return their children to the countryside.

Billy's dad had been very relieved to send Billy away, and made no attempt to bring him back, as did many parents in the more impoverished families. Of those who had brought their children back to the East End, it was mainly the better-off families who kept their children at home for Christmas. Molly, therefore, arranged a Christmas party in Chipping Norton Town Hall for the children from the poorest families, enlisting the help of many of the shops in the town to provide little Christmas presents for the children. She needed someone to be Father Christmas.

"No!" exclaimed Robert at the bank when she approached him. "I can't imagine anything worse. I'm no good with small children. I still haven't lost that image of all those little boys pissing when they got off the train. I'm not the right person to have them all sitting on my lap, all wanting Tommy guns."

A couple of weeks later, Robert Evans was seated behind the curtain, on a large chair, on the stage of the Town Hall, fully dressed as Father Christmas, in an outfit supplied by the Co-op, a big white wig and extraordinarily uncomfortable beard, muttering, "I don't know how I was persuaded to do this."

Vicky, dressed as an elf stood at his side. "I'll look after you," she grinned. "We've got a bag of boys' presents, and a bag of girls' presents. Rosemary spent three evenings this week wrapping them. The boys' presents are mainly cap guns, and the girls' presents are rag dolls."

"Cap guns?" said Robert. "Does Father Christmas approve of giving out weapons even if they are toys?"

"There is a war on," smiled Vicky. "It's what they all want. There's probably a few girls would rather have a gun than a doll."

At the side of the stage, a queue was forming, headed, predictably, by Billy McCann. His friend Mike was right behind him. "We never had a Father Christmas before," said Mike. "It's only 'cos you Silver kids is 'ere."

"We never had one at 'ome, neither," said Billy. "It's good this 'vacuation lark, innit?"

Vicky opened the little door at the side of the stage and the line of children shuffled up the short staircase to the stage. Billy peeped round the curtain.

"He's there," he reported to the rest of the line. "I seen 'im."

"And what's your name, little boy?" said Robert, once Billy was settled on his lap.

"Well," said Billy, drawing a big breath, and ignoring Robert's question, "I'd like a Tommy gun and a machine gun and lots of bullets, you know the sort that you put in a big strap on your shoulder, and a tank of me own, and a sword and a shield like Robin Hood, we read a book about 'im at school, and one of those spear things like the Romans had, and me dad to come to Chippy for Christmas."

"Gosh," said Robert, "I don't know about all that. Have you been a good boy?"

Glancing at Vicky, Billy replied, "Course, I'm always a good boy, ain't I miss?" Turning back to Robert and staring him in the face, he went on, "and I'm good at climbing trees now I live 'ere at Mike's 'ouse."

Vicky handed Robert a small parcel. "Here's a present for you," he said faintly. "Be a good boy."

"Thanks, mate," said Billy, "and of all those things, the best would be for me dad to come 'ere."

Billy jumped down, and ran back past the line of waiting children. "Got a presi!" he shouted to the world in general, and rushed to show Mrs Thomas.

"Let's save it for Christmas Day," said Mrs Thomas, taking the little box from Billy.

"OK, mum, now where's the buns?"

Robert looked with alarm at Vicky. "Are they all going to be like that?" he said.

"No," grinned Vicky, "you got the hardest one first. The rest will be easy. The only trick is to watch out for kids who try to come again. I bet Billy will try it, but I'll catch him." She beckoned to Mike to come forward, but her thoughts were with what Billy had said. Could she ever get Billy's dad to come to Chipping Norton for Christmas?

By Christmas Eve, the Anderson-Grey household had received countless Christmas cards, mostly for the Major and Mrs Anderson-Grey, but also a few for Rosemary, and one or two for Vicky.

"After all," reflected Vicky, as they sat together in the parlour, "hardly anyone knows my address, so I can't expect them to send me a card."

"It would be jolly if the Major and the boys had come home for Christmas," said Marjorie.

"There are lots of families thinking much the same," said Rosemary.

Amongst the cards delivered that day, was an envelope which Marjorie recognised as coming from the Army mail service. "Something from the Major, at last," she said, and slit the thin envelope open with her paper knife. Buster sniffed the envelope as if he could smell his master's hand upon it.

Marjorie unfolded the letter, and two postcards fell out. "Cards from the boys!" exclaimed Marjorie.

"Read the letter," urged Rosemary.

Marjorie read. *"Can't tell you where we are, except somewhere in France. All quiet on the journey here, but lots of shelling around us now. Both boys deployed, and trying to engineer to keep them together, so far so good, although that might not last. All letters will be censored, and anyway I'm not going to write any confidential information. You can tell the others we're in France, billeted in a grand chateau, but that's all for the time being. Keep cheerful, old girl. Happy Christmas."*

Rosemary and Vicky giggled.

"Old girl?" said Marjorie. "He's never said that before. Oh well, no news is good news I suppose. What a strange Christmas this is going to be."

Lizzie and Molly worked together to make Christmas lunch at the Harding house. Edward opened a bottle of sweet sherry, and they shared a drink before the meal.

"Here's to victory," he said.

"And to all the boys in the forces wherever they are," said Stanley, "especially those in France."

"Missing their families," said Molly. "Cold and scared, most of them: won't be much of a Christmas."

Although designed for carrying milk bottles, the carrier was good for wine, and it clanked as Major Anderson-Grey walked across the gravel yard of the chateau. It was a frosty morning, and steam rose from the kitchen of the chateau where the officer's lunch was being prepared. He knew his sons were billeted in one of the outbuildings, and he was determined to find them. "Christmas Day," he thought, "let's hope Marjorie's found a good bone for Buster!"

The various middle ranks jumped to attention as their major entered the barn. "At ease chaps," he said, "just brought you a drop of Christmas cheer. Found these in the cellar, thought you'd enjoy them." He held up the milk carrier. "Hope it's a good vintage. I've brought a corkscrew, but no glasses. You'll have to drink from your tin mugs."

Once the bottles were opened and the wine poured, the Major spoke again. "It's Christmas Day, chaps. Let's hope it's the only Christmas we spend in France. Happy Christmas boys."

As they clanged the mugs together, Bobby whispered to Henry, "Nice to have a senior officer in the family." They turned to the small crew of junior officers, "Happy Christmas Major! Happy Christmas Dad!"

Billy had woken up early, and shaken Mike awake.

"He's been," he said, "Look, there's your stocking."

Rushing downstairs, the two boys excitedly showed their stockings to Mrs Thomas, who acted very surprised despite having been the person who had crept into the bedroom to deliver them.

"Happy Christmas, boys," she said. "Proper big Christmas breakfast today: bacon and egg, baked beans, and fried bread."

"What's that nice smell?" said Billy.

"That's the turkey. It's been in the oven since half-past five."

"Can I see it?" said Billy, and when Mrs Thomas opened the oven for Billy to have a peep, he was astonished. "Bloody hell," he exclaimed, "that's a bloody whopper!"

Soon Mr Thomas had joined them, and they were about to sit down to breakfast, when Billy noticed that an extra place had been laid on the kitchen table.

"Who's that for?" he asked.

"Oh," said Mrs Thomas, "it's just in case Father Christmas wants some breakfast on the way back to Lapland."

At that moment, there was a loud knocking on the front door of the cottage.

"Billy, darling, go and see who that is. I'm still frying the eggs."

"Me?" said Billy.

"Go on boy," said Mr Thomas, "might be Father Christmas come for breakfast."

They listened as Billy went to the door.

"Blimey, Miss Jones, what you doing 'ere? 'appy Christmas Miss. Mike and me, we got stockings from Father Christmas."

They heard Vicky laugh, and then she said, "Happy Christmas Billy. I've brought you an extra Christmas present."

And then they heard an extraordinary noise from Billy: a kind of screaming yelp: "Daddy! My Daddy!"

Mike and his mum and dad hurried into the front hall. There stood Mr McCann, his big physique filling the door frame, with Billy clinging round his neck.

"Come in, come in," called Mrs Thomas. "Breakfast is ready."

In the middle of the introductions and exclamations, Vicky quietly said, "I'll leave you to it," and slipped away, back to the formal breakfast promised by Rosemary at The Manse.

Billy's dad was a big man, and the Thomas's cottage was small. The kitchen seemed very full as Mrs Thomas continued to fry eggs in one pan, and soak bread in hot dripping in another. Billy climbed onto his dad's lap, and clung tightly for a while, but at last the smell of the breakfast tempted him away. No sumptuous breakfast in any palatial house was as brilliant, or as enjoyed, as the humble bread-fried-in-dripping breakfast in the Thomas's cottage

Mr McCann explained that a couple of weeks ago, he had received a letter from Miss Jones. He had left work on Christmas Eve, and rushed to Paddington, where he managed to catch the last train of the day. He'd phoned The Manse from the call box on Oxford Station, and had heard Marjorie calling Vicky to the phone. He apologised that he would be arriving very late at Chipping Norton Station. Marjorie and Rosemary were aware of the plot, and had a camp bed ready for Mr McCann when Vicky brought him from the station.

"And so 'ere I am!" he grinned. "I've not brought much, but I got this for you." He presented a big brown paper bag to Mrs Thomas; a small parcel for Billy; a similar parcel for Mike, and even a little packet for Mr Thomas.

"It is as if Father Christmas has come to breakfast!" said Billy. "We all got something!"

Mrs Thomas went to her pantry, and produced a big mixing bowl, the one they'd mixed the pudding in a month before. Placing it in the middle of the kitchen table, she poured out the contents of the brown paper bag. Out tumbled some strange orange fruit. "What's them?" said Mike.

"Mandarins," said Mr McCann. "They come into the quay from Spain, and they sell them in London shops. I helped unload this lot myself. One of the boxes broke open, so I could get a bagful for you. They only come at Christmas."

Marjorie and Rosemary waited for Vicky to return before making breakfast. "Scrambled eggs and smoked salmon," said Marjorie. "There will always be plenty of eggs, as long as the hens keep laying, but it's getting harder to get the salmon."

Marjorie approached Christmas lunch the way her husband approached a military campaign. The turkey had been stuffed on Christmas Eve, and the ham boiled, and the onions put into the milk to soak overnight for the bread sauce. With breakfast finished, Rosemary and Vicky were sent to the kitchen garden for potatoes, carrots and parsnips. They sat at the kitchen table to peel the vegetables, and to cut little crosses into the bases of Brussels sprouts. At the same time, Marjorie produced a small jar of red currants to make sauce, and began the mysterious art of her personal gravy-making.

Mary, Mr Harper, and the postman had been given their gifts on Christmas Eve, but the rest of the parcels under the tree in the hall remained untouched. Vicky wondered when they would open their presents. At home, when her parents were alive, they had presents immediately after breakfast, but Marjorie showed no sign of opening anything before lunch.

Just when everything seemed ready, Marjorie announced that they would go to church. She and Rosemary had been regular church-goers, but Vicky had never joined them.

"It's Christmas, Miss Jones," announced Marjorie. "I think you should accompany us this morning."

In the Thomas cottage, Mr Thomas and Mr McCann were exchanging stories about ferrets; they'd discovered a mutual interest, and although neither owned a ferret, they'd followed ferret hunting, Mr Thomas in Oxfordshire and Mr McCann in Essex. Billy and Mike, having opened their presents, were now well armed for the war, as almost every parcel and box had contained a gun or similar weapon. The general hubbub of the cottage was interrupted by sudden bursts of gunfire as the boys played with the cap guns they'd got from Father Christmas at the town hall.

At last all was set and Billy and his dad, and the Thomas family sat round the kitchen table. Mr Thomas produced bottles of stout ale, and the boys were given home-made ginger beer. Raising his glass, Mr McCann said, "This is the best Christmas since Billy's mum died. Thank you for having me, and for all you do for Billy. Let's raise a glass to new friends, and victory in 1940!"

"Victory in 1940!" was the toast in the Harding household as Lizzie and Molly brought the lunch into the dining room.

"Victory in 1940!" was the toast at The Manse, with Marjorie adding, "And may the Major and the boys come home safely."

"Safely," echoed Rosemary and Vicky.

Retiring to the parlour after the excesses of the lunch, Marjorie announced that Vicky, as the youngest, should act as postman, and bring the presents from under the tree. "Please open your gifts very carefully, as we always save the Christmas paper for next year," Marjorie said. "Some of this wrapping paper is several years old."

Vicky carefully undid the string around a box from Rosemary, and smoothed the paper. Opening the box, she found a bracelet of small gem stones, which she delightedly put on her wrist. The exchange of gifts continued in a kind of subdued truce from the usual frosty relationships, until Vicky came to the long box given to her by Marjorie. Once more untying the knots in the string, and smoothing out the paper, she found a long box, which opened to reveal a selection of knitting needles.

"Just what I was hoping for," she said through gritted teeth, and with a forced smile.

"Now you've no excuse," said Marjorie. "You can start knitting for our troops."

CHAPTER FIVE

On Monday 8th January, Rosemary joined the queue outside the Co-operative grocery shop. There was a lot of curiosity about the new system they were about to experience.

The women had become used to the habit of sitting together in the parlour in the evening, listening to the radio. Vicky, coming late from school, would have some supper in the kitchen before creeping in to the room and listening to the dispiriting messages coming from the BBC. It seemed that no progress was being made by British forces, and with some reluctance, the news reports described the successes of the Nazi troops in Europe. The BBC tried to make light of Nazi advances, but it was difficult to keep morale up in the British listeners.

Marjorie was frustrated at the lack of news from her husband or the whereabouts of her sons, and her regular comment, "Well .... no news is good news," seemed increasingly desperate. "Whatever is going on?" she would ask at the end of another rather vague news report. "Surely we've enough fire power and troops to turn back the Nazis?"

Neither Vicky nor Rosemary had any answer to her questions.

As the New Year 1940 dawned, the effects of the war had started to become apparent on the home front. The smoked salmon they enjoyed on Christmas morning was the last they'd see for a very long time; and many more basic foods were in short supply. During the run-up to Christmas, the Co-operative grocery, which was the most important shop in Chipping Norton, would have signs stating, "Sorry – no biscuits today." Or "We regret that supplies of sugar are very limited, so no more than one bag per customer."

Government ration books had been distributed, and the people waited for the instructions to use them.

With the New Year came a message on the BBC announcing the beginning of rationing. On 8th January, bacon, butter and sugar were rationed. Marjorie scoured the kitchen for any hidden sugar; Vicky was surprised that the many cupboards and drawers contained all kinds of goods bought and forgotten about, something which could never happen in a cash-strapped working-class home. She remembered Billy telling her on the train, that there'd been nothing in the house to eat except bread and dripping. Marjorie, however, found all kinds of luxury foods in odd corners, and assembled them all on the kitchen table.

On the Monday, whilst Vicky was at school, Rosemary was sent with the ration books, to go and investigate how the rationing system would work. She found that half of the housewives of Chipping Norton had had the same thought, and the queue at the Co-op was long and slow. Mid-morning, the manager of the Co-op had come out to the street to talk to the women in the queue, and to apologise for the slowness of the system. Many in the queue realised that queuing was going to become a way of life as long as the phoney war dragged on.

Marjorie was horrified when Rosemary returned home with a small screw of sugar in a small brown bag, and a modest nugget of butter in greaseproof paper. "You queued all that time, for this?" said Marjorie. "Thank goodness we have a very productive garden, or else we shall surely starve."

A few days later, the BBC announced that the government had added to the list of rationed foods, which now included meat, jam, tea, biscuits, breakfast cereals, cheese, eggs, lard, milk, canned fruit and dried fruit. "We'll survive this war relying on our garden," said Marjorie. "Heaven help those without gardens: it will be a real struggle to survive just on the rations. I suppose the working classes are used to being hungry, so it won't be so bad for them."

Vicky rolled her eyes; she had given up rising to Marjorie's provocations, although she knew the day would come when she would explode again. A few days later, she received a letter from her landlady in Silvertown. She read it privately, and then decided to read it to Marjorie and Rosemary:

"Dear Vicky,

"I'm not sure how much you know about what's been happening in East London, and I'm free this afternoon, so I'm writing to you. First, let me tell you about the docks, where so many of our neighbours are working. It's very strange down there, with far fewer ships, and lots of very scared sailors. We're not being bombed at home, but we know it's only a matter of time. The boats, however, are having a very difficult time, with the German navy blowing them up in the middle of the sea. We're hearing terrible stories of ships being sunk, and sailors drowning.

"I bet it's all quiet in the countryside. But it's very different out at sea. We've been calling it the phoney war since September, but there's nothing phoney about what's happening in the oceans. And some of the warehouses round here are very empty. I'm told that there's not much sugar at Tate and Lyle's. That's why they've started the rationing.

"The other thing we have to cope with is the blackout. I expect you'll have to do it in the countryside sooner or later, but we now have a total blackout at night here. When it gets dark, it gets totally dark, and pretty scarey in the streets.

"We have a lovely air-raid warden, and guess what, when I spoke to him the other day, it turns out he used to be a teacher at your school. I expect you remember him: his name is Eric. It turns out he volunteered for the airforce, but failed the medical because he had rheumatic fever when he was a teenager. So they made him an air-raid warden. He doesn't have a uniform, *but they've given him a tin hat, a bicycle and a rattle, like those rattles they take to football matches. I told him I'd be writing to you, and he wants me to remember him to you. He also said to tell you that Frank is training to be a pilot in the RAF.*

"*Another thing is the sandbags. Ever since September, they've been gradually appearing. They've put them in front of the post office and the bank – I'm not sure why – and at the station. We also have a concrete air-raid shelter built in the middle of the road, and loads of sand bags all around it. Eric has organised us practising going and sitting in it, which is quite jolly as we know it's a practice, but we know the real thing won't be fun. I've put tape on all the windows, just like they told us in the News Chronicle, but again I'm not sure if it will do much good. At least sitting together in the shelter will be better than sitting alone under the stairs.*

"*I must stop, and hope all is well with you. You're much better off there than here. Keep those kiddies safe. Very best wishes from Mrs M.*"

Edward Harding arrived home one day towards the end of January, to find that the materials to build an Anderson shelter had been stacked in the street, one collection of parts per household. Lizzie met him at the door with the instructions. "You start by digging a big hole in the garden," she grinned at him.

That evening, Stanley helped him carry all the components for the shelter into the back garden, and at the weekend the two headmasters started the construction. Lizzie and Molly kept them supplied with tea. It took the whole of Saturday to dig the hole for the shelter, but by the end of the day they had managed a rectangular excavation more than a yard deep, and created a very large pile of earth next to it.

Filthy and tired, they sat in the kitchen, and prayed that all this exertion would prove to be unnecessary. "After all," said Stanley, "we must do the best we can to stay safe, but let us hope we never have to spend a night in this shelter and listen to bombing overhead. We should be safe here in the country, but I would not want to be back in Silvertown at this time."

On Sunday they built the shelter. The pile of parts they had carried in from the street included bunk beds as well as the large sheets of corrugated steel, a bag containing a spanner, and a handful of nuts and bolts, as well as lots of rivets. With a drawing to guide them, they built the shelter, placing the bunk beds on either side.

"It's just a dirt floor," said Lizzie. "I'll find an old carpet so it's not so cold."

That evening, the four of them sat in the shelter, to try it out for size. "It's very small," said Molly, "especially for two tall people like Stan and me."

"Climbing down isn't easy," said Lizzie, "and that will be quite difficult for older people."

"We've been told to pack a suitcase each with spare clothes and valuables," said Edward. "We can use the suitcases and make steps for climbing down into the shelter."

"What's that thing with a long hose attached?" said Lizzie.

"It's a stirrup pump, to put fires out with," replied Stanley.

"I shouldn't think you'd put out much of a fire with that little thing," said Lizzie.

"No, you wouldn't," said Stanley, "but it's better than nothing."

"What if the door got blocked from the outside?" asked Molly.

"There's an escape hatch at the other end," explained Edward.

"I've been thinking," said Stanley. "Building this thing has been quite a marathon, and we're young-ish, and fit. We've got elderly neighbours: we must find out which of them needs help.

By the end of February, by which time they had completed their fourth shelter in the street, the men really had got the system worked out, and had come home with several bottles of home-made wine, from the grateful neighbours they'd helped.

Billy and Mike had been very enthusiastic helpers for Mr Thomas.

"It's like building a den," said Mike.

"Digging a bloody big 'ole!" exclaimed Billy.

Mr Thomas was used to manual work, and they dug their hole quicker than the two headmasters. Soon the shelter was finished in the Thomas's garden, and Billy and Mike were inside planning their "den".

"Have you seen all these people building air-raid shelters?" asked Rosemary.

"It looks like hard work," said Marjorie. "Mr Harper would have found it rather a challenge at his age. Thankfully we have an excellent cellar to go down into, if there's an air-raid."

"Is it likely?" said Vicky. "I thought we were evacuated here to avoid air-raids."

"I am sure everyone building these shelters, hopes they never have to spend time in them," said Rosemary.

"And they seem to be such unsightly things," said Marjorie. "I wouldn't want one of those cluttering up the garden."

Lizzie, Molly, Edward and Stanley completed their shelter. A piece of old carpet was laid on the earth floor, and their emergency suitcases were packed and stored just inside the door. Bottles of water, and tins of food were stacked on a little old bookcase they fitted in, and a slightly battered Tilly lamp was primed ready for use.

"With a tin opener," laughed Lizzie, "or else we'd look pretty silly unable to open the tins."

The four of them sat in the shelter. A heavy silence descended upon them as they tried to imagine the unimaginable. Edward spoke haltingly: "We've been getting this shelter ready in a spirit of light-heartedness, but sitting it, cramped and squashed together, we hate to think of needing it in an air-raid. We may be lucky here in Chippy, but there are thousands of these shelters in tiny back yards, all around the country. Imagine...."

He trailed off, and Stanley took up the theme: "Imagine sitting here like this, all squashed together, all night, with the noise of warfare outside, not knowing what you'd find when you climbed out..... it doesn't bear thinking about."

Marjorie was sitting at the kitchen table, her head in her hands, when Vicky got home from school. Rosemary was sitting with her, a cup of tea gone cold on the table.

"Are you alright, Mrs Anderson-Grey? You look as if you've seen a ghost."

"Please don't joke, Miss Jones. I've had a letter from the Major. It came in the afternoon post. It's very short and rather ambiguous. Here, read it and tell us what you think it means."

Vicky sat and read. *"Dear Marjorie, I have a chance to write a short note to you. The bombardments have been very severe, and the Frenchies are in trouble. We keep moving our HQ, every time nearer the Channel: it is withdrawal. The boys' divisions are regrouping, and we are all involved in a degree of consolidation, but I can't say more. Chin up, and watch the news. I may be home sooner than I expect."*

Vicky looked up. "He may be home? That's odd. Bombardments severe; Frenchies in trouble; moving nearer the Channel: sounds like they're retreating."

"That's what I thought," said Marjorie. "The letter is in code, but over the years, I've learned what the Major means. Withdrawal is clearly retreat; regrouping means they're in a big muddle, and disorganised; and consolidation, that's the worst – it means disaster impending. It must be very grim, if they're heading back to the coast. That letter means we're going to lose France. Hitler will be looking at us from the French coast."

"The radio said the Nazi forces were very strong," said Rosemary. "If they are pushing our troops back to the Channel, the boys will be trapped in France."

"And they're under fire," said Marjorie. "That's what he meant by bombardments severe. I think this letter is a warning to expect the worst."

"Listening to the BBC every evening is getting a bit depressing," said Vicky, "but we must keep listening, and try to work out what's going on."

"Thank goodness we've now got Churchill," said Marjorie. "Poor man: he takes over as Prime Minister in our hour of need. He'll give us leadership, but I feel very worried by all these rumours."

Lawrence Powell was agitated when he walked into the staffroom. "There's all kinds of rumours flying around," he said. "The kids wouldn't settle to anything until I let them tell me what they've heard."

"Mine are too little to worry about what's happening," said Vicky, "but they were still inquisitive. Billy, as usual, was the one who blurted it out. 'Are the Germans coming, Miss?' he said."

"Yes," said Lawrence. "That sums it up. They're all listening to their parents talking, and everyone is buzzing with talk of the Nazis occupying France. When they listen to the radio, the children understand more than we give them credit for."

"Has Mrs Anderson-Grey heard from the Major? He's in France isn't he?" said Stanley.

"Yes he is," said Vicky. "She had a letter the other day. You had to read between the lines, but it seems the British troops are in retreat. Marjorie thinks that soon there will be swastikas flying in Paris. She's very worried about the Major and her boys."

In all the homes in the town, everyone was listening to the radio. In his first broadcast to the nation since becoming Prime Minister, Churchill was struggling to keep up morale in the face of disastrous news. Aware of the impending disaster in Northern France, he spoke boldly to the nation. He spoke of how Britain and France were fighting together, but "the time may come when Britain might find itself fighting alone."

"That's it, "said Marjorie. "He expects the Germans to overwhelm France any day now. That was what the Major was hinting at."

Churchill continued that the battle will be "for our islands, for all that Britain is, and Britain means."

"That's fighting talk," said Vicky. "He's telling us that the Germans will invade as soon as they reach the Channel ports."

"Arm yourselves, and be ye men of valour," continued the Prime Minister, *"and be in readiness for the conflict: for it is better for us to perish in battle than to look upon the outrage of our nation."*

"Is that Shakespeare he's quoting? Henry the Fifth?" said Rosemary.

"I don't think so," said Vicky. "Sounds more like the Bible to me."

"But where's it from? I'll ask the vicar," said Marjorie.

Edward and Stanley could scarcely continue with regular lessons the following day, especially with the older children, who were all clamouring to talk about the news. Vicky was sent down the road to buy the daily papers, and the teachers of the older children improvised lessons about the impending crisis. Maps of France were found, and the proximity to the Kent coast measured.

Although the meaning of Churchill's speech was clear, no-one could place the obscure quotation, and finally Edward telephoned the vicar.

"Yes, it taxed me," replied the vicar, "but I found the quotation in the first book of the Maccabees. Not a text I've ever used for a sermon; in fact not a book of the Bible which many people know about."

The consensus in the staffroom was that Churchill had stepped into the breach at a particularly difficult time, but had made an astonishingly good start in his first broadcast address.

"The vicar says it's from the First Book of the Maccabees," said Marjorie, returning from the telephone in the hall. "He says he's been asked several times, as no-one knew the quotation."

The week was tense: and by Saturday 25th, everyone knew that the British forces were on the beaches of Northern France, trapped between the German army and the sea.

"I wish I had a message from the Major, or one of the boys," said Marjorie. "It's very hard sitting here, in the comfort of our home, knowing they're in danger, but not knowing anything."

Churchill continued to broadcast on the BBC, and the Archbishop of Canterbury called for a day of national prayer on Sunday 26th. The women were grim-faced as they walked to church. Vicky recognised that these two women, despite their airs and graces of class, were desperate for their loved ones, and needed her support.

The vicar read again that much-rehearsed quotation from the Book of Maccabees, focussing particularly on the phrase 'be ye men of valour'. The vicar struggled to be encouraging and hopeful at a time when the news was particularly bleak, and he spent some time praising the new Prime Minister, Winston Churchill, for his up-lifting speeches during the week. He ended his sermon with a prayer for a miracle, that the men on the beach would be saved. The congregation sang lustily:

"Oh God our help in ages past, our help for years to come,

Our shelter from the stormy blast, and our eternal home."

As they entered the house, Rosemary burst into tears. "That wonderful smell of the Sunday roast in the oven!" she exclaimed. "Will our boys ever smell that again?"

"It is truly British, isn't it?" said Marjorie. "I suppose that's what they're fighting for."

Major Anderson-Grey sat in his jeep, and surveyed the beach before him. In his many years as a professional soldier, he'd never seen anything like it. He turned to the officer beside him.

"It's chaos. We've lost control of our own men," he said quietly, "and we've lost this battle. It's every man for himself in the ranks."

"Thank God for the ships," said the officer. "Look, there's hundreds of them."

"But there's thousands of us," said the Major. "My own two sons are somewhere in all that mass of men."

"Oh God, here they come again," said the officer as a formation of small planes roared down the beach, machine-gunning the unprotected soldiers. They watched as men fell, as if at random, within the crowds of soldiers.

"God Almighty, I have never been so frightened in my life; frightened for my men, frightened for my sons, frightened for myself. Are we to sit here and be machined-gunned to death? Is this what it's come down to? I should be with my men, not watching from the top of a sand dune."

"Shall I drive down onto the beach, sir?" said the officer.

"Yes. No. We'll stay here and watch. We can't do anything down there. It's every man for himself. As senior officers, we must see that as many men as possible are rescued before we try to save ourselves. The captain stays with his sinking ship....."

They continued to watch as more men scrambled down the sand dunes, staggered across the beach, discarding their equipment as they went, and waded into the sea. They saw men die on the sand; and drown as they clamoured to get into a boat; and then they saw men rescued, carried away from the beach and taken out of the jaws of defeat.

The BBC continued to report the chaotic retreat for all of the next day, and into the evening. "Turn the radio off," said Marjorie, wearily. "It's time for bed, and we'll not hear anything new tonight. Let's go on praying for that miracle, although right now, my faith is sorely tested."

Marjorie was on the stairs, with Rosemary close behind. Vicky had gone to the kitchen with the cocoa cups, and to say goodnight to Buster, when there was a thunderous hammering on the front door.

"What the hell, at this time of night?" said Vicky as she shot out of the kitchen. Marjorie and Rosemary were frozen with fear, when the tumultuous pummelling was repeated.

Vicky ran to open the door, with the dog at her heels. A man staggered into the hall: filthy and stinking, and collapsed onto the floor. Marjorie made a kind of weird shriek, as she rushed to the prone body. "Henry!"

The man looked up with a very slight grin, and whispered, "No, I'm Bobby," and fainted.

"Run for the doctor, Rosie," said Marjorie, her usual calm momentarily deserting her. "Can we move him, Vicky?"

"No, let him be," said Vicky closing the door behind Rosemary. "He's too big to move. I'll get a cloth to wipe his face."

Returning from the kitchen with a cloth, she found Marjorie kneeling at her son's head.

"Why is he so dirty?" she said. "It's not ordinary grime, it's almost putrid."

"It's oil of some sort," said Vicky, "he's covered in oil."

They heard the crunch of feet running across the gravel, and Vicky opened the door to the doctor and Rosemary.

"It's Bobby. He just fell through the door. He's fainted," said Marjorie. "Is he OK?"

The doctor knelt beside the young man, and pulled his begrimed clothes away from his face. He dragged one glove off to reveal a blackened hand, and felt for a pulse. "He's OK," he said, "probably completely exhausted. God knows how he got here, but his strength kept him going until he fell into the house."

"Can we move him?" said his mother.

"Probably not," said the doctor, "he's too heavy for me, or you, and anyway with all this diesel oil over him, he'll make a fearful mess."

"Let me put a cushion under his head," said Marjorie.

"It will ruin the cushion," said the doctor.

"Does that matter? I think not. Is he sleeping?"

"Yes," said the doctor. "I think he is. We should leave him here to sleep."

As if by way of understanding, Bobby gave a slight snore. Marjorie smiled, "That's my boy. I'll stay here with him tonight, and be here when he wakes."

"I'll stay with you if you would like me to," said Vicky.

"No, I'll call if I need anything. You've got to go to school in the morning, so you must go to bed. Rosemary, too, you get some sleep, I'll need your help in the morning. Thank you, doctor, for coming so quickly." She looked down at her sleeping son. "Where's your brother? Does he sleep somewhere safe tonight? And your father? You are the first miracle, but I need two more."

The dog lay down close beside Bobby, ignoring the rancid smell of diesel oil, and let out a long sigh.

"I'll be back in the morning," said the doctor, "just to make sure he's alright."

When Vicky tiptoed downstairs the next morning, she found Bobby in the same place, still snoring gently, and Marjorie in a chair, also asleep. Rosemary crept downstairs just as Buster stood and stretched. The three of them went into the kitchen and quietly closed the door.

"Oh, Buster," said Rosemary, "you stink as well. You'll have to have a bath before the end of the day. You'd better go out into the garden." Turning to Vicky, she said, "Well you've certainly got a story to tell them at school this morning. I wonder how long he'll sleep?"

"Good luck," said Vicky, letting herself out of the back door. "You've got quite a clean-up to do today, and I can't wait to hear Bobby's story."

When she got home that evening, she found Bobby sitting in his dressing-gown, the very one she'd worn when she first came to The Manse, cleaned-up and eating a plate of sandwiches. Marjorie was sitting close, as if worried that Bobby would vanish if she took her eyes off of him. He turned as Vicky came into the room.

"Wotcha, little teacher," he said. "How are you doing?"

"I'm well," she stammered, "but what about you?"

"Not supposed to be here," he grinned. "I should have reported to barracks, but once I got to the harbour – it turned out to be a small town called Ramsgate, I got a lift in the back of an empty truck, and when he said he was going to Birmingham, I said via Chipping Norton, and he said yes, so I just lay in the back of the truck and jumped out, up at the Quiet Woman, and kind of half-ran, half-staggered down the hill and home. And I'm not going back to the barracks until tomorrow. Mother's going to phone this evening and say I'm not fit enough to travel."

"Which you're not!" exclaimed Marjorie.

"And you are Bobby, aren't you?" said Vicky, making Marjorie and Rosemary laugh.

"Yes, I'm Bobby, I promise. Oh, and don't worry, I'll sleep in Henry's bed tonight, you can stay in my bed."

Marjorie had regained much of her poise, and told Vicky how Bobby and Henry had got to the Dunkirk beach together, but had been separated in the chaos. She explained how thick diesel oil floated on the sea water, spilled from sunken vessels, coating the unfortunate men with the stinking stuff.

"And of dad," said Bobby, "the Major, there was no sign. He would have had a driver and jeep to get to the beach – the rest of us walked there – but we didn't see him."

"I'll phone now," said Marjorie.

They all listened as she went to the receiver in the hall and dialled Aldershot. They heard her explain that Bobby was safe at home, and "utterly exhausted", and then they heard her voice drop an octave. "I understand," she said.

Coming back into the room, she was grim-faced once more. "No news," she said. "Nothing from either of them."

Vicky had been in bed a few minutes, when there was a quiet knock on her door; the door opened and Bobby crept in.

"Don't be alarmed," he said, "there's nothing funny going on."

Vicky sat up, and Bobby went and sat on the bed facing her. Slow tears were trickling down his face. "What if I'm the only one to survive?" he said in a whisper. "So many men died on that beach, and more in the sea. It was terrible. I lost sight of Henry, and I'd no idea where dad was. What if I'm the only one, what if I left both of them to die on that bloody beach?"

"You don't know," said Vicky. "Your mother always says no news is good news. That's what Aldershot told her. No news is good news."

"But what if I'm the only one? I left them there to die," said Bobby, and the tears continued to flow.

"Come here," said Vicky, thinking that this big soldier was no different from a little boy, upset in the playground at school. "Come here, and let me hug you. You need a hug, don't you?"

Bobby fell forward into Vicky's arms, and he snuggled against her. She stroked his hair back from his face, and the tears seemed to stop. "Perhaps tomorrow, you could come to school, and tell us all about your adventure," she said, but he didn't hear her: he was asleep.

CHAPTER SIX

"What's this?" said Mr Thomas.

"A new kind of pie," said his wife. "I got the recipe from the wireless."

"I like it," said Mike, "but why are we having it?"

"It's Lord Woolton's pie, and it's made entirely with ingredients not on the ration – in fact all grown in the garden."

"It's lovely," said Billy, digging into the pie with a big spoon, "nice and easy to shovel in. Mind you, I bet we'll do a lot of bloody farting!"

Marjorie paced up and down the hall, unable to decide if she would telephone Aldershot again. She jumped when the phone rang, and picked it up quickly. Rosemary hurried to the hall to overhear the conversation.

"That's wonderful, wonderful," said Marjorie, and then after a pause, "Oh ..... is he coming home to recover? Bobby's leaving tomorrow, but perhaps he'll be able to stay and see his brother before he leaves."

There was another pause, then Marjorie said, "No news of the Major?"

She nodded, and then replaced the receiver. Rosemary said "Henry?"

"Yes," said Marjorie. "He's at the barracks, with a broken arm. They're sending him home for a bit whilst his arm heals, but he's not leaving for a day or two. Bobby will be able to see him at Aldershot."

"I hope you like it", said Lizzie. "I've made quite a lot, and it's all vegetables from the garden."

"Nothing on the ration," said Molly. "That's good, I suppose."

"Is this the Lord Woolton's pie everyone's talking about?" said Stanley.

"It is," said Lizzie. "Easy to make. I think we might be having it, or versions of it, quite regularly."

"Needs quite a lot of pepper and salt," said Edward. "Let's hope they don't get rationed."

"I don't think they will, but you know what the BBC was talking about this morning? Clothing may be rationed. I don't know how it will work, but we're going to have to collect coupons."

When the time came for Bobby to leave, Vicky gave him another big hug. Neither had mentioned the night they'd spent together, but as they hugged, Bobby whispered, "Thanks Auntie Vicky, for looking after me." Quickly he was out of the door before Vicky could reply. 'Auntie Vicky?' she thought, 'I suppose I am a few years older than him. Cheeky boy!'

She watched him marching up Church Street, swinging his arms, reflecting his Sandhurst training. Marjorie turned and briskly walked indoors. "Well that's one sorted out," she said, "and next week we'll sort out the next one; still no news of the Major."

"I'm going to have a go at that Lord Woolton's pie," said Rosemary. "I copied the recipe down from the radio, and it's quite straight forward. Vicky, come and help me get the vegetables from the garden."

Once out of Marjorie's earshot, Rosemary was very inquisitive. "What did Bobby whisper just as he was leaving?" she said.

"Just said thanks for helping him recover," said Vicky casually.

"Is that all?" said Rosemary.

Vicky smiled, and said, "Now which vegetables do you want?"

The newspapers and the BBC told the nation that Dunkirk had been a victory, and that God had answered their prayers and delivered the miracle of Dunkirk.

"I'm not so sure," said Stanley. "It sounds like a retreat to me. No war was ever won by retreating."

"We must be thankful that so many soldiers were saved," said Molly. "Did you hear that both of Mrs Anderson-Grey's boys survived?"

"But still no news of her husband," said Stanley. "Odd that, a senior officer is missing. Perhaps he got captured."

Marjorie could not resist telephoning Aldershot each day, but when Henry finally arrived home, he tried to stop her making the calls. "They'll let us know as soon as there's news of dad," he said. "Calling the barracks will only annoy them – there's hundreds of chaps listed missing, and father is only one of them."

Whilst Bobby had been obliged to go back to the barracks by train, Henry had the luxury of an army ambulance to bring him home. He arrived with his arm in a sling, which he wore as a badge of honour. Where Bobby had been subdued, Henry was full of bravado as he told his story.

"The beach was a scene out of hell. Most of the chaps were exhausted, some had walked for days, often under enemy fire. We were hungry, and dirty, and hadn't washed or shaved for ages. At first we didn't know what would happen when we got to the beach, but once we got to the top of the dunes, there we saw all the little ships. We couldn't believe our eyes, and some of the chaps started running into the sea. There was no discipline; don't let anyone tell you we queued up patiently like at a chip shop; it was every man for himself."

"Although, of course, all over the beach there were little acts of bravery, as the fit and strong helped the exhausted and injured. No-one left a mate behind if they could help it. Sometimes a line would form to get into a boat, but they quickly broke ranks and pushed forward. I saw some men shoved back into the sea when the tub they were trying to get into was full."

"We were under fire all the time – the Huns had brought some pretty big guns on railway trucks and were shelling the beach. Constantly shells would fall with a terrible thumping noise, literally deafening, and we'd fall over and get a mouthful of sand, and some unlucky blighter would have copped it right next to where you were lying, and we'd pick ourselves up and struggle on towards the sea."

"Just as we thought we'd be safe, a clutch of Hun planes came screaming in, machine guns blazing. There was no cover, but we instinctively fell flat to the ground again. The noise was horrendous, and a sudden pain in my arm made me scream out and groan. Just as quickly as they'd come, they were gone again. The man next to me, half on top of me, was dead, and the bullet that killed him had gone clean through his body and into my arm, smashing the bone just above my wrist."

"I pulled out from under the poor bugger, and tried to walk down to the sea, but the pain made me stumble quite a lot. I hooked my hand into my uniform, and made it into the water. I'd no idea where Bobby was, and I'd not seen dad all day.

"I saw someone, it might have been Bobby, clambering into what looked like a cabin cruiser," he went on, "the sort we used to see on the river at Radley, but I was too far away to keep up with him. The boat was very overloaded as it was, and it turned and chugged away. The next chance came with another little boat, a small passenger ferry from Poole."

"By this time I was covered in the stinking diesel oil. God knows where so much came from, but it was foul. I couldn't climb onto the Poole boat, but a couple of chaps dragged me into it. God knows how many of us were in the boat, it could have been fifty or sixty. We were low in the water and I thought we might sink. The engine struggled and we made it out to deeper water and a British frigate."

"Getting on the navy boat was hard, but the sailors dragged us up, regardless of how filthy and stinking we were. I was taken to a kind of sick bay, which was crowded with blokes with all kinds of injuries, and some who'd taken in too much sea water. I can't tell you how hellish it was in that room, men groaning, one or two dying, and everyone in some kind of agony. The ship was so full of men, we'd no idea how many, hundreds, perhaps thousands."

"It was a retreat, not a bloody miracle as some say it was, but a total shambles. We were numb with the pain and the knowledge that we were running away. We'd no fire power left, nothing. The Hun had beaten us, and we were lucky to be alive. The trip back to Blighty seemed to take for ever, and now and again planes screamed overhead, firing at the poor buggers on the deck."

"When we pulled into a British port, we didn't know where we were at first, but amazing, there was a train waiting for us on the quayside. We staggered down the gangplank, and stood around drinking big mugs of tea. Those old ladies who made the tea, they must have wondered what was happening, this horde of weary, unwashed, stinking men, lurching from the ship towards them. But I can tell you, that tea tasted good."

Henry smiled. "We knew we were safe, and we climbed onto the train with no idea where it was going. We must have made the carriages disgusting sitting covered in all that filth. I can't tell you what it was like to arrive at Victoria. More tea ladies, and current buns! There were transports to take us back to barracks, and then at last, they took me into sickbay, unwrapped my bloody arm, cleaned me up and I was quickly into the operating theatre. By the time I got to Aldershot, my hand was numb and blue, and I wondered if I'd lose it, but it's still there. I have to wait a month, and then report back to the army hospital for them to take off the plaster and see what the damage is."

"Does it hurt?" asked Marjorie.

"Throbs a bit, and is bloody inconvenient, but I'll survive." Henry looked at the three women who were staring at him, and smiled. "You're all looking as if you've seen a ghost!"

"It feels bit like that," said Rosemary. "You really have come back from the dead."

"And what about you, Miss Vicky Jones? What have you to say?"

"I'm speechless," said Vicky. "I can't imagine what you've been through. Bobby didn't tell us much about what happened, although we knew it was terrible."

"The most terrible thing is dad," said Henry. "Knowing him, he'll have watched his men getting off the beach, and not saved himself until....."

".....until it was too late," said Marjorie. "That would have been what the Major would do."

The newspapers continued to carry stories of the 'little ships of Dunkirk', continuing the image of the whole retreat being somehow a victory achieved out of the jaws of defeat. Billy collected the smudged photographs of the little ships, and Mrs Thomas let him paste them on the bedroom wall.

"I bet it was fun sailing back from France," he said.

"I don't think so," said Mrs Thomas as she put them to bed. "I'm sure those soldiers were pleased to be escaping, but they were all very tired and hungry."

"Like me after playing out," said Billy.

"No, much more tired, and much hungrier, young man."

"When I grow up, I ain't gonna be a soldier, I'm gonna be a pilot, and learn to fly," said Billy.

"Then you must work hard at school, Billy, or you'll never be a pilot."

"I do work hard, mum, but sometimes it's boring."

"That Miss Jones is lovely," said Mrs Thomas. "I can't imagine being in her class is boring."

"She brought that soldier with a broken arm to school today," said Billy. "He didn't say much, but told us the same – work hard and grow up to be soldiers. He was one of them from Dunkirk. I wonder if he was in one of these boats in the photos?"

"Perhaps he was, Billy, perhaps he was. Now go to sleep. It's school tomorrow."

Billy hugged Golly and snuggled down. He liked having a mum.

"Henry Anderson-Grey came into school today," Edward said to Lizzie. "He's the son of the woman where Vicky Jones is lodging. Nice young man, had a very rough time, but wouldn't say much. When you asked him a question, he'd give a smile and say, 'official secrets, can't answer that'. Nasty break in his arm, hope it mends OK."

"He's expecting to go back to the army," said Molly. "I made him a cup of tea, and he said it was just as good as the mugs of tea they got at Folkestone."

Later the same evening the four were sitting as usual listening to the BBC. Alvar Lidell's familiar voice was reading the news, when they heard a distinctly unfamiliar tremor in his voice. "I have just been handed a news bulletin," he said. "The government has announced that earlier today Nazi troops entered Paris without a shot being fired. France has now officially fallen to the German invader. We go over to Downing Street for a message from the Prime Minister."

Addressing the nation, following the fall of France, Churchill's voice was grave: *"We shall defend our island, whatever the cost may be; we shall fight on the beaches, we shall fight on the landing grounds, we shall fight in the fields and in the streets, we shall fight in the hills; we shall never surrender."*

"I am thinking of tomorrow's newspapers," said Stanley. "Are we to see pictures of Herr Hitler at the Arc de Triomphe, and at the Eiffel Tower?"

"Perhaps we will," said Molly, "but he'll walk into Buckingham Palace over my dead body!"

The afternoon post produced a large brown envelope, with unfamiliar stamps, addressed to Marjorie. "Rosemary," she called, "come quickly, and see what this is with me. It's seems to be from Geneva." She opened the envelope with shaking hands. Inside was a thin envelope with her name, and the address of the Manse.

"Red Cross!" exclaimed Rosemary, "It's a Red Cross Letter."

Trembling, Marjorie slit open the thin blue envelope. "It's from the Major! He's alive!" Looking at the postmark, she went on, "or he was a month ago."

"Read it," said Rosemary.

"I can't, I'm shaking too much. You read it to me."

"I was taken prisoner on the beach at Dunkirk; now in POW camp near Dieppe. Hope to see you soon. Anthony."

"Is that all?" said Marjorie. "Here, let me see." Taking the brief note, she read it again.

"Look, there's something else," said Rosemary, returning to the bigger envelope. "It's a message from the Red Cross."

Pulling out the second sheet, Rosemary read that the Red Cross was supervising the treatment of prisoners of war throughout Europe, and that prisoners were allowed to send letters of no more than twenty-five words. 'Don't be upset if the message is brief,' said the note, 'but prisoners are strictly limited in what they write, and their letters are censored. You can write a short reply, again of no more than twenty-five words.' The note went on to say how to address replies to prisoners of war via the Red Cross Headquarters in Geneva.

Marjorie sat on the hall chair re-reading the brief letter, whilst Rosemary ran to the garden where Henry was enjoying the sun. "Henry, Henry, we've had a Red Cross letter. Your father's safe."

Henry jumped up, and ran to his mother. "Where is he?"

"In Dieppe, in a prisoner of war camp."

"Excellent," said Henry. "He'll escape, I'm sure. All officers are expected to try to escape, and Dieppe is right on the coast. You know him: he'll get out somehow and get a boat. Wow, good old dad!"

CHAPTER SEVEN

Lawrence Powell was an experienced teacher, much loved by his fourth year pupils, and unused to losing control of his class. It was thus a great shock when the entire room suddenly rushed to the windows and then out of the door. He could hardly blame them: the noise had been extraordinary.

Although they were quickly in the playground, there was nothing to be seen, but a distinct exhaust smell lingered in the air. "Planes, sir," said the class, "loads of them, really low."

Billy McCann, in Vicky's class, had been staring out of the window as usual, and seen what had flown over.

"Miss, look, look," he'd shouted out, making the entire sleepy class jump, "look at all them planes!"

The noise of the fourth years rushing out into the yard had further disrupted the whole school, but slowly order was restored. Lawrence shepherded his flock back into their room, but all chance of returning to a lesson about the Vikings was lost.

"My dad says there's a really big RAF base at Rissington," said one boy.

"Yes," said another, "and something's going on."

"What do you think it is?" said Lawrence.

"My mum said, 'with Hitler and his army conquering France, it won't be long before they come over here'," said someone else. "That's our planes getting ready to defend us."

In Vicky's class there was a younger view of events. "That's our boys going out to get Germans."

"Rat-a-tat-tat!" said Billy. "We'll soon see them killing the Huns!"

Henry had been in the garden. With the heavy and awkward plaster cast on his arm, he was restricted in what he could do, and had spent a lot of time reading in a deckchair. He looked up at the aircraft noise, and was astonished to see the sky momentarily filled with small planes.

"Spitfires," he told Rosemary later. "I think they were delivering them from the factory to Rissington. Something's happening."

"How many planes was it?" Rosemary had run outside and seen the last disappearing south.

"Hard to say," said Henry. "Thirty? Perhaps forty? Seems a lot, but we're going to need more than that to make any progress in this war."

Molly and Lizzie had been into Banbury, and were waiting for the return bus when the phalanx of planes had roared over.

"They were low," said Molly.

"Just taken off, I expect," said Lizzie. "There's a factory on the edge of Banbury where they make Spitfires. I suppose they have to deliver them to the airfields for the boys to fly them."

"Ever since Dunkirk, I've been on edge, waiting for something to happen," said Molly.

"We all have been," said Lizzie. "They must be scared to death on the south coast. They say Hitler can see Dover from the cliffs at Boulogne. They'll be an invasion any day now, heaven help us."

"That's what I'm gonna do," said Billy. "Fly one of them Spitfires. How old d'you have to be to join the RAF?"

"Seventeen or eighteen," said Mrs Thomas. "You've got quite a long time before you're big enough."

Billy counted on his fingers: "Nine years? I can't wait that long. Why, the war might be finished."

"I hope it is," said Mrs Thomas.

"I'm gonna eat loads of carrots, mum, so I get twenty-twenty vision. Miss Jones says you've got to have good eyes to be a pilot, and carrots are good for your peepers."

Henry came away from the telephone confirming that he would be going back to barracks the next day. The doctors were hopeful that they could put a smaller, lighter cast on his arm, and he could resume some duties at Aldershot. He'd been able to speak briefly to Bobby, who'd agreed that 'something was happening', but he still didn't know what.

The radio that evening announced that the Germans had attempted a bombing raid in South Wales, and there had been some damage. The population were warned about further attacks, and to ensure their air-raid shelters were fully equipped and stocked, as they may need them soon.

The next day the newspapers covered the Welsh bombing raid, but it had not been too serious. They also reported that the Luftwaffe had attacked ships in the English Channel.

"This is it," said Marjorie. "it's started."

"I'll try and phone from Aldershot," said Henry as he was leaving, "but I can't promise."

"South Wales?" said Vicki. "I thought they said the first bombs would be Silvertown."

She and Lawrence were in their usual position on the playground, enjoying the summer sun, in the last few days of the summer term.

"I'm going to go and see my parents," said Lawrence, "but I'll come back to Chippy. They live in Coventry, and they've been told to expect air-raids there. So far it's been peaceful, although they've had the blackout every night."

"I'll go down and see Mrs M," said Vicky, "stay a few days I suppose, but I'll come back as well. There's quite a few kids staying here during the holidays, and it would be good to be around."

"And who knows," said Lawrence, "It might be Silvertown next. Billy McCann, don't do that."

"It's so peaceful here in the Cotswolds," said Vicky. "Most of the time you'd never know there was a war on. The children seem to be very happy."

"Have you heard the rhymes they chant when they're skipping?" said Lawrence. "I held the end of the long rope yesterday, and could hardly believe my ears."

"You mean the Littler-Hitler one? Those girls in your class are singing it now."

"Who is this geyser Hitler? We don't want 'im here.

If he were any littler, he would disappear.

Like goosey-goosey gander, he's climbing up the stairs.

If he goes any 'igher, he'll meet the Rooshan bears.

One, two, three, four, bang, bang, bang, the door, and you're out!"

"Wherever did they get that from?" said Lawrence.

Later in the staffroom, the staff talked about their summer holiday plans. It seemed everyone was heading home, mainly to parents, but intended to return to Chipping Norton during the summer to help keep an eye on the Silvertown kids who were still with their evacuation hosts.

Stanley and Molly were heading for Tenterden in Kent. "I didn't know you come from there," exclaimed Vicky. "I always thought you were East Enders."

Molly smiled. "Stan and I are both proper East Enders, but when my dad retired a couple of years ago, my parents decided to move out of London, and now live in Tenterden. I know it sounds posh, but it isn't really."

"It is a bit," grinned Stanley, "but they like it there. It's very peaceful after a lifetime in London."

"How do you get there?" asked Lawrence.

"It's quite easy: a train from Charing Cross to a place called Headcorn, then change onto a little branch line to Tenterden. Mum and dad rent a house on the road from the station up to the market. It's very rural."

A few parents arrived to take their children home to Silvertown when the school broke up for the summer holiday, but most just visited, and left their children in the country.

"After all," said one, "now Hitler's watching us from France, anything could happen. He's had a go at Wales, so next time it could be us. We've spent many nights in the air-raid shelter, and it's not very nice. The kids are far better off in the country."

Coventry was peaceful, and Lawrence returned reassured that his parents would be safe there; Vicky had a few very unpleasant nights in the shelter in Mrs M's street, and was relieved to return to The Manse; and Molly and Stanley settled into the routine of sleepy life in Tenterden.

Of all the unlikely places, it was Tenterden which received the most unexpected blow. The siren had sounded, and they'd climbed down into Molly's parents'

Anderson, and tried to get comfortable. Suddenly the peace was shattered by multiple explosions.

"Whatever is going on?" said Molly.

"I think that's a bombing raid," said her mother. "Here? Of all places?"

The noise died down, but the all-clear was not sounded, and they realised they were going to spend the night in the shelter. Twice more in the night, just as they were fitfully dozing, came the thunderous sound of bombing. Twice more they shuddered in the tiny shelter, and hoped they'd survive the night.

In the early hours of the morning, the all-clear sounded, and they clambered out to find that the sun had already risen. Looking around, they were shocked to see that a house at the end of their street, near the station, had disappeared, collapsed into a heap of dusty rubble. A small crowd was gathering, and Stanley went to see if he could offer any help.

"They were in their shelter," he reported, "and they've survived; but they've lost everything except the clothes they're standing in."

"Poor souls," said Molly. "Is this what this war is coming to? Ordinary people seeing their homes destroyed, just like that?"

At that moment, a squadron of Spitfires raced over head.

"Spitfires," said Stanley, "like the ones based at Rissington, near us in Chipping Norton. I wonder what they're up to, heading towards the coast?"

High in the sky appeared a group of different planes. "Those aren't Spitfires," said Molly. "I can't identify them."

"Perhaps they're German planes," said Stanley.

The group of Spitfires came screaming back at a higher level, aiming straight into the cluster of unidentified planes, and the people of Tenterden could clearly hear the rattle of machine guns as the planes tore into one another.

"Oh my God," said Molly. "They're fighting one another. Oh those poor boys."

The aerial skirmishes were repeated day after day. It was a wonderful summer, with hot sunshine and clear blue skies, and it seemed beyond belief that overhead young men were trying to kill one another in their tiny war planes. Stanley had expected a week or two of peace with the elderly in-laws, but instead discovered he had a grandstand view of the war in the skies. The population of the small town took to watching the aerial dog fights, and small boys excelled at identifying the different aeroplanes taking part.

With the dog fights continuing overhead, the population had become used to burning planes plummeting out of the sky. Each time, they'd screw up their faces, put their fingers in their ears and hold their breath waiting for the 'crump' as the plane crashed. There was no celebration when a German plane crashed – the people watching knew another young man had died a horrible death, but there was a quiet acknowledgement that the RAF appeared to be winning the battles.

Molly's mother had started to volunteer at a big house called Kench Hill, on the outskirts of the town, which had previously been a maternity hospital, but was now being used as a convalescent home for the armed forces. One afternoon, she was sitting on a deckchair on the lawn talking to two of the recovering soldiers, remembering the horrors of the Dunkirk evacuation, when a dog fight came dangerously close to them. Squinting up into the blue, they watched as a Messerschmitt roared overhead, chasing a lone Hurricane. Suddenly the Hurricane turned back towards them. The Messerschmitt banked abruptly and opened fire and they watched with horror as the British plane burst into flames, and started to spiral down towards them.

Paralysed with horror, they watched as the plane crashed into the orchard of Kench Hill House. A huge plume of black smoke arose, and many of the staff, and some of the patients, rushed out to see what the dreadful noise had been.

In the town, Stanley had watched the same calamity. Turning to Molly, he said, "That's gone down very close to that place where your mother is working. We should go and see if she's alright."

They heard the bells of the fire engines rushing to Kench Hill, and they hurried out of the town towards the billowing smoke. They arrived to find that the fire engines had driven across the lawn, and had almost finished putting out the fire. They were damping down a number of bushes and small trees which had burned in the conflagration. Molly's mother and the two injured soldiers were still sitting in their deckchairs.

"Whatever are you doing sitting here?" said Molly.

"A plane just crashed in the orchard," said her mother. "We watched it."

"You just sat and watched it? Are you crazy? You shouldn't have stayed watching!"

"We've watched many of these so-called 'dog-fights', and we've never thought of the dangers to ourselves," said her mother. "We were mesmerised by the sight, and just stared. We couldn't move, and anyway, it was all over too quickly to take cover."

"I think you're lucky to be alive," said Stanley.

"We're lucky the house wasn't damaged, with the crash so close." Molly's mother started to shake a little. "I feel a bit shocked now, perhaps we can go inside and get a cup of tea."

"I think that would be a very good idea," said Molly, "and then you'd better come home with us."

Vicky had enjoyed a few peaceful days with Mrs M. She had disliked spending time in the ugly brick shelter that had been built in the street, but she'd been to several of the little local shops which knew her, and she'd met several parents of evacuated children, and been able to reassure them that their children were thriving. Mrs M had been delighted by the bag of vegetables that Vicky had brought from Rosemary, and Vicky had packed a bag of her things ready to take back to Chipping Norton.

The BBC broadcast the results of the fighting over Kent as if it was football results, telling listeners how many German planes had been shot down, and how few British planes had been lost.

"My headmaster and his wife are in Tenterden. I wonder if they're seeing any of this fighting in the sky?"

"Not very nice for them to go on a holiday, and find themselves in the front line of the fighting," said Mrs M.

"It's not really a holiday," said Vicky. "No-one's really having a holiday are they? They've gone to make sure her mum and dad are OK. They left Plaistow when her dad retired for a quiet life in the country."

"It's not a very quiet life now, is it?" said Mrs M. "Look at all these pictures in the paper."

Lawrence was having a similar conversation with his parents in Coventry.

"Just look at these photographs," he was saying, "in the paper. Such tiny planes in the sky. Since Dunkirk, it seems our only defence is these little fighter planes."

"There's been so much talk of bombing, and so many nights in the Anderson which were false alarms, it will be a relief when the real thing starts," said his father.

"I know it feels like that," replied Lawrence, "but when it comes, if it comes, it will be very frightening. The idea of spending the night in the shelter, with all hell letting lose above, fills me with horror. Are you sure you'll be safe here in Coventry?"

"We'll be out of harm's way here in Coventry," said his father. "It's not like in London, where the docks will be a target, or even places like South Wales which the damned Furher tried to bomb recently. We're inland, and away from danger. You wait and see: Coventry will be all right."

"I hope you're right," said Lawrence, with a sense of foreboding.

CHAPTER EIGHT

Marjorie and Rosemary were reading the papers, sitting in deckchairs on the lawn.

"I don't like the look of this," said Marjorie. "It seems we're relying on a small number of RAF personnel to stop an invasion. I'm sure the army will be champing at the bit to get involved. Hitler's standing on the French cliffs laughing at us, trying to stop him with a squadron of little fighter planes."

"Not if we win in the air," said Rosemary. "He'll not invade if we show him we're superior in the air."

"Let us hope to God those boys in the Air Force know what they're doing."

Billy McCann was having the time of his life. No school, and endless days of tree climbing, and building dens, and learning what to eat from the hedgerows. Mike was not as adventurous, but knew just where to find wild plums, and hazelnuts, and fat blackberries. One day, high in an old oak tree near the common, Billy shouted,

"I can see into the garden where that posh woman lives, you know the 'ouse where Miss Jones lives."

"Come down," said Mike, "you're too high."

"Come up," called Billy, "you can see the whole world."

"Come down," shouted Mike again.

"You sound just like mum!" laughed Billy, but the next thing he knew was a sudden cracking, as he slipped and fell, bouncing against lower branches, and landing with a thump on the grass.

Mike stared in dismay. "Billy! Are you OK? Are you dead?"

Billy opened one eye and grinned. "I meant to do that," he lied.

"No you didn't," said Mike. "You fell. And you've ripped your shirt. Mum's not going to be very happy about that."

When Lawrence and Vicky returned from their trips, they were pleased to receive an invitation to tea with Edward and Lizzie Harding. They arrived together, and were delighted to see the tea things ready in the garden. Stanley and Edward had carried the dining room table and chairs out to the lawn, and Lizzie and Molly had baked scones and cake.

"Make the most of it," said Lizzie. "With more and more rationing, it will get hard to make a tea like this."

"It's funny, isn't it, "said Molly. "Living in the country, some things are plentiful, especially with what you can grow in your garden; but other things like flour and sugar are getting very scarce."

"Londoners have started to dig up the parks and plant vegetables," said Stanley. "That's the only way they'll get enough to eat."

Vicky told them that the East End was still living in a strange limbo, waiting for something to happen. She described the big communal air raid shelter built in Mrs M's street. "Very smelly, with all those people, and very hard to get any sleep; and that was without any enemy action."

"My parent's Anderson wasn't very nice either," said Lawrence, "but they don't expect the war to go to Coventry, so they're hoping for the best. Their Anderson is just like yours," he continued, "quite crowded with three of us; it must be difficult with all four of you in yours."

Vicky suddenly looked at Molly. "I've just realised that you went to see your mother and father in Kent. Did you see anything of these dog-fights in the sky we've been hearing about?"

Molly nodded and looked serious as she said, "We saw too much. Let me tell you what happened."

"My arm hurts," said Billy that evening. "It's gone all stiff."

"Let me see," said Mrs Thomas.

"It hurts when you touch it, and it's sort of puffed-up."

"It's down to the cottage hospital for you, my boy. You did something to it when you fell out of that tree."

"I don't want to go to no 'ospital," said Billy. "I 'ate 'ospitals."

"But you have to go to see what's wrong with your wrist, darling. They'll make it better."

"No they won't, they'll make it worse."

"Why do you say that, Billy?" said Mrs Thomas. "They're there to make you better."

"My mum died in an 'ospital. You die if you go there. I ain't going."

"This is different," said Mrs Thomas, desperately trying to think of the right thing to say. "Ours is only a little hospital, called a cottage hospital, and they only do things to make people better. And when you come home, you might have your arm in a sling, like a proper soldier."

Billy's resistance started to crumble. "Are you sure? Promise? Like a soldier?"

"Promise, Billy. Now come on, soldier, let's get you sorted out."

Lizzie and Molly were checking the Anderson shelter. "We must change the water more often," said Lizzie. "Even if we don't drink it, the day might come when we'll need it, and we don't want to find it's gone horrible."

"And the matches," said Molly. "It's always a bit damp, even during these dry summer days. We want matches that will strike when we need them."

"I don't like it in the shelter," said Lizzie. "We sit there, and it's quiet and peaceful, but I keep imagining what it would be like with planes overhead and bombing."

"I can tell you from the plane crash in Tenterden," said Molly, "that the noises of war are terrible, and we only saw one crash. I think it's the noise which makes it so frightening."

"Let us hope, here in Chippy, we never have to endure a raid," said Lizzie.

"Thank goodness the news is a bit more positive," said Molly. "It seems those dreadful dog fights over Kent have done the trick. The BBC says that Hitler has hesitated. There's not been an invasion."

"Yet," added Lizzie ominously.

Stanley peered apprehensively at the letter. It had been rare to receive anything posted in Plaistow, and he had a premonition that this was going to contain bad news. He recognised the handwriting, but for a moment could not think whose it was. He slit the envelope, and pulled out a single sheet of paper. Glancing at the end, he saw it was from his young staff member, Eric. He read:

Dear Mr Wykes,

I regret to have to tell you some very sad news. Our dear colleague Frank is dead. He was excited to join the Royal Air Force, and the last I heard from him was that he'd completed twenty-one flights over Kent and the Channel, fighting in the Battle of Britain. I have just heard, quite by chance, that he didn't return from his twenty-second flight. As far as I can tell, he was shot down over the channel, so lies at peace in the depths of the sea.

It's hell here in Silvertown, and I hate being the ARP Warden, but I am safe and surviving. I did not realise how much I would be upset by losing Frank. I am so sorry that you will have to tell the rest of the staff. Pleased tell them I love them all.

Yours in sadness, Eric.

Edward walked into the small office shared by the two headmasters. "Are you alright?" he asked.

"No," said Stanley. "I've just read a letter giving me the worst possible news. I don't know how to tell the others. Here, you read it."

Edward read Eric's letter, and turned. "I'm so sorry."

Stanley looked at him. "And to think I was in Tenterden just a few weeks ago. Molly and I watched the dog fights in the sky. We'd no idea Frank was up there. It was bad enough to watch, and Molly's parents were very close to a British plane crashing. Oh, Edward, this war is terrible. We have a staff meeting tomorrow and the new term opens next week. What a dreadful piece of news to tell everyone."

The staff was numb from the shock of Frank's death, as they approached the new term at the school. The Battle of Britain was reported as a great success, but it didn't feel like that to the teachers. Little did they realise that worse was to come.

The headline left no doubt about what had happened. The Express stated blankly, "Blitz bombing of London goes on all night."

The school had opened for the Autumn Term just a few days earlier. Despite the devastating news of the death of Frank, Stanley was pleased to see so many children arrive: a lot of the parents who had taken their children back to London earlier in the year, had taken the government's advice and sent them back to the country. The children were buzzing with stories about the Battle of Britain, as the aerial dog-fights over Kent had become known.

With great difficulty, Stanley had talked to the assembled children at their first assembly. They listened with rapt attention when Stanley started by welcoming them back, but then he told them that one of their teachers had been killed in the Battle of Britain. There was a profound silence even amongst the youngest children as they heard the dreadful news.

Stanley also spoke about his and Molly's experiences in Tenterden. He tried to bring a note of compassion into what he said, reminding the children that a life was lost every time a plane was shot down. He told them that both British lives and German lives were precious, but the message fell on deaf ears. The children, both boys and girls, had seen the dog-fights as exciting, and had cheered when a German fighter was lost.

The first few days of the term passed quietly, with the children pleased to see old friends, and exchange war stories. Billy tried to persuade everyone that he'd broken his wrist in a dog-fight over Kent, but no-one was fooled. "I bet you fell out of a tree!" was the usual response. Nevertheless, he was very proud of the plaster cast, which had not stayed white for very long; and although the sling was a badge of honour for a while, "Just like that soldier who came 'ere miss," he soon discarded it when rushing around in the playground, or once more up a tree.

The storm broke at the weekend. The three women, sitting listening as usual to the BBC, were startled to hear the first report of the bombing of the East End, and felt very uneasy when they went to bed. Sunday brought alarming news on the radio, but it was Monday before the true horror of the night was reported in the newspapers.

Vicky held the newspaper with trembling hands. There was no mistaking the photograph which dominated the front page: the Pig and Whistle, the local public house near to Mrs M's, where she lived. The remains of the pub were on fire, but worse showed behind it – a scene of devastation: most of the street obliterated.

Vicky had bought the Express on the way to school, and was in the playground, as usual, with Lawrence supervising the Silvertown children before their lessons began. "Blitz bombing of London goes on all night," she read again. "That's the pub at the end of the road where I live," she told Lawrence, "and Mrs M's house is just down there."

It was difficult for Lawrence to know what to say. The photograph showed complete devastation – it appeared that there was very little left of the houses in the street, and the vague reports of some deaths were very chilling. "I'm still upset by Frank's death," he said, "and now this. It doesn't look good."

"I should go down as see if Mrs M's alright," said Vicky.

"No," replied Lawrence. "The BBC says the raids are coming every night; you'd just be walking into the most dangerous place, and we need you here with the kids. We must stick together to cope with losing Frank. You must not put yourself into unnecessary danger. Some of our children will have lost their homes, and perhaps their parents, who knows? They will need us even more. I think the news will be slow to filter through."

"It's pretty clear what's happened," said Vicky.

"Yes, but we need the details. We need to know exactly which houses are lost, if anyone's been killed, and who's survived. We could ask Stan to phone the town hall, or police, or someone: I'm not sure who."

Lizzie could play the piano, but not very well. She was, however, the only person around to help with some singing, and Edward had brought her into the school once a week to play for the children's singing. The repertoire was very limited, and old-fashioned, with the children learning songs like 'The Lass of Richmond Hill'.

Music at Silvertown School was equally limited. Stanley had got Molly to help with some unaccompanied songs, using her background from being in the Girl Guides. Lawrence had been a Boy Scout, but his repertoire was also limited, and similar to Molly's. Thus the school had developed a bizarre stock of songs, mainly of the 'Ging-gang-gooly' type.

Thankfully, there was one kind of singing which both schools relished, which Vicky particularly loved, and which Lizzie could roughly master on the piano: the patriotic songs of Vera Lynn. Lizzie had been into

Oxford and bought a book with simple piano versions of several of Vera's songs, and had been working hard to play them. Vicky took the lead, bringing both schools together, squeezed into the St Mary's assembly hall. Lizzie sat at the piano, and nervously started 'There'll Always be an England."

To the delighted astonishment of the teachers, the entire gathering of children started to sing, gingerly at first, but with Vicky's encouragement with growing enthusiasm. They didn't all know the words all the way through, and after a while the song faltered. Vicky, continued to sing, her clear soprano ringing out, full of the emotion contained in the song. She was singing for Frank, and all the airmen, and her eyes filled with tears. When they reached the end, the children clapped.

"No, no," said Vicky, "don't clap me. I want you all to sing, all the words. Now Mrs Harding, let's start again, and see how far we can go without help."

After several false starts, and stops, when Vicky helped with the words, the children seemed to know the song quite well. Vicky turned to Lizzie, leaned close over the piano and whispered, "This is harder than I expected, I keep thinking of Frank." She took a breath, turned to the children, and managed a smile. "OK, one more time, all the way through."

"Wait a minute," said Lawrence. "I think it would be better if everyone stood up."

With all the windows open for the hot Indian summer, the lusty singing rang out into the Chipping Norton air.

I give you a toast Ladies and Gentlemen,

I give you a toast Ladies and Gentlemen,

May this fair land we love so well in dignity and freedom dwell.

While worlds may change and go awry,

There'll always be an England, while there's a country lane,

Wherever there's a cottage small beside a field of grain,

There'll always be an England, while there's a busy street,

Wherever there's a turning wheel, a million marching feet.

Red, white and blue, what does it mean to you?

Surely you're proud, shout it a-loud, Britons awake!

The Empire too, we can depend on you,

Freedom remains, these are the chains, nothing can break.

There'll always be an England, and England shall be free,

If England means as much to you as England means to me!

It was completely by chance that Rosemary happened to be passing the school at that moment, and suddenly there was a deluge of singing. She stopped to listen. Music was pouring from every window of the school.

Whilst the combined schools were singing, Stanley had been making telephone calls. He finally got through to the Town Clerk at Plaistow Town Hall. The connection was very slow, and when he did get through, he found it hard to hear what was said. There had been several deaths in Silvertown, and many homes destroyed. The situation was chaotic. The Saturday night raid had been a terrible shock, and had been followed by an equally horrific raid on Sunday night. "We'd not cleared up from Saturday, when nightfall brought more bombs on Sunday," said the Town Clerk. "Heaven help us if they come again tonight."

"Do you have any names of the injured or killed?" asked Stanley fearfully.

"We can't give names until we've identified the victims and informed their next of kin."

"But I've got nearly two hundred children, evacuated here, who might be the next of kin," said Stanley.

"I understand," said the Town Clerk. "Once the picture is clearer, I'll try to get a list of names to you. I promise I will telephone, if I can, but it may not be for a few days, everything is so confused."

"There's a telegram for you," said Marjorie as Vicky walked through the door. The young teacher's ebullient mood vanished. "It came just half an hour ago."

Rosemary watched from the kitchen door, and even Buster sensed the seriousness of the occasion and sat quietly.

Shakily, Vicky opened the tiny envelope, and pulled out the message. *'Terrible here – stop – I'm OK – stop – house lost – stop – will write – stop – MrsM.'*

Vicky sank into the hall chair. "Thank God she's alive."

"It's quite a shock, isn't it?" said Marjorie. "Rosemary, I think we need a cup of tea."

Later, sitting at the kitchen table with the tea, Vicky said, "I feel so helpless. I wondered if I should go and see if I can help, but everyone at school said it's my job to look after the children here. They're right, of course, but it's the not knowing. Thankfully Mrs M's alright, but what about the others?"

"And only an hour ago, there was all that wonderful singing," said Rosemary.

"How do you know about that?" said Vicky.

"I was passing the school. The sound was wonderful."

"I wonder how many of our kids, singing with such pleasure and full of life, and happy, are actually orphans, and they don't know it?" said Vicky.

Edward and Stanley sat late in the office they shared.

"Staring at the phone won't make it ring," said Edward.

"I know," said Stanley, "but I feel a heavy burden. I've brought all these children out here to the country to save their lives; but their parents remained behind to face unknown terrors."

"And now we know what those terrors are," said Edward, "or at least we know about them, even if we are lucky enough not to have that dreadful experience. We should go home, and listen to the BBC."

"And go home to congratulate Lizzie. The singing this afternoon was wonderful, and Lizzie did a good job on the piano."

"Your Vicky did pretty well leading the singing," said Edward. "How ironic that at such a time of fearfulness, our two schools should unite so well in singing together."

Mr and Mrs Thomas were taken aback. As usual during supper, they had the BBC on, and were listening to one of the many patriotic music programmes. When Vera Lynn came on to sing 'There'll always be an England', Billy and Mike leapt to their feet in mid-mouthful, and joined in very loudly with 'I give you a toast, ladies and gentlemen', and continued to sing lustily all the way through the song.

At the end they collapsed in fits of giggles. "How do you know that so well?" said Mrs Thomas, smiling and clapping.

"We did it in school," said Mike.

"Both schools together, all crammed together in the hall. Miss Jones did it, with Mr Harding's wife playing the piano. Miss Jones can't 'arf sing! My dad said she used to sing down the Pig and Whistle, but I wasn't allowed to go in there."

After Vera Lynn, it was time for the early evening news.

"Here is the news, and this is Alvar Liddell reading it. Following the raids on London's docklands at the weekend, the Nazi bombers have returned this evening. Air raid warnings sounded throughout the London area around four o'clock this afternoon, and queues formed at the public shelters. With clear skies, and a bright full moon, the silver ribbon of the River Thames is leading the Nazi hordes directly into the centre of the city. A particular focus seems once more to be the docklands and the area known as Silvertown."

"Turn it off, father," said Mrs Thomas. "We'll listen again later, but we don't want the boys hearing that."

Mrs Thomas had spoken too late. "He just said Silvertown, didn't he?" said Billy. "That's where me dad is. Is 'e gonna be OK?"

"I'm sure he will be, Billy. Now finish you tea, and let's get you into bed.

Later Mrs Thomas peeped into the boys' bedroom. Mike was obviously asleep, but Billy was talking quietly to Golly. "The Nazi hordes and the silver ribbon: bloody 'ell, Golly, dad'ud better be careful." Suddenly he shouted out, "Dad! Dad! Don't let 'em get you!"

Mrs Thomas tiptoed into the room and leaned over Billy. "Golly says, 'Dad's OK, Billy'. Now try to go to sleep."

"Mum?" said Billy. "Will he be OK?"

"I'm sure your dad knows how to look after himself, Billy. Now go to sleep."

"Where's Miss Jones?" said Marjorie. "She should have had her supper by now, and joined us in the parlour. She's usually very attentive to the evening news, but she's not here."

"I'll go and see if she's had her supper," said Rosemary.

At first Rosemary could not see where Vicky was in the kitchen. The remains of her supper were on the table, but she was not sitting there. Rosemary looked around, and heard a very soft sighing. Looking under the table, she found Vicky and Buster, curled up together.

"Whatever's the matter?" said Rosemary, kneeling.

"I can't stand it," said Vicky softly. "All these news bulletins reporting night after night of bombing, night after night of people's homes and lives being destroyed. I don't want to listen to any more of it."

"I know," said Rosemary. "It's hard for us all. But worse for you, knowing those streets, those homes, those people....."

Vicky smoothed Buster's warm coat. "How lovely to be a dog, with no worries, no cares, just a contented life." Vicky paused. "Do you think Buster could come and sleep on my bed, with me?"

"Certainly not!" came Marjorie's voice from the doorway. "Now pull yourself together young lady. You have responsibility for all those children: you can't afford to be sentimental."

"Actually, Buster often sleeps on my bed," said Rosemary, still kneeling on the floor. "I'd happily share him with Vicky."

"If you do, I'd rather not know about it," snapped Marjorie. "Now I'm returning to the parlour to listen to the BBC, and when you are ready you may join me."

For several days, Stanley had a sense of foreboding. His staff were keeping the children happy and working well in the classrooms, and they played joyfully in the play-ground; but with no message from Plaistow Town Clerk, he was left helplessly worrying who had been killed and injured, and which of his pupils was affected.

Vicky, Lawrence, and all of the staff were living a double life, jolly and enthusiastic with the children, worried sick away from the classroom. Each day that passed brought further horror stories as the relentless bombing of docklands extended over much of London.

A week after the London blitz started, the people of Chipping Norton were startled by an air-raid warning in their own small town. It was late evening, when they hurried into their Anderson shelters.

"Surely it's not coming here?" said Lizzie as they squashed into the Harding's shelter.

"Got the dog?" said Rosemary, as the residents of the Manse clambered down the steep steps into the cellar.

"Come on boys," said Mrs Thomas. "We're going to sleep in your den tonight."

"Under the stairs?" said Lawrence. "Is that all?"

The town held its collective breath, and waited in silence. Slowly, faint at first, came the distinctive rumble of heavy aircraft.

"Bombers," whispered Billy.

The noise grew and grew. It was clear that a very large number of big planes were rumbling overhear, frighteningly low.

"This is what they hear at home, before the bombs drop," said Vicky.

"But they're not dropping bombs," said Molly. "Just flying over us and onwards, north I think."

"North?" said Marjorie. "Birmingham or Coventry?"

The grotesque rumbling grew to a crescendo. Billy and Mike put their hands over their ears.

"I don't like it," wailed Mike.

"None of us do," said Mrs Thomas, "but they will pass."

And to the astonishment and relief of the town, they did pass, but the all-clear did not sound.

"Do we go back to bed?" said Edward.

"Not yet," said Stanley. "We must wait for the all-clear."

"What's going on?" said Rosemary. "Where have they gone?"

"North, as I said," said Marjorie. "Someone's getting it all tonight."

"I'm looking out," declared Edward. "It's quiet now."

The two headmasters stood together on the Harding's lawn. It was a clear, warm night, with a bright moon. "You can see for miles," said Stanley, "even though it's two in the morning."

"And the bombers could see for miles, as well," said Edward. "Oh, for a cloudy night."

As he spoke, a new distant rumbling started in the north. "They're coming back," said Stanley. "We should go back to the ladies."

The new sound was different. "They're higher," said Rosemary, "and lighter."

"They've dropped their loads. Someone, somewhere else, has suffered tonight," shuddered Vicky.

"Some poor blighters north of here have copped it tonight," said Stanley.

"Birmingham?" said Edward.

The BBC was more sombre than ever the next morning. "Last night, the Blitz came to Coventry."

CHAPTER NINE

As the children and their teachers arrived for school, Lawrence was in a considerable state of anxiety. "To think I thought they were safe," he said of his parents. "I didn't think Coventry would be a target. How stupid am I?"

"Have you heard anything from them?" asked Vicky.

Lawrence shook his head, and then looked up to the top of the tallest tree. "Billy McCann, be careful. Come down, you're far too high!" Turning to Vicky, he said, "Whatever happens in our lives, we've still got these kids to look after."

Billy scrambled down the tree, and ran across the yard to Vicky and Lawrence.

"Miss, from up there you can see all the way up to the big school, and they're building something real weird up there, and it looks like a zoo."

"A zoo, Billy? I don't think so. That's where the allotments are, where people grow vegetables," replied Vicky.

"But it's little huts and sort of cages, miss – real weird."

"Perhaps we'll find out after school, Billy. Now stay down from the trees: it will soon be time to go into school."

The strange developments near the Grammar School were forgotten, however, when Vicky got home to find a letter from Mrs M.

"Afternoon post again," said Marjorie. "Funny how important letters always arrive in the afternoon."

Vicky sat at the kitchen table to open the letter. She scanned through the three pages of neat handwriting, and then read it to Marjorie and Rosemary.

"Dear Vicky,

I hope you are well and surviving these difficult times. You'll be surprised that I'm writing to you sitting in your old classroom at Silvertown School. For the time being, this is where I am. We are suffering these God-awful raids every night, and spend the nights in the shelter, but during the day we come out and those with homes to go to, go home. They've opened the school for those of us with nowhere to go.

"The house was lost that very first night of the Blitz. I suppose some street had to be first, and it seems our street was. The siren sounded and we all went quite

calmly into the street shelter. I carried my little suitcase, and a big handbag, and we sat there in the dark listening to hell over our heads. It's like the worst kind of thunder, but it's non-stop. There's no breaks between the roaring barrage, just non-stop booming and crashing. You sit there as if the end of the world has come.

"That first morning, it was a Sunday, we got the all-clear just as dawn was breaking, and we staggered out of the shelter into bright sunlight. The sky was clear, as if no enemy had been near; but then we saw what had happened. The Pig and Whistle was still burning, and beyond it, our street was wrecked. I just stood there, kind of numb, holding my little suitcase and my handbag, and found tears were trickling down my face, although I didn't know I was crying.

"That nice teacher from your school, the one called Eric, who is now our ARP warden, found me and put his arm round me. I don't know how he knew my name, but he said, 'Come on Mrs M, we'll look after you.' and I let him lead me down the road.

"The house was gone. A great pile of bricks and dust and splintered wood, my bedroom curtains blowing in the breeze. When I packed my suitcase I looked at my best cut glass vase on the front room mantel, but I couldn't fit it in. It's gone now, of course. And across the road, there was a piano. It had been dragged out onto the pavement, and someone started to play 'roll out the barrel' but no-one joined in, and the piano player stopped.

"They got me to your old school. They'd painted a big red cross to show it was a kind of first aid post, but most of us were just bewildered old people. We didn't need sticking plaster, just a cup of tea, and somewhere to lie down. I just wanted to sleep, to shut my eyes, and pretend it hadn't happened. I don't remember what was next: I think I had a cuppa, then slept somewhere.

"When I woke up, the air-raid was sounding again, and we were shepherded back into the smelly shelter, and the noise started all over again. I think that second night, my mind was a bit clearer. 'I'm alive,' I said to myself, 'and not hurt. Pull yourself together, Gladys, and get on with it.'

"Monday morning, I went back to look at the house, but it wasn't safe to go climbing on the rubble, so I couldn't salvage anything. I stood in the street, and said goodbye to the poor old house, and walked to the school. I'm sorry, but all your stuff's gone too. There's nothing left. I hope you've got your precious things with you. I sit and look though my handbag. You remember there was some photos in frames in the front room? I took them out of the frames, and put them in my handbag. Thank God I did. It's all I've got left of my family.

"And here I am, sitting in your old classroom. I've got a sister in Chingford, married a publican, and I'm going there tomorrow. I've never written such a long letter in all my life, but there's not been anything else to do. I don't know what Chingford will be like, if they've got the bombing up there. I'll try and write again, when I get there.

"Yours truly, Gladys Merchant."

"I didn't even know her name was Gladys," said Vicky. "We don't know half it, out here in Chippy. Just think of it, night after night. We hear it on the BBC, but it takes a letter to really bring it home."

As usual, Marjorie allowed Buster to put his front paws up on the counter at the bank, so that he could pant at Robert.

"It's a prisoner of war camp," said Robert, when Marjorie quizzed him. "As your ARP Warden, I'm informed about developments which are supposed to be secrets, although everyone's talking about it."

"Prisoners of war?" said Marjorie. "That's the last thing we need. Isn't it bad enough to have all these East End urchins clogging up our streets, without a gathering of the enemy on our doorstep?"

"I don't think the children are really clogging up the streets, Mrs Anderson-Grey," said Robert, "and I understand it will be a fairly small prison camp, designated for Italians."

"And when they escape? Will we be safe in our beds? Remember my own husband is a prisoner of war in Germany, and it is his duty to escape. As a matter of fact, I expect him to walk though my front door any day now. Presumably these Italians will think the same."

"And are the German ladies safe in their beds when your husband escapes?" smiled Robert, becoming bolder with this line of conversation.

"My husband would not dream of anything untoward," said Mrs Anderson-Grey sharply. "He's made of stronger moral stuff than any German or Italian."

Robert could not be sure, but he thought Buster winked at him.

"There's so much happening," said Lizzie over supper. "It's hard to keep up with it all, even though we seem to be lucky here in the Cotswolds."

"What a job for the War Cabinet and Mr Churchill," said Molly, "so many dreadful issues to deal with, and on so many fronts."

"Lawrence hasn't heard anything from his parents," said Stanley. "He keeps telling everyone how much he feels a fool for thinking them safe in Coventry. Of course the big industrial places are in Hitler's sights, as they are all devoted to arms, guns, tanks, planes. The whole of industry is given over to the war effort."

"Vicky let us read her letter from her landlady," said Molly. "I met Mrs M once or twice. She came to the school when we had a jumble sale. I've never been to Chingford, but I'll bet it's very different from Plaistow. By the way, what do you know about this prison camp up by the Grammar School?"

Edward frowned. "Not much more than you do. I gather that there are small prisoner of war camps being built all over the country, and that the idea is to make each one house prisoners from a different country. Apparently, ours is to be Italian."

"I'm still waiting for more information from Plaistow. It's clear from the BBC that this dreadful bombing is going on night after night. I hope and pray that most people are safe in their shelters, or the big public ones, but I dread how many casualties there might be," said Stanley.

"It's the Anderson-Grey woman I feel sorry for," said Molly. "She's a snob, and not an easy woman, but there must be some feelings under that tough exterior. Vicky says that her husband is a prisoner of war, and she's got two boys, both in the army, and she's heard nothing from them for months. Apparently she believes that her husband will try to escape, and might show up at her front door any day."

"I bin up to see, Miss," said Billy, importantly. "It's a prison camp. Gonna be full of Eye-ties. What's them Miss?"

"Italians, Billy. It's not good to call them what you said, you must call them Italians."

"There's only a few of 'em. Young blokes, speaking a funny Eye-tie lingo."

"Italian language, Billy."

"Yes Miss, and one of 'em speaks English, although it sounds all funny. 'E said they ain't gonna escape 'cos they don't wanna go back to the fighting."

"I'm sure anyone would be pleased to avoid the fighting."

"I wouldn't be Miss, I'd wanna get back in there and give these Gerrys a good bashing! Wait a minute though, they ain't Gerrys, are they, so why are these Eye-ties enemies?"

"I showed you on the big map on the classroom wall. They're part of what's called the Axis, that's Germany, Italy and Japan. They're fighting together and they are all our enemies. When we get back to the classroom, we'll all look at the map again."

The air-raid siren sounded nightly in Chipping Norton. Robert Evans, the ARP warden would close the bank, and wait for the telephone call to sound the alarm. As dusk fell, he would collect his bicycle and set off round the deserted town. Occasionally he'd see a light showing, or a late pedestrian hurrying home to take shelter, but generally it was a lonely job. His tin hat felt heavy, and strangely unnecessary, and his gas mask in its little cardboard box would jolt against his knees. He'd pass the darkened Fox, and think longingly of a pint, but instead would pedal back to the bank, and sit gloomily in the vault, his personal air-raid shelter, with the door open so he'd hear the all-clear telephone call.

The ominous drone of the enemy bombers would grow nearer, and the startling racket of the ack-ack guns up by the Silent Woman would start. He'd rigged up a radio in the vault, and would listen to the sounds of the Blitz, first in London, and then Birmingham, Plymouth, Southampton, and Coventry again. In Chipping Norton he would hear the heavy planes with their lethal loads, grinding their way to the Midlands, and on the radio he'd hear the devastating noise of the bombs dropping, followed by the return of the planes with their higher, lighter sound. Witnessing this ghastly sequence, night after night, seemed to Robert to be standing on the sidelines of hell; and the ritual of his nightly chores stretched endlessly into the future.

Often he'd sound the all-clear at about four o'clock in the morning, after the last of the enemy planes had flown home, and the ack-ack guns silenced. He'd cycle the short distance to his cottage, and fall into bed for a couple of hours.

Sometimes Stanley and Molly wondered if it was even worth getting into bed. The precious time between the all-clear and the time to get up was often no more than two hours: and that was all the sleep they had.

"Hitler's worst weapon is to deprive us of sleep," said Molly. "I don't know how long we can go on with just a couple of hours a night." She smiled a grim smile. "But we will go on, and we'll never let him win. One day, when this is all over, we will sleep for a week!"

Buster had learned the sounds of the air-raid and all-clear siren; and was often the first at the cellar door when the air-raid sounded. Spending most of every night in the cellar, Rosemary had set up a bed for him, and added dog treats to the growing stock of supplies to get them through the night. The dog had also mastered getting back up the ladder-like steps when the all-clear sounded. With one bound he'd be up the steps and rushing to the kitchen, to bark at the last of the ack-ack guns.

Buster was not enjoying the war, since he took a very dim view of the vegetables he was given to eat. Marjorie would look at him as he sniffed and worried at the mess of carrots and potatoes Rosemary had cooked for him, hunting for the tiny scrap of horse meat hidden in the bowl. Marjorie would tell him to count his blessings. "Lots of other dogs, and cats, were put down because of the war, because there was nothing for them to eat. You're lucky we kept you."

It was in the autumn of 1940, that Marjorie finally received a letter from the Major, delivered via the Red Cross.

"It's November and I'm still alive, old girl, and still a prisoner. I sent you a message after the Dieppe Camp, that I escaped from, but was caught very quickly on the beach trying to find a boat. Then a long train journey, far away from the sea, to a camp near Nuremburg called 'Weiden'. Seemed to be no more than a farm they'd commandeered, way off the beaten track, and

not visited by the Red Cross – hence no letters. Easy to escape, just walked away when no-one was looking. Nice little Bavarian town. But I didn't get far. I was hanging around near the station wondering if there would be any trains, when I felt a gun in my back. I've learned to put my hands up to stay alive, and I was captured by some young boy with a nasty-looking ancient blunderbuss in his hands. So now I'm in Colditz, and the Red Cross is here, and apparently will deliver this letter to you. It seems this castle is reserved for officers. Chin up, Marjie, we'll win in the end even if it takes a very long time – we'll never be beaten."

"Chin up, Marjie!" laughed Vicky, joining in the general relief that the Major was at least alive.

Marjorie looked over the top of her reading glasses. "That's for the Major to say, not you, Victoria."

"But it's good news, isn't it? He is still alive."

"Where's Colditz?" said Rosemary.

"Never heard of it, said Marjorie. "I think this is one for Arthur Mee. Victoria, the boys' encyclopaedia is in your room. Could you go and fetch the volume for Colditz, and we'll see what it says."

"Look Miss, he give me a badge," said Billy.

"What do you mean, Billy?" said Vicky.

"One of them Eye-ties," said Billy impatiently. "I took 'im some apples from mum's garden, she said I could, and 'e give me this badge. They're just ordinary blokes, Miss, s'funny to think they's the enemy."

"Most of the men fighting are 'ordinary blokes', Billy, like you say. But we're at war, and in war, ordinary blokes kill ordinary blokes."

"They don't want to go back to the war," said Billy. "They said they're pleased they got captured and they're 'appy just to wait for the war to finish."

"Colditz Castle, it says here, is 'a Renaissance castle in the town of Colditz near Leipzig, Dresden and Chemnitz in the state of Saxony in Germany.' That's east of Berlin," said Vicky looking up from the encyclopaedia. "There's a photograph, although it's not a very good one. Looks a very big place."

"It's huge," said Rosemary, looking over Vicky's shoulder.

"I'm sure the Major will not be there long," declared Marjorie. "He's escaped from two other prisoner of war camps, he'll soon be out of this one. I understand that the Red Cross will deliver a letter from me, and also take a parcel. I wonder what he'd like me to send?"

"I expect he'd like some of the nice fresh things from the garden and orchard," said Rosemary, "but we don't know how long it will take for a parcel to get there. It would be terrible for him to open a parcel and find a lot of mouldy and shrivelled-up fruit and vegetables."

"You're right, Rosemary. We must send food that will travel well and keep in tins and jars. I'll look though the pantry. I'm sure we can find things he particularly likes."

"Pilchards!" said Rosemary. "They're in tins, and he always likes pilchards on toast when he comes home."

"Assuming they can have toast in that castle prison," said Vicky.

"Of course they'll have toast," said Marjorie. "He says it's a prison for officers, so of course they'll have toast. Mind you, although we'll send a parcel, I expect he'll be home by Christmas."

Billy knew he'd be in trouble, as he'd stayed out late, and it was getting dark. It was a Thursday evening in November. He'd wandered as far as the station, and was perched in a tree, curiously watching to see if any trains came. Just as he was turning to go home, he heard a train in the tunnel, and from his vantage point in the tree, saw it come thundering out of the tunnel. The tank engine and its three carriages came to a screeching stop, and just one lone figure alighted.

"Sir!" shouted Billy, "Sir, Sir!" and he scrambled down the tree as fast as he could.

Eric looked around to see where the boy's voice was coming from, and then he saw Billy running towards him.

"Sir! Wotcher doing 'ere? I thought you was in London."

"Billy McCann," laughed Eric, "of all the kids in the school, you're the one I meet."

"I'm probably the only one still out at this time of night," said Billy. "Wotcher doing 'ere?"

"I've come to see you and all the others," said Eric. "Perhaps we could start with Miss Jones. Apparently she's staying in a big house and I might be able to stay there."

"I'll take you there," said Billy. "It is a big 'ouse, biggest in the town. You 'ave to watch that one there, she's proper posh."

"You mean Mrs Anderson-Grey? I've heard about her," said Eric.

"It's just down this lane," said Billy. "Look, we go under this arch, Mr Powell lives there, and down this lane. You don't think it's spooky to go through the graveyard in the dark, do you?"

"No Billy, as long as you're not leading me up the garden path!"

"No, I'm taking you the proper way," said Billy, not understanding Eric's joke. "Look, it's there. Go and ring that bell. I must run 'ome, as I'm dead late. See you in school tomorrow, Sir," and with that Billy vanished.

It was already dark, when the front door bell jangled at The Manse. "Whoever could this be at this hour?" said Marjorie.

Getting up, Rosemary said, "If we don't go, we'll never know."

"She always says that," said Marjorie.

They listened, but could only work out that Rosemary seemed to be saying, "Yes," over and over again. After a moment or two, she returned to the parlour. "It's a friend of yours," she said to Vicky.

Vicky went into the hall. "Eric!" she exclaimed. "I never expected to see you here! Are you OK?"

"Vicky," said Eric, "It's so good to see you; and no, I'm not OK, but much better for seeing you."

"Come in and meet the others," said Vicky.

"Can I speak to you privately first?" said Eric.

"Yes, of course. Come into the kitchen. I'll make you a cup of tea."

Seated at the big kitchen table, Eric blurted out, "I've had some kind of nervous breakdown. I'm not really ill, or anything, but just need a few days to escape. The bombing seems to have stopped, at least for a while. Did you know we had fifty-seven nights, fifty-seven on the trot, night after night, with no let-up? I've been to hell and not really come back, we all have. Now it's stopped, I asked for leave. I can stay for a week if I can find somewhere to stay. Just to recover. Just to try and get some sanity back."

"You poor thing," said Vicky. "We've had air-raid alerts, lots of them, but that's because the bombers are going overheard to Birmingham and Coventry and other places. So far, no bomb has dropped on Chipping Norton."

"It just went on and on, night after night, and I didn't realise that I would miss Frank until he was gone. I miss him so much, and still can't believe he was shot down in his Spitfire. I had to carry on for all the people of Silvertown. People like your landlady, Mrs M, who lost everything, but it hit me hard when the bombing stopped, and I stopped sounding the air-raid siren. Frank's gone, and it was only by chance I found out."

Rosemary appeared in the doorway. "Would you like to come through to the parlour?"

Eric looked up. "I'm sorry, I'm being very rude. I should say hello properly. Are you Mrs Anderson-Grey?"

"No that's my sister. Come and meet her."

Marjorie was standing in front of the fireplace, and shook hands solemnly with Eric. "Victoria told us about you," she said. "We were so sorry to hear about the death of your colleague. The brave boys who died in the Battle of Britain will be remembered for ever more."

"I'm sorry to intrude at this time of the evening," said Eric, "but the train took far longer than I expected. At one stage, I thought we would be waiting in Oxford all night."

"How did you find the house in the blackout?" said Marjorie.

Eric smiled. "One of the children from school was train-spotting at the station, and he brought me here. It seemed he knew where Miss Jones lived."

"Billy!" laughed Vicky. "He's the only one likely to be out in the dark, and probably the only one who knows where I live."

"He was up a tree at the station, when he saw me and shouted at me. That was quite a shock: I didn't expect a voice to shout at me from the top of a tree, especially a voice I recognised. He showed me where Lawrence is lodging as well."

"There's nothing much escapes Billy," said Vicky. "Did he tell you they've only just taken the plaster cast off of his arm? He broke it falling out of a tree. Actually, he loves being here."

"Where are you staying, Eric?" asked Rosemary.

Eric looked helplessly at Vicky. "I haven't got anything arranged."

"Then, Marjorie, perhaps he could stay here. He could have Henry's room, couldn't he?" said Rosemary.

Marjorie had decided she liked Eric. He had a good home-counties accent, and seemed to be a well-mannered young man. She gave a hint of a smile. "Have you brought your ration book?" Eric nodded. "And it's for how long?"

"Only a week, Mrs Anderson-Grey. I must report back to the ARP post in a week."

"Then I think you can stay. Have you had any supper?"

"No, nothing since Paddington, ages ago."

"Then, Vicky must find you something from the pantry. I know: there are some very large potatoes and you could bake one for Eric, it won't take more than an hour in the Aga, and we might even find a tiny piece of cheese to go in it when it's done. Vicky, go and see to the potato, and Rosemary, take Eric to Henry's room. And, Vicky, be a love and make me a fresh cup of tea, would you. This one's gone cold."

In the hall, Rosemary and Vicky burst into giggles. "She called you Vicky!" said Rosemary.

"It won't last," said Vicky. "I'll be Victoria again tomorrow, you'll see."

"What's the joke?" said Eric.

"That's a long story," said Vicky.

The next morning, Vicky took Eric to school. Stanley and Molly were delighted to see him, and when he walked into the school assembly, the children clapped and cheered at the sight of their long-lost friend. Eric shook his head. "If only Frank was here to see all these smiling faces," he said quietly to Molly.

Later in the staffroom, he talked a little about the Blitz. "Your Mrs M was right in the thick of it. First street hit by a bombing raid, on the first night of the raids. The Pig and Whistle pub burned to the ground, and most of the street flattened. Your Mrs M was very shocked when I found her, just wandering about the street, and surprised that I knew who she was; but I recognised her from when she visited the school jumble sales. She's was one of the ones who I took to the school when her house was bombed."

"She wrote to me from the school," said Vicky.

"I know she did. I posted the letter for her. That's how I knew where you were. She wrote 'care of Mrs Anderson-Grey' on the envelope, and I couldn't forget a name like that."

"And Billy McCann was down at the station when you arrived?" said Lawrence.

"Yes, and very helpful he was too. It was just getting dark, and I'd no idea where to go. He took me to Mrs Anderson-Grey's front door, and then scarpered home."

Friday afternoon was the time for singing, and Lizzie had worked on a new song for the schools to learn: 'The white cliffs of Dover'. As with all the wartime songs, Vicky knew it well, and led the singing:

There'll be blue birds over the white cliffs of Dover,
Tomorrow, just you wait and see.

I'll never forget the people I met, braving those
angry skies.
I remember well as the shadows fell, the light of
hope in their eyes.

And though I'm far away, I still can hear them say:
Bombs up...but when the dawn comes up...

There'll be bluebirds over the white cliffs of Dover,
Tomorrow, just you wait and see.

There'll be love and laughter, and peace ever after,
Tomorrow, when the world is free.

The shepherd will tend his sheep, the valley will
bloom again,
And Jimmy will go to sleep in his own little room
again.

There'll be bluebirds over the white cliffs of Dover,
Tomorrow, just you wait and see.

Eric's emotions were in turmoil. He was delighted to hear the singing, with Vicky's brilliant voice leading the combined schools, and he was bowled over by the enthusiasm with which the children sang. At the same time, he couldn't get Frank out of his mind, and the singing brought him to tears. He fled to the staffroom, where Molly caught up with him.

"Have you cried since you knew Frank was gone?" she said.

Eric shook his head. "There was too much to do, what with the bombs and the air-raid siren, and keeping everyone blacked-out. I couldn't stop to think, and it was only when the bombing stopped, and for a moment all was quiet, that I felt so tearful."

"It's good to cry," said Molly.

"But I'm supposed to be a grown-up. I'm a teacher, and an ARP warden. I can't go blubbing like a little kid."

"No, you can't once you've started to get over it, but for the time being, you're missing your friend. We're all missing him, and we've all cried for Frank at some time."

"That song, of all to chose today: that was Frank, those lines 'never forget the people I met, braving those angry skies,' that was Frank." Eric looked up. "This bloody war," he said. "How long will we have to endure it?"

"As long as it takes to win," said Molly grimly. "As long as it takes."

Vicky took Eric back to the Manse for supper that evening. "It will be yet another variation on Lord Woolton's pie," she said, "but with a great big garden, we've a non-stop supply of vegetables, and thus much luckier than most people."

To Vicky's surprise, Rosemary had laid the dining room table for supper, and made a particular fuss of Eric.

"Just for tonight," she said, "to welcome this charming young man. Tomorrow it will be back to normal."

"I bet it's still Lord W's pie," said Vicky.

"I'm sure it will be lovely," said Eric. "A real treat after the stuff I've been managing at home."

"Tell us your story," said Marjorie. "You're not an East End boy, are you? Yet you are working in the same school as Victoria."

"Well," said Eric, "No, I'm not an East End boy: I was born in Guildford, and went to Guildford Grammar School. I decided to be a teacher whilst at school, and got very keen on working with the younger children, what we used to call prep-school children. I trained at Goldsmith's college, and did some work in the area there in South London, with some children from quite deprived homes, and got interested in working with kids like that, to see them do their best, and reach their potential. So I decided to work in the East End, and finished up at Silvertown School."

"Where you met me, and Frank and all the others," said Vicky.

"Yes, Frank was already there. He'd been there a couple of years before me, and was looking for someone to share his flat; I was looking for somewhere to live, so it was a great opportunity. We've been best friends ever since."

"How did you find out about Frank?" said Vicky.

"It was just chance really. After the school left on evacuation day, Frank and I went to the recruitment office in Stratford. We both applied to join the RAF, and quite quickly we were given medicals. It had not occurred to me that the rheumatic fever I'd had when I was fifteen would be a problem, but it was, and I was rejected, and immediately directed to join the ARP team. Frank was very excited, and was soon training on Spitfires."

"In fact, the training was very short, and I was shocked how quickly he was flying missions. I didn't hear much from him then: he was too busy to write, and we didn't have a telephone."

"The mail started to pile up, and I didn't know how to send it to him, so I found his parent's address and wrote to them. That's how I got the news, in a letter from his parents. You see, when he was killed, they sent a telegram to his parents; and that was all. If I'd not written to them about the letters piling up, I'd have still not known, and nor would any of us."

"That was hard for you," said Rosemary.

"Yes, but not as hard as enduring the Blitz. I try to stay calm. We lost some lovely men in the Battle of Britain, but not so many as the people we're losing in the blitz. And the nightly bombing and the feeling of helplessness sitting under the bombers as they rain down death and destruction, it's really dreadful."

"We must thank God that Hitler has not invaded," said Marjorie. "Your friend Frank, and all the other boys of the RAF gave everything to stop the invasion, and they succeeded."

"We don't understand what war is like until we meet it first hand," said Vicky. "Mrs M's letter told us more than the radio or newspapers, and seeing how it's affected you, and taken Frank away from us, brings it home to us all."

"I'm sorry to be so gloomy," said Eric.

"Not at all," said Marjorie. "We must all pull together and support one another. Now Rosemary, if I'm not mistaken, there's a bottle of sherry in the sideboard. I was saving it for Christmas, but it won't do any harm to open it early. Victoria, can you get some sherry glasses from the kitchen? Rosemary, have you found the sherry? Now, I propose a toast: to the memory of Frank."

"To the memory of Frank," they replied, and sipped the sweet liquid.

"He was a very good teacher," said Molly. "I went into his classroom a few times, and it was always a very happy place. The children loved him."

"Yes, he was good. They both were, he and Eric, and all of my team. I just pray that this war doesn't take anyone else away from us," said Stanley.

Edward looked at Molly and Stanley. "You know, it's been a rare experience for us. Little more than a year ago, we were strangers, thrown together by the most awful circumstances; and now we have become very good friends. Could we ever say that good can come out of war?"

"Good has come for us," said Molly, "but the price is too high. You are right, we have discovered two very good friends in you and Lizzie, friends we will never forget; but the price? Without this war, we would never have met you, but we would still have Frank, we wouldn't have children in our school who have lost parents or grandparents; we wouldn't have half the population terrorised by bombing and all the horrors of the Blitz."

"It's getting harder to make many of the things we like," said Rosemary. "The ration for butter is so small, and I can't make pastry at the moment. When they rationed biscuits, I thought, 'never mind, I can make very nice biscuits', but I can't. We're lucky with so much fruit and vegetables from the garden, but it's ages since I made an apple pie."

Eric was sitting in the kitchen watching Rosemary make the lunch. He had been amazed at the variety of produce growing in the garden, and Rosemary had proudly shown him the jars of jam and fruit lined up on the pantry shelves. He'd even recognised Vicky's handwriting.

"It is getting harder and harder to feed people in London. It's all very well for those who can afford it to go to restaurants, and thankfully we've now got a few affordable people's restaurants opening; but for most people it's a struggle. We used the school, our school, Silvertown, as a Red Cross centre, and it's still vital as a shelter for people bombed out in the area. Stan would be very surprised to see a huge red cross has been painted on the wall just beside his office window. People like Vicky's landlady, Mrs M, who lost everything, are given day-time shelter in the school, and we tried to open up the school kitchen and make school dinners for them; but we had little ingredients."

"We've a surplus growing in the garden. Even Marjorie is thinking we should sell some of it, but I'm inclined to give it away. When you go back, we'll definitely load you up with whatever you can carry." Rosemary looked out of the window as Mr Harper, the gardener, walked across the lawn with a basket of potatoes.

"You could put a table of surplus vegetables at the front gate," said Eric, "and just ask for voluntary donations."

"Marjorie wouldn't like that," said Rosemary.

"She would if it was for the Spitfire fund, or some other wartime charity."

"Which reminds me, we're supposed to be putting together a parcel for the Major. Apparently the Red Cross will deliver it to Colditz Castle, where they're holding the Major."

"So collect money for the Red Cross and for Spitfires from your surplus vegetables!"

Marjorie had sent Rosemary to the Co-operative Shop to beg for a box, and she had returned triumphant with a strong box which had once had a dozen bottle of Scotch in it. Mr Harper had brought a bundle of hay to pack around the various jars and tins which they assembled for the Major. As well as several tins of pilchards, they had some jars of home-made jam, some tinned ham, and some very small jars of meat-paste. They had giggled a little when Marjorie found a tin of caviar at the back of a cupboard, and imagined the inmates of the castle prison sharing it. "I don't know why that's funny," said Marjorie. "The men are all senior officers, so caviar will not be such a novelty – and it should cheer them up." She did, of course, remind them that the ever-resourceful Major "Will have escaped by now, and will walk through that door at any minute!"

Billy McCann was very intrigued by the small group of Italian prisoners of war. He visited them regularly and spoke to them through the barbed wire. "There's only a couple of old men guarding them," he told Mrs Thomas. "They could easily escape."

"Those men are not as old as you think, and they are members of the Home Guard," said Mrs Thomas. "I assume they have guns."

"They don't look very fierce," said Billy, "but the Eye-ties have said they don't want to escape. I wonder what it will be like for them at Christmas? We should give them Christmas presents as they are a long way away from home."

"They're prisoners because they are the enemy, Billy, they're not our friends."

"I'm going to ask in school about them. You never know what Miss Jones might think of."

"Oh well," said Lizzie, "we'll do our best for a Christmas lunch, but it won't be like last year. Plenty of vegetables and lots of potatoes, because they're all in the garden, but not much chance of a turkey, and no pudding."

"Why aren't there any turkeys?" said Molly. "Surely, Hitler's not got them all!"

"No," laughed Lizzie, "but the butcher at the Co-op says the shortage of stuff to feed the turkeys on, means there are very few available. It's like so many people killed their pets last year, thinking there would be no way for feeding them."

"Vicky says that Mrs Anderson-Grey's dog has become a vegetarian."

"I wonder what the dog thinks about that," said Lizzie.

"Better than being put to death," said Molly, "but it's not so bad if we have to have a chicken for Christmas. There seem to be a few local ones about."

"No," said Lizzie. "I've got a better plan, but I'm keeping it for a surprise in case it doesn't work."

"Miss Jones," said Billy, in his most wheedling way, "you know those Eye-ties up at the prison camp? There's only a few, and they're quite nice men, and they don't want to escape...."

"Yes, Billy, what about them?"

"Well you know we've been learning these Christmas Carols in school, and Mr Wykes says we're going to have a Carol Concert...."

"Go on Billy."

"Well," he paused and took a breath, "why not invite them to the concert. They'd like that."

"They're our enemies Billy, I'm not sure the people in the town would be very pleased to sing carols with the enemy. The concert's going to be in the Town Hall, with the Mayor and everybody. What would they think if a group of Italian enemies are allowed in?"

"Mum said the same, Miss Jones. She said they're our enemies, but you keep going on about 'goodwill to all men'. They're men, ain't they."

"I'll talk to Mr Wykes. Perhaps we'll talk about it at a staff meeting."

CHAPTER TEN

Marjorie was both delighted and crestfallen to receive a letter from Colditz Castle: pleased to hear from the Major; but disappointed that he was still there, and had not escaped.

"He says that it is the duty of every British prisoner of war to escape, but, *"This is Colditz. We've discovered that we have all been brought here because we've escaped from other prisoner of war camps, and have finished up here because the Nazis think it's impossible to escape. It certainly looks pretty tricky, and we are mightily challenged to think about an escape method. I won't say more, as I'm sure they read our letters before they give them to the Red Cross."*

"Our daily life is tolerable but very boring. The food is adequate, but also very boring. Now and again a Red Cross parcel arrives, and we share it between us, bringing great relief from the dreary fare. It surprises me that these parcels get through, and I'm looking forward to one from Chipping Norton."

"I've heard nothing of the boys. If you get news, please write to me. It will be a great relief to know they're safe."

"You may not hear from me again before Christmas, so I send my best wishes to you old girl, and to Rosemary, and that little teacher you've got there."

"If only," sighed Marjorie. "I wish I knew about the boys. This war seems to have spread all over the world: they could be anywhere."

"It's strange, isn't it," said Rosemary. "The Major is safe because he's locked up in a German castle. The Italians are safe in a make-shift prison camp up by the allotments. It's the ones not captured that are in the greatest danger."

"The boys will be doing their duty," said Marjorie, "and I daresay they're far too busy to write, but it would be a relief to hear from them, especially with Christmas coming."

"Speaking of Christmas and the Italians," said Vicky, "there's a great discussion going on at school at the moment. A group of the children want to invite the Italian prisoners of war to the carol concert in the Town Hall. We cannot decide if this is a goodwill gesture, or foolhardy, or even stupid."

"Good Lord!" exclaimed Marjorie. "You certainly know how to stir up trouble. I am sure the Mayor will have something to say about this, and Mr Evans our ARP warden."

"I think it's a remarkable idea," said Rosemary, "but I can't imagine that Mr Evans has anything to do with the decision. The Mayor will be the guest of honour, and I suppose it's his Town Hall, so perhaps he should be consulted, but it seems to me to be an extraordinary act of reconciliation."

"Reconciliation!" said Marjorie. "With the Major locked up in a Nazi castle, and the boys God knows where, you talk of reconciliation! If these enemies are invited to the carol concert, I certainly will not be going."

Lizzie knew that one of her neighbours was a beater at a local pheasant shoot, although she was unsure what time of year this happened. Without telling anyone else, she walked down the hill to Jacob Brown and knocked on his door.

"You're not the first," he smiled, "and I'll add you to the list. I can't promise, but what I get, I'll pass on."

How long is your list?" said Lizzie.

Jacob smiled again. "I'll not tell you, but I'll come knocking on your door a few days before Christmas, if I've got anything for you. If there's no sign of me by about the twentieth, it means I've not got enough and you're out of luck.

"Many thanks, Mr Brown," said Lizzie. "It would be wonderful if you did manage some for us."

"You know you'll have to pluck and pull the birds, don't you? They'll arrive just as they were shot."

"I've done it before," said Lizzie, "but it will be quite a shock for Mr and Mrs Wykes – I bet they've never plucked a bird in Silvertown."

The Town Council met in the council chamber at the Town Hall. Edward Harding, Stanley Wykes, and Marjorie Anderson-Grey were squeezed into the tiny space allotted for the public. Councillor Hannant, the Mayor, called the meeting to order, and announced that they would deal with a particularly controversial item first, before the usual business. Clearing his throat dramatically, the Mayor announced that he would read a letter received from the two head-masters who were in attendance:

"To the worshipful, the Mayor, dear sir,

"You will be aware that we have planned a large Christmas Carol event to be staged in the Town Hall including the children from both our own local school, Saint Mary's, and the evacuated school, Silvertown. It is now over a year since our two schools met to share our premises, and we have formed many close friendships. In particular, our children have enjoyed singing together and recently have been learning a number of Christmas Carols.

"A suggestion has been received from the children, that we invite the Italian internees from the prison camp on the edge of the town. Our joint staff have debated this issue and decided in a spirit of goodwill to

all men, that we would like to go ahead with the invitation. We are sure the Home Guard can provide sufficient security, and we are told that the Italians have no intention to try to escape.

"We emphasise that the suggestion has come from the children, and we believe it should be supported. Edward Harding and Stanley Wykes."

The Mayor paused and looked around the assembled councillors. "I was taught that this is the season of goodwill to all men," he said. "I am happy to support this invitation to the Italians, but I need to know that I am, in turn, supported by my fellow councillors."

The short debate was polite, punctuated by loud snorting from Marjorie when she disapproved of someone's point of view. The argument was evenly balanced until one of the councillors read a letter from his own son, who was currently in a prisoner of war camp. The son had written to his father that the camp was planning a Christmas Carol concert, and that all the nations represented in both prisoners and their guards, would be taking part. "It gives hope for the future," said the young soldier in his letter, "if we can all come together in this way."

Marjorie had a sudden thought. What if the Major had written a similar letter? What if Colditz Castle was holding a similar carol concert? How could she tell the Major that she'd opposed a similar event in Chipping Norton? She looked at the Mayor, who was summing up the discussion, and asking for a show of hands. The young soldier's letter had swayed the argument, and the town council unanimously agreed that the head masters could invite the Italians to the concert. Edward and Stanley shook hands, nodded to the Mayor, and left the chamber.

It was dusk as Marjorie walked slowly home down the Church Street hill. Soon the town would descend into the darkness of the blackout. Marjorie wondered how she would save face with Rosemary and Vicky.

When Molly opened the door for Edward and Stanley, she knew they had good news, and she called to Lizzie to join them. "And to think," said Stanley, "that this all came from a chance remark by Billy McCann."

"I've got a surprise as well," said Lizzie. "Come into the kitchen."

There on the table were four pheasants. "Two brace!" exclaimed Edward, "how amazing."

"We have to hang them until Christmas Eve, then pluck and draw them," said Lizzie.

"That will be .... er .... fun," said Molly, her eyes rolling.

"Well done Lizzie," said Edward. "We will have something special for Christmas, after all."

Although there were very few Christmas Cards in the shops – the only ones available being left over from previous years – a few started to arrive on doormats. One of the first was for Vicky, and she was very pleased to find enclosed a letter from Mrs M.

"Happy Christmas my dear Vicky", she wrote. *"Another Christmas at war, and we all hoped it would be over by now. This war seems to drag on and on, and there's not much good news."*

"I'm now living with my sister and her husband in their pub in Chingford. We still have to deal with the blackout and air-raids, but the bombing is not as intense as in the East End. Some nights we stand in the garden and watch the explosions and fires. It's terrible to think of the people still living there. I'm so thankful that you took all those kiddies to the country. No child should ever live through what is happening in London.

"I expect you saw in the paper that the John Lewis shop on Oxford Street was destroyed in September. There were many people sheltering in the basement, and thankfully they survived. The shop has re-opened in the basement, and on dry days, they sell what they can from trestle tables in the street. I went down to see it. The old store stands as a burnt out wreck and very sad it is to see. So many bomb sites, so many destroyed homes. Our beautiful city will never be the same again.

"I hope life is better for you in the country, and all those children are growing up healthy and fit, and not too frightened by this terrible war.

"Best wishes, Gladys Merchant"

"We don't know how lucky we are, living in this corner of England," said Rosemary.

"John Lewis in September, then that awful bombing of Coventry Cathedral in November," said Vicky. "It seems there is no end to the devastation this war will bring, so many cities being hit: Sheffield, Liverpool, no-one escapes."

"And it stretches before us, perhaps for years and years. We must make the most of this Christmas – it may be the last we ever have," said Rosemary.

"Nonsense, Rosemary, you lumpkin. With boys like Bobby and Henry, and all the thousands like them, we will never be defeated. Hitler may think he has the upper hand, but he will never be seen in our green and pleasant land."

A couple of days later, it was Marjorie's turn to find a letter on the doormat. She had just returned from a rather heated discussion at the butcher's shop, and found the envelope, delivered in the afternoon post. She slit it open impatiently with her paper knife, and found a home-made Christmas Card. She called to Rosemary to come quickly.

"It's from the boys," she exclaimed. "Listen."

"Dear Mother, we are both in Aldershot. Bobby has been on all kinds of ops, but they're secret, so we can't

tell you what. I, Henry, have been stuck here doing desk jobs as my smashed arm is still not quite right. Thank goodness it's my left hand that's affected and not my right. We'll tell you all kinds of stories when we see you, because <u>we're coming home for Christmas!</u> Love from Henry and Bobby."

"The boys are home for Christmas!" exclaimed Marjorie, "they underlined it! And I can't find a turkey."

"Where will they sleep?" asked Rosemary.

"Don't worry about that," said Marjorie. "We'll work our all the details, but the best news, is the boys coming home for Christmas. After all these months of hearing nothing, not knowing if they were alive or dead, they're coming home for Christmas!"

That evening they gathered round the radio as usual, but could not concentrate on the BBC, with discussion of the arrangements for Christmas.

"Now Victoria, we'll bring up the camp bed from the cellar and put you in here, so the boys can have their rooms," said Marjorie.

Rosemary interrupted. "No, that's not fair. Vicky's been with us for a long time, and got used to her own room. The boys can share Henry's room, like they did when they were little." Marjorie opened her mouth to speak, but Rosemary carried on. "I daresay they shared rooms at Sandhurst, and still do at the barracks, so it won't be a hardship."

Marjorie looked at the two women. "Very well," she sighed. "Victoria you may remain in Bobby's room, and Bobby will have the camp bed in Henry's room." She glared at Rosemary. "And if they don't like it, I'll blame you."

"I'm sure Bobby will be very happy to be here," said Vicky.

Rosemary turned to the other two with a serious look. "I've got a favour to ask," she said nervously. "I'd like to ask that nice ARP man, Eric, for Christmas. You remember the man who used to be one of your teachers, Vicky?"

"And one day, I hope, he will be back teaching Silvertown children again," said Vicky.

"Yes," said Rosemary. "He was so sad when he came before, and he liked being here. It would be a good gesture to ask him back."

"This is a little unexpected, Rosemary," said Marjorie, "but I don't see why not." Turning to Vicky, she went on "Would you be happy with Eric coming for Christmas?"

"Certainly," said Vicky. "He's a very nice man. He was very near some kind of breakdown when he was here before, and it would be good to bring him back at a time, we hope, of happiness."

"By the way," said Rosemary, "What did you mean about the turkey?"

"I talked about this with the butcher. I reminded him what loyal customers we've been for a very long time, and said even if he can't get turkeys for other people, he should jolly well get one for us."

"What did he say?"

"He told me there is a war on, as if I didn't know, impertinent man. I'm afraid I was rather cross with him after that, so you will have to go and buy the meat from now on, Rosemary."

"Not that there's much to get these days," said Rosemary, "with the rationing."

"I don't mind if you can't get a turkey," said Vicky.

"But I mind, especially now that we know the boys, and your friend Eric, will be here. I will have to think about it."

The BBC news programme had started on the radio, and Vicky was half-listening. "Stop, for a moment," she said, "and listen." The BBC was announcing the start of bombing raids over Germany.

"At last," said Marjorie, "giving them some of their own medicine."

"Where's Mannheim?" said Rosemary.

"South, I think," said Vicky, "not far from France. I suppose there must be factories or something there."

"Factories making tanks or weapons, I suppose," said Rosemary.

"Such good news," said Marjorie. "Perhaps the tide is turning."

Friday the twentieth was the last day of the school term. The children had enjoyed a Christmas party on Thursday, when Robert had once more been Father Christmas. The party food was mainly vegetables, but with Lizzie Harding working hard at the piano, they had sung lots of songs, and played many boisterous party games. On Friday morning they had a rehearsal in the Town Hall, and then returned to school to get ready for the evening performance of their Carol Concert.

It was already getting dark when the crocodile of children set off from the school. Stanley and Edward led the line, with Molly and Lizzie at the rear. "Just like the day we left Silvertown," said Molly. "Doesn't that seem a long time ago?"

At the Town Hall, the audience had started to arrive. They saw the small pen at the back of the hall reserved for the Italians: a dozen chairs were surrounded by a wire fence, rather like a chicken run, and a nervous member of the Home Guard stood restlessly holding his gun.

"Where's Billy McCann?" said Vicky.

"Isn't he with you?" said Lawrence.

"No," said Vicky, "I thought he was with you. It's not like him to miss something like this, and I know Mrs Thomas is going to be in the audience. There's Mike, I'll ask him where Billy is."

Mike grinned. "He made me swear I wouldn't tell."

"There's no time to go and look for him now," said Vicky. "We just have to hope for the best. I'll wait outside for him."

The children squeezed onto the small stage, with an overflow in front of it. Lizzie went to the piano, and arranged her music. She had never done anything like this before, and was trying not to show how anxious she felt. The hall was rapidly filling with parents and grandparents, and a buzz of anticipation filled the air.

Vicky was watching up the hill towards the Italian prison camp, when she heard the sound of marching boots. Around the corner of the Co-operative Store, came the small platoon of Italians. Marching in front was a Home Guard officer, and marching alongside him was a very proud Billy McCann, with his dad's air gun on his shoulder. Vicky shook her head, and stood to one side as the strange contingent mounted the steps.

There was a silence in the hall as the dozen men were shepherded into the cage at the back, where they sat. Vicky walked to the front of the children, and signalled to them stand up. She nodded to Lizzie, then turned to the audience and gave them a signal to stand. The Italians stood, unsure of what to expect.

Without any announcement, Lizzie played an introduction for "God Save the King", and the entire hall sang with fervour. At the end, the audience and the children applauded with enthusiasm. The Italians stood timidly and watched the patriotic British gathering.

Next the children sang: "Once in Royal David's city." After the first verse, Vicky signalled to the audience to join in. At first they sang quietly, but gradually the volume increased until the hall was filled with singing. The Italians looked at one another, and slowly began to smile. They did not know the English words, but could sing quietly in Italian.

After the opening carol, it was the Mayor's turn to speak:

"The Lady Mayoress and I are pleased to welcome the children and staff of Silvertown School to our Carol Concert for 1940. We also welcome the children, staff and parents of our own St Mary's School. We know that the children of both schools have been working hard to prepare for this evening. The town of Chipping Norton remains firm in its loyalty to the King and our country. I am also delighted to announce that at the end of the concert, there will be a collection at the door for the town's Spitfire Fund. We will all do our part to ensure we win this war. At this season of goodwill to all men, we also welcome the group of men from Italy, who are now living alongside us, in our community."

There was some scattered applause, although many in the audience remained unsure about these representatives of the enemy being in their midst at this time. The singing continued with several well-known carols, and in addition to carols for audience, the children sang "Jingle Bells" – working hard with all the words for the verses.

It was after "While shepherds watched their flocks by night", that Vicky nodded to the Italian prisoners in the cage at the back of the hall. Recognising their cue, the men stood and, unaccompanied, sang "Silent Night" in Italian.

"Astro del ciel, Pargol divin, mite Agnello Redentor."

Unexpectedly, many of the audience hummed the familiar tune as the Italians sang. The atmosphere in the Town Hall was hushed and calm. At the end of the singing, there was a scattering of applause.

During the carol, Lawrence had quietly gone to the piano, and as the applause died away, he nodded to Lizzie. In an abrupt change of mood, she played the introduction to "There'll always be an England," and in his clear tenor voice, Lawrence sang the opening line, "I give you a toast, ladies and gentlemen!"

Some of the children were tempted to join in, but nudged by others, kept quiet until the rousing chorus. Almost all of the audience sang the chorus as loudly as the children, bringing the concert to a noisy and rousing close.

The mayor and his wife rose and walked to the back of the hall, and as the Italians with their Home Guard escort left the cage, he shook hands with each of them.

"That was all very nice and sentimental," Marjorie said later at home, "but I remain unsure. I will write to the Major and see what he says."

"The children did very well," said Rosemary.

"I was very pleased with them," said Vicky, "and I had no idea Lawrence had such a nice voice. I think ending as we did with 'There'll always be' redressed the balance for those unsure about the Italians. When we go back to school after Christmas, I want to teach some more of Vera Lynn's songs, and other patriotic songs as well. I hope Lizzie can play 'Rule Britannia' as that will be excellent for the children to sing."

"So have you finished at school now for the Christmas holiday?" said Marjorie.

"Almost," said Vicky. "Staff are all going in on Monday to take down the Christmas decorations, such as they were. We don't like to take them down on the children's last day, as they are still looking forward to Christmas, but we don't want them up when we return for the new term in the new year; and then Tuesday will be Christmas Eve, and the holiday really starts."

Marjorie was determined that she would provide a tra-ditional Christmas lunch for her sons, as well as the others, and had decided against her better judgement that they should go to a restaurant on Christmas Day. She had considered both the Fox Inn and the Blue Boar, but shuddered at the thought of Christmas in a public house; so she visited the Crown and Cushion Hotel.

She interviewed the head waiter and inspected the restaurant. "We shall be a total of six on Christmas Day," she said, "and we want the best table in your restaurant."

"You may be happier in a private dining room," said the waiter, "as the main dining room will be quite busy. Everyone who can afford it, is escaping from the problems of rationing by eating in our restaurant. We have never been busier."

"I will be very happy with a private room," said Marjorie. "A little privacy and exclusivity will be welcome."

On Christmas Eve, Edward, Stanley, Lizzie and Molly sat in a circle in Lizzie's kitchen wearing aprons. Each had a pheasant on their lap. Edward took the lead, with Stanley trying hard to pretend he knew what he was doing, and Molly feeling faintly alarmed.

"The feathers come out very easily," said Edward, "and I expect you'll speed up as you go. We've spread this big table cloth on the floor, so you can just let the feathers fall to the floor. Now watch how I get started, then have a go."

Molly, despite feeling squeamish at first, soon mastered the technique, and feathers were flying in all directions from her bird. Stanley was much slower to understand what to do, and his bird became naked much more slowly. Eventually there was a huge pile of feathers on the floor, and four plucked pheasants lay on four dusty laps.

Molly had put her misgivings to one side, and decided she liked the experience. "I never thought I'd ever be a pheasant plucker!" she chuckled.

They bundled up the cloth with the feathers, and sat down again ready for the next stage.

"Now we must pull them," said Lizzie.

The smile vanished from Molly's face. "You mean, pull out the guts?" she said.

"Yes," said Lizzie. "You put your hand in, like this, and twist and pull." She demonstrated as she spoke and the birds innards came spilling out. "Don't forget we want to keep the liver, and heart. The liver will fry wonderfully for breakfast, and if you don't want to eat the heart, we'll give it to someone who will."

After much grunting, the four birds were pulled, and they faced the final horror: cutting off the heads and feet.

Rosemary had received a brief letter from Eric saying that he would apply for leave from his post as ARP warden and was extremely grateful for the invitation for Christmas. He aimed to arrive on Christmas Eve, and promised to phone from a call box at Paddington, if one was working, to tell them what time he'd arrive. Rosemary was downhearted that no call had come; but her mood changed abruptly when Eric himself pulled the brass handle of the front door bell.

Impetuously, Rosemary kissed him. "Happy Christmas!"

"Thank you for inviting me," said Eric. "It is very good to be away from the troubles of London, even though I can only stay for a couple of days. You have a lovely Christmas tree."

"My sister always puts the tree in the hall, she thinks it's welcoming to see it when you come in the front door. Thankfully our gardener was able to find a good tree this year, and the decorations have been in the family for years. Leave your bag in the hall, and come into the parlour: we're about to have tea."

Marjorie and Vicky had hardly greeted Eric, when there was another furious ringing of the door bell. "That will be the boys," said Marjorie. "They always swing on the bell pull like that." Rushing to open the door, they heard the noisy greetings as the two soldiers embraced their mother. "Here they are," she announced, and suddenly the parlour seemed very full of excited people.

Bobby picked up Vicky and twirled her around. "Hello, my little Auntie Vicky," he said, "Happy Christmas!"

"Bobby," she replied, "how lovely that you're here."

"Put her down Bobby," laughed Henry, "and let us kiss everybody."

"Have you two been drinking?" said Marjorie. "You are certainly very full of Christmas Spirit!"

Once Eric had been introduced, they sat down for tea. Eric was rather overwhelmed by these two big young men and their public school confidence, and watched with some trepidation as they dominated the room, the conversation and their usually formidable mother.

"Where have you been, and what have you been doing?" said Marjorie.

Bobby smiled. "You know I won't tell you. I'm an officer, and get involved in all kinds of ops. I have travelled around, and been very busy, but that's all you'll get from me."

"And I've been in Aldershot and other places," said Henry, "with this wrist of mine. I am so tired of having my arm in a sling, but it's not right yet, and it may never be quite right." Turning to Vicky, he went on: "I'm sure the little boys in your school will admire a war wound, and think I'm a hero, but there's nothing good about a smashed arm. There are plenty of desk jobs for me to do, in fact I've been very busy in my office, but it's not why I joined the army."

"Have you heard from Father?" said Bobby.

"Not recently," said Marjorie. "The last letter came from a place called Colditz Castle."

Bobby almost choked. "Colditz? Dad's in Colditz?"

"I'm sure he'll be doing everything he can to escape," said Marjorie. "I still think it's possible he'll walk through the door at any moment."

Henry gave a small laugh. "Sorry Mother, but if he's in Colditz, you'll not see him until the end of the war. It's the Nazi High Command's most secure prisoner of war camp; almost an honour to be incarcerated there. Father will probably be quite proud to have ended up in Colditz. It's reserved for officers who have successfully escaped from other camps."

"We sent a Christmas parcel to him through the Red Cross," said Rosemary. "I hope he's got it in time."

"I expect he has," said Henry. "The Red Cross seems to be very successful at getting letters and parcels through. Did you write to him, in addition to the parcel?"

"I sent him a Christmas card," said Marjorie, "hoping he'd be home for Christmas."

"I'm sure he will," said Bobby, "but it won't be this Christmas."

CHAPTER ELEVEN

When he arrived at Colditz, the Major had no idea he would be incarcerated with a number of other senior officers who would be famous by the end of the war. He had heard of Wing Commander Douglas Bader, although they had never met. He did not know Captain Pat Reid, nor Lieutenant Airey Neave, but they quickly became friends. There were only thirty men in the British contingent imprisoned in the castle: they were the elite of officers who had tried to escape from the Nazis.

The Major met several of the French officers and the small group of Belgians, but he had little to do with the large group of Polish officers, who seemed reconciled that their escaping days were over, and would simply sit out the war.

The British, however, never stopped thinking about escape. The atmosphere was like it had been at the public schools that they had all attended, and they called one another by their surnames: Bader, Reid and Neave. They baulked at Anderson-Grey, and resolved to call the Major, simply 'Grey'.

The winter had brought deep snow, and to some the castle may even have looked picturesque; but to the inmates, the snow signalled frustration and the post-ponement of escape endeavours.

"It is Christmas Eve," announced the Commandant, "and we will together sing. One day, when we this war have won, carols together we will sing. There is no reason that we should not this season celebrate. And we shall in our best uniforms it do."

The guards shepherded their charges into the chapel. The Major joked to his companion as they walked down the stone steps, "God, how these Germans mangle our language. We from the chapel to look for escape routes, will do!"

At first the singing was lack-lustre, but gradually the atmosphere changed. The creaking old pipe organ wheezed its way through several familiar tunes, and the Germans sang in German, and the English sang in English, mingling with the French, Belgian and Polish of the other officers. Neither the German guards, nor the international inmates were expecting the air of calm and peace which descended as the singing became clearer and more tuneful.

"That was extraordinary," said Bader as he struggled back up the steps to the British quarters. "I don't think our fellow officers in London would believe that such an atmosphere would develop."

"It won't last," said Reid, "we'll still be plotting to escape tomorrow, even if it is Christmas Day, and they'll still be trying to keep us here. We might sing carols together tonight, but they'll be ready to shoot us in the back tomorrow."

When they reached their quarters, a number of Red Cross parcels had been put upon the central table. The Major was pleased to receive the parcel from Marjorie. "Typical of the old girl to get the timing just right!" he said. "Let's hope her choice of food is as good as her timing."

Fishing amongst the dry hay, he found the jars of fruit from his garden in Chipping Norton, and the jams his wife had made for him. He found several tins of sardines, and there was much laughter when he discovered the little pot of caviar.

Several of the men had received food parcels for Christmas, and they put all the preserves and goodies on the makeshift table. "It might be a rather strange combination of luxury food and grey Nazi rations," said the Major, "but I think we can have a rather jolly feast tomorrow."

"Save the boxes and the straw," said Reid. "We never know what we might use anything like that for."

"A glider made of cardboard boxes, to sail away over the roof tops," said Bader.

"Don't joke," said Neave.

"Reid, you tunnelled out of your last place, didn't you?" said the Major, addressing the Captain.

"Yes," said Reid, "Digging the tunnel was easy there, and didn't have to be too long. We came up in someone's garden shed, just outside the wire. We had a few days on the run, but obviously I was caught and finished up here. Did you do any tunnelling, Grey?"

"Didn't need to. First chance, just walked out of the camp. It was in the chaos of the Dunkirk evacuation. I'd been watching my boys get to the boats which would save them, and stupidly didn't hear the Nazi captain coming up behind me. They weren't ready for prisoners, so we were in a flimsy barbed-wire enclosure, not much more than a field, just outside Calais. I waited my chance, and just scrambled over the barbed wire."

"Too easy," said Reid, "but you didn't get away."

"No: I thought I'd try and get a boat, but got caught by a patrol on the beach. Probably a good thing, as I'd have had very little chance of rowing across the Channel."

"And then?" said Reid.

"Another camp, deep in the countryside: it was an old farm, and once more I just waited until the coast was clear, and walked out. That didn't succeed either, as I had no disguise, and was very obviously a British Officer when I tried to find the station. Two escapes and I was brought here."

"I bet I'll be out of here within a year," boasted Neave.

"A year!" exclaimed the Major. "I'm hoping the war won't last that long."

"It may," said Reid. "I'm as anxious as anyone to get out, but as your escape officer, we must co-ordinate and work together. No individual heroics."

"I've written to my wife," said the Major. "It's very hard to know what to say that will get past the Nazi censorship."

Marjorie led her extended family to church on Christmas morning. She had found it very strange to have Christmas without the house full of the aroma of a roasting turkey, but had quite enjoyed not having to work quite so hard in the kitchen. Rosemary was even more grateful.

Dressed in their best, with the two young men in their uniforms, the group processed directly from the church, up the hill and across the market place to the Crown and Cushion.

Marjorie led, arm in arm with Henry. His crude sling had been replaced by one of his mother's Hermes scarves, a slash of crimson and gold against the drab khaki of his uniform. Bobby followed with Vicky, he proud in uniform to have such a pretty girl on his arm, and she hoping he didn't know that she was wearing one of Rosemary's old dresses under her worn winter coat. Rosemary and Eric completed the little procession, Eric feeling very self-conscious that he wasn't in uniform, and Rosemary walking in a cloud of her best perfume.

A few curtains twitched as the group walked past. Most of Chipping Norton was sitting down to a small chicken, or tiny piece of ham. Although there were plenty of vegetables from gardens and allotments, it did not seem like a Christmas feast in many homes. The old ladies in the Almshouses turned back to their carefully warmed potatoes; the butcher himself, behind the lace curtains of his living room over his shop, watched, and then looked at the platter of sausages which would be his Christmas lunch; and Dr Gripper, seated near the window of his grand town house, returned to trying to slice a very small joint of beef.

Marjorie was met at the door of the Crown and Cushion by the manager. A few wealthier farmers from outlying villages and farms, who could afford to eat in the town's best restaurant, looked up as the Anderson-Grey party were escorted to the private dining room. Entering, Vicky and Eric gasped. The table was laden with Marjorie's best elegant china from The Manse, and the best silver cutlery.

Marjorie smiled at her astonished family. "We might not be having our lunch at home," she said, "but that doesn't mean we can't have our best china and cutlery."

"And these are our napkins," said Rosemary.

Marjorie handed a box of matches to Bobby. "Light the candles, darling, would you?"

"This is our candelabra, isn't it?" said Bobby, "and to think I didn't notice it was gone from the sideboard. Can you afford to use all five candles? Shouldn't they be down in the cellar?"

Marjorie smiled. "Everything has been planned for this day," she said. "Mrs Wheeler was sworn to secrecy. She helped by washing and starching the cloth, and packing the china. Mr Harper was in on the plan, as well, as he helped carry everything up here without anyone noticing."

"It's a pity Mrs Wheeler and Mr Harper aren't joining us for lunch," said Vicky.

"What a strange suggestion," said Marjorie. "I'm sure they will be much happier in their own cottages."

A waiter arrived with six glasses of sweet sherry. "The hotel's glasses, not our best cut glass," said Marjorie, "there had to be a limit. Happy Christmas everyone, and a special toast to the Major."

"I expect he's toasting us in Colditz Castle," said Henry.

Christmas morning in Colditz started no differently from any other morning: the men had their usual ration of porridge and the very watery mint tea, which was at least hot, but then started to bring out the various goodies they had hidden away in preparation for Christmas lunch.

Red Cross parcels provided them with tinned meat and fish, and they were able to make something resembling a British Christmas dinner with potatoes and carrots from the dull daily rations provided by the Germans. From parcels sent from home, they found jam and honey, and a little dried fruit. Marjorie's small jar of caviar was spread very thinly between them all.

One officer produced something in a big tin can. "Be careful," he said. "This is the hooch I made from those Australian raisins that had gone a bit mouldy." The men had endured all kinds of odd smells coming from the strange can of liquid, and were apprehensive of the resulting drink. The officer continued, "The mould was like yeast, as I expected, and I managed to ferment the mixture. It tastes like nothing on earth, but it is alcoholic."

With all food spread out on the trestle table, it appeared that the men would have a good Christmas lunch, although the table was hardly festive. The battered tin plates and cups, with the beaten-up spoons and forks, mixed with all kinds of foods in random containers, reflected an image of the chaotic life in the castle. A feeble light bulb hung mournfully over the table. Despite the strange combinations of foodstuffs, and the gloomy environment, the men had an enjoyable meal, leaving their daily privations to one side for an hour.

Lifting the tin mugs to their lips, they toasted "absent friends" and sipped the strange brown liquid. "Christ, it's got kick," said Reid. "Well done that man!"

Lizzie lifted the sizzling birds from the oven. Molly had been busy all morning with vegetables, and Lizzie's roast was surrounded by golden potatoes. Lizzie called to Edward to carve the pheasants whilst Molly made the gravy.

"It will be a bit thin", she said, "with nothing to thicken it."

"It was lucky I still had a couple of Oxo cubes," said Lizzie, "as there aren't any in the Co-op at the moment."

"I expect they're reserved for the troops," said Stanley. "They were used in the last war to help keep our boys nourished."

"We shall carve two of the birds now, and save the other two for a pie," said Lizzie. "I'll save the dripping from the roast, and should be able to make some sort of pastry. Pheasant pie for Boxing Day."

"Such luxury," said Molly. "It is amazing that in time of rationing, we are having such a wonderful Christmas lunch."

"With two courses," said Edward. "The vegetable soup you've made, Molly, is an excellent way to start our meal, but this year, there's no pudding."

"That's hardly a hardship," said Molly. "Few families are as lucky as us."

Edward had pulled some ivy from a hedge in his garden and draped it across the table. Lizzie lit a single candle, and the scene was set for their Christmas lunch.

After the soup, Lizzie and Molly carried several steaming dishes to the table: there were carrots and parsnips, the roast potatoes, cabbage and boiled beetroot, all from Edward's garden, and the festive table was strangely jolly in the circumstances. The pheasant was a special treat for Molly and Stanley who had never tasted it before.

Marjorie invited everyone to be seated. "My good sons on either side of me," she demanded, and you, Eric, opposite, then we will be in proper order around the table." She nodded to the nervous waiter, and he started to bring the plates of smoked salmon.

"I didn't expect to taste this before the end of the war," said Rosemary. "We've not had it at home for a very long time."

When the fish plates were cleared away, the waiter brought hot tureens to the table with wisps of steam escaping from under the lids. "They're mostly our own vegetables from our garden," said Marjorie. "Mr Harper brought them up yesterday; but it remains to be seen if we've Brussels sprouts, as we didn't have any in the garden."

The waiter then delivered the plates of meat. There were generous helpings of turkey, with a slice of beef and a slice of ham, accompanied by a thin chipolata sausage, and a sphere of stuffing. Vicky could not stop herself from exclaiming: "Bloody hell, I thought there was a war on. What a spread! Is this how the upper classes always live?"

"Restaurants are not restricted by rationing," said Rosemary, "so they can buy almost anything they want, in any quantity."

"And those with enough money, can eat like this every day," said Bobby. "It doesn't seem very fair, does it?"

"I hear they're thinking of restricting restaurants in the future, if the war lasts much longer," said Henry.

The scene was picture-perfect. All sense of being at war was left outside the Crown and Cushion Hotel, as Marjorie glowed in the light from her own candelabra. As dusk began to fall in Chipping Norton, the table glimmered with the candlelight reflecting in the gold rims of Marjorie's best plates.

"Me dad's not coming, is he?" said Billy.

"No darling," said Mrs Thomas, "we've not heard from him this time. I expect he's really busy."

"This is Christmas Day, isn't it? Can Golly come to lunch?"

Mrs Thomas looked at her husband, then said, "I think so. Golly can be in your dad's place today."

Billy ran upstairs, pulled Golly from his bed, and ran back down. With the black doll in place on a chair of its own, Mrs Thomas brought the lunch to the table. There was a very small chicken, and a very big bowl of potatoes. Mr Thomas had successfully grown some huge cabbages, and one of these provided another big bowl of vegetables.

The gingham cloth was decorated with little chocolate Father Christmases – but Mrs Thomas warned them not to eat them, as they were several years old. The plates were piled high with home-grown vegetables, topped with the small portion of chicken.

"I'm sorry there's no proper Christmas pudding," said Mrs Thomas, "but we have got some hot pears. I saved one of the Kilner jars we did in September, especially for today."

"It looks dead good, mum," said Billy, "better'n we used to get at 'ome. My dad was a lousy cook, but it would've been nice if 'e was 'ere."

"Wherever he is, he's thinking about you, Billy, and I expect he's missing you."

The Italians were shivering. Christmas was not as significant to them; the highlight of the season for them had been the carol concert in the town hall, the previous week. A number of the people of Chipping Norton had visited them and left small food parcels, and their

Christmas consisted of sitting in a small group huddled round the stove, feeling cold and miserable.

"We must ask them to let us do some work," said one. "There's all that space for growing vegetables just beyond the barbed wire. If we can convince them that we won't try to escape, we could start gardening. I'm sure tomatoes would grow even in this dreary weather, and once we got things going, the town would start to trust us more. We could even go and help some of the women, whose men are gone fighting. The mayor, who was kind to us, said something about 'goodwill to all men', so let's show we deserve his trust."

The men looked at one another and at the dull lunch laid out on the table. "Tomatoes?" said another. "It would be good to grow some. Of all the things from home, it's the tomatoes I miss the most."

The men all laughed. "I wouldn't tell your wife that when you get home," they joked.

The rough table carried a meagre selection of winter vegetables: parsnips, carrots and potatoes, all thoroughly boiled, but hardly appetising, or sufficient, for a group of young Italian men. The enamel plates and mugs were placed in a circle, and the men solemnly shared the hot meal. "Buon Natale ragazzi," they said gravely. They drank the water that the vegetables had been boiled in.

"I've said it before, and I'll say it again," said Neave. "I'll be home before next Christmas."

"I wonder what Christmas has been like in Chipping Norton," said the Major. "I daresay rationing's hit them quite hard. They've got plenty of supplies growing in the garden, potatoes and so on, but they'll be stuck like everyone else with rationing of meat and other things. I expect their Christmas lunch was a bit different this year."

"Who is that?" said Billy.

"Sh-sh," said Mrs Thomas. "That's the King. He's talking to you from Buckingham Palace. He does it every year. That's why we were in a hurry to wash up, so we could sit down to listen to the King."

"My dad saw 'im once," said Billy. "He was going down the river in 'is boat, and all the stev'dores was standing watching."

In days of peace the feast of Christmas is a time when we all gather together in our homes, young and old, to enjoy the happy festivity and good will which the Christmas message brings. It is, above all, the children's day, and I am sure that we shall all do our best to make it a happy one for them wherever they may be.

"Yes," said Billy, "it's a children's day, but also for mums and dads and Gollys."

"War brings, among other sorrows, the sadness of separation. But how many more children are there here who have been moved from their homes to safer quarters?

"To all of them, at home and abroad, who are separated from their fathers and mothers, to their kind friends and hosts, and to all who love them, and to parents who will be lonely without them, I wish every happiness that Christmas can bring. May the New Year carry us towards victory and to happier Christmas days, when everyone will be at home together in the years to come.

"That's you, Billy, he's wishing you a happy Christmas."

"Time and again during these last few months I have seen for myself the battered towns and cities of England, and I have seen the British people facing their ordeal. I can say to them that they may be justly proud of their race and nation. On every side I have seen a new and splendid spirit of good fellowship springing up in adversity, a real desire to share burdens and resources alike. Out of all this suffering there is a growing harmony which we must carry forward into the days to come when we have endured to the end, and ours is the victory.

"Ours will be the victory," said Mr Thomas, "however long it takes."

"And now I wish you all a happy Christmas and a happier New Year. We may look forward to it with

sober confidence. We have surmounted a grave crisis. We do not underrate the dangers and difficulties which confront us still, but we take courage and comfort from the successes which our fighting men and their Allies have won at heavy odds by land and air and sea.

"The future will be hard, but our feet are planted on the path of victory, and with the help of God we shall make our way to justice and to peace."

"I didn't get all of what 'e said," said Billy, "but 'e sounds a nice man. I bet my dad was listenin' too."

"He's got two little girls, not much older than you," said Mrs Thomas. "They are princesses."

"I wouldn't mind being a prince when I grow up," said Billy. "Miss Jones read us a story about a little prince."

"That was amazing," said Vicky, as they staggered, replete, into the parlour. "I never had a Christmas dinner like that, not even in peacetime: the beef and ham, as well as the turkey, why I've eaten enough for three people."

"Goodness knows if we will ever eat like that again," said Marjorie. "I was determined to give the boys, and the rest of you of course, a wonderful lunch; and I suddenly thought about all of the good china. I remembered your landlady, Victoria, telling us about her best cut glass.

I thought, we are lucky to have all these lovely things, what if the house was bombed and it was all destroyed? We should use them: and then I discovered that the only way to have a turkey was to go to the hotel. What a dilemma – so I arranged for our own good china and silver to go to the hotel.

"I didn't risk the cut glass – some of the wine glasses are very delicate, and it would have been perverse to risk them, and break them, taking them up to the town. So we are going to have an evening drink here, with the good crystal. There's half a bottle of sherry – we drank the other half before Christmas – and the last surprise: a bottle of sloe gin. The Major and I made this from hedgerow sloes, about five years ago. I hope it's still good."

Rosemary poured the last of the sherry into the best wine glasses, and they sipped the sweet drink. "Perhaps this is a good time to say thank you," said Eric. "This has been a very special occasion for me, and I am very lucky. Many thanks, all of you."

Marjorie then went to the kitchen and brought back the sloe gin. "What is it?" said Vicky, staring at the large bottle with its ruby liquid.

"Sloes grow in the hedges around here – they're bitter little berries, no good to eat," said Rosemary, "but you prick them and drop them into gin. And then you just wait for the sloes to do their magic."

"Rosemary," said Marjorie, "you shall be our taster. Take a small drop and see if it's drinkable." Rosemary drank the last of her sherry, and then poured a tiny drop of the liquid. It lay like a jewel in the crystal glass. Rosemary sipped it, her eyes opening unusually wide.

"S'wonderful!" she gasped, "but I think you need to drink it sitting down!"

At that there was a great jangling of the front door bell, and Buster began barking enthusiastically. The dog had become rather confused by everyone leaving him alone at lunch time, and was puzzled that the usual smells of cooking were not coming from the kitchen. The bell rang again.

"Oh dear," said Marjorie, "In a rash moment I invited the vicar and his wife for a cup of tea. Whatever will he think, finding us attacking a bottle of sloe gin? Rosemary, you'd better let him in."

Marjorie was desperately making sure the room was immaculately tidy, when the vicar and his wife came in. "You catch us investigating the Major's sloe gin," said Marjorie. "I'm afraid it's not afternoon tea."

"God would not have invented sloes if he did not expect us to drop them into gin!" laughed the vicar. "I saw your jolly little house party in church this morning. Thank you all for coming. Now you can introduce me properly, and when you've done that, I would love a very tiny taste of your delicious-looking liquid."

Both the vicar and his wife thought the sloe gin was delightful, and both had rather more than a very tiny taste. In fact everyone in the room relished it, and eventually the bottle was empty.

"Good Lord, it's quite dark," said the vicar. "I shudder to think what time it is. I really must be moving. We are promised to visit a couple of other parishioners this evening. I will leave you to your festivities. Don't get up – we'll find our own way out."

When the vicar had left, Vicky looked round the room. She had Bobby sitting on the floor at her feet, with his head on her lap; Rosemary was sitting very close to Eric, engaged in a mysterious whispered conversation; and Marjorie and Henry were actually giggling at some shared secret joke. Buster wandered from person to person, sniffing the empty wine glasses, and wondering if anyone would give him some dinner. "Just look at what a bottle of slow gin will do," she thought. "I hope the vicar can find his way home. Party games!" she announced brightly.

"Oh no," said Rosemary, "I can't even stand up."

"Please feel free, Victoria dear, but count me out," said Marjorie. "I'll go and feed the dog." She stood up, and abruptly sat down. "Perhaps a little later." Buster looked at her with something approaching resignation, and lay down at her feet. With a loud sigh, he stretched his legs and settled down to wait, remaining on Marjorie's feet, so that she could not move without being reminded about him.

"The King's speech!" said Marjorie suddenly, startling the dog, "We missed it. O dear, I've never missed it before, and this year of all years. I hope it's repeated during the evening. Quickly put the wireless on!"

After a prolonged recital of Christmas carols, the BBC repeated the King's speech, but by this time both Henry and Bobby had fallen asleep. "Henry, wake up," said Marjorie, shaking Henry. "And poke Bobby, please, Victoria. We can't have Grenadier guards asleep when the King himself is addressing the nation."

"I think they were awake during the actual speech," said Rosemary indistinctly, "because that's when we were having the pudding up at the hotel, and it's OK to sleep in the repeat, and anyway, they weren't wearing their bearskins, that would have been very naughty...."

"Rosemary," said Marjorie severely, "you're rambling and making no sense. Go and make cocoa for us all, and feed the poor dog."

Rosemary rose and wobbled a little. "Yes," she said, "six dog dinners coming up, and the dog's cocoa."

Eventually Marjorie gave up on making any conversation with her inebriated family and went to bed. Rosemary followed, and soon Vicky went upstairs. The three young men were left alone.

"My bloody arm hurts when I'm tired," said Henry. "It's strange to go to bed so early, but with nothing left to drink, I think I'll turn in."

Eric stood and tottered into the front room, where he had slept on the sofa the night before. To his surprise, Rosemary was sitting on the sofa. "It's not very comfortable," she said quietly. "Come upstairs, my bed is much nicer."

"Rosemary," began Eric, but she put her finger to his lips.

"Don't say anything; there's a war on, you know."

Bobby instinctively tip-toed to his old room, and opened the door as silently as he could. "Auntie Vicky," he whispered, "just making sure you're OK; time for a cuddle?" Soon he was sleeping contentedly in Vicky's arms.

The Hardings and the Wykes had washed up and sat ready for the King's speech. They listened solemnly, and nodded sagely at the end. "He got that right," said Edward. "No-one is pretending that the road ahead is easy, but he'll see us through to victory."

"Him and Winnie," said Stanley. "You know, I was never sure why we fought the last war; but this time it's clear. Hitler and the Nazi war machine is nothing but evil, and we're clearly fighting for right."

Molly looked at her companions. "We're hearing some terrible rumours coming out of Germany," she said. "We pray that they are not true, but if they are, these Nazis are even worse than we could imagine."

"Yes," said Lizzie, "dreadful stories of arrests and mass murder. Heaven help the world if the stories are true."

The Italians were still cold, despite several layers of clothing and a stove in the centre of their hut. "how long does the winter last in this place? asked one.

"It can't go on for ever," said his companion. "Let's sleep; perhaps it will be Spring when we wake up."

The officers in Colditz were cold despite the unusually large lunch. "As soon as this snow melts," said Neave, "I'm out of here."

"Are you going to learn to fly?" said the Major.

"I don't know yet," said Neave, "but I promise you, I'll find a way. Sweet dreams, everyone."

In the early hours of Boxing day, Eric met Bobby (or was it Henry?) on the upstairs landing. "Just heading for the bathroom," muttered Eric.

"Just been," muttered Henry, (or was it Bobby?)

CHAPTER TWELVE

1941 brought sad news. Stanley was unfamiliar with the official-looking letter, as it was not from the Ministry of Education, nor from the Education offices in Plaistow. It seemed to be from the Home Office.

"As the headmaster of Silvertown Primary School, we understand you will know the whereabouts of a minor called William McCann, known as Billy. We regret to inform you that his father, Sean McCann, previously employed as a stevedore, was killed during an air-raid on 26th December 1940, at his place of work in the docks. Details are vague, but it seems he was hit by falling masonry. At this stage, we are unable to trace any known relatives of the minor William McCann. Please acknowledge receipt of this letter, and if possible, inform the above office of the whereabouts of said minor."

Stanley's heart sank. The previous evening they had toasted the new year, with hopes for peace, and the first news of January was this hammer-blow. He called to Molly for her advice.

"I'll go and talk to Mrs Thomas," said Molly. "I know her a little from jumble sales and other times when she's been to the school. She's taken quite a shine to our Billy, and he's certainly been a much more settled kid since he was with her. He calls her 'mum', you know."

When Molly got to the Thomas's house, Billy and Mike were playing in the garden. Mrs Thomas went to get them in, but Molly stopped her. "It's you I need to talk to," she said, "on your own."

Mrs Thomas sat down. "You make it sound very serious," she said.

"It is," said Molly. "It couldn't be more serious. I bring very bad news. Billy's dad was killed on Boxing Day." Mrs Thomas gasped, and her eyes filled with tears. "You know he has no mother, I understand she died in childbirth, and we don't know of any other family. His dad was all he had."

"This cruel war," said Mrs Thomas. "This cruel war."

"Do you want me to tell him?" asked Molly.

"No," said Mrs Thomas. "I'll do it, but you might stay with me for moral support."

Calling Billy from the garden, she told Mike to stay outside. "I want to talk to Billy on his own," she said.

When Billy saw Molly sitting in the kitchen, he thought he was in trouble, but she reassured him quickly. "No, you're not in trouble Billy. We just want a little talk."

"Billy," said Mrs Thomas, "you know you came to live with me here because it was very dangerous to stay in Silvertown?"

Billy nodded, "Because of the war."

"Well, we've had a bad message today, Billy. It was very dangerous in Silvertown, and your dad has been killed. He died a few days ago."

"Oh," said Billy, unmoved, "few days ago?"

"Yes," said Molly, and there was a silence.

Billy looked up. "I'll go and get Golly," he said.

They heard him walk slowly up the stairs, and back down with Golly.

"Tell Golly," he said.

"Well," said Mrs Thomas, "Billy's dad died a few days ago. It's because of the war. There were lots of bombs dropped on the docks and in Silvertown."

Billy looked at the black doll. "Golly don't believe you," he said.

Mrs Thomas looked at Molly. "This is worse than I expected," she said.

Molly looked at the little boy. "Billy," she said, "I think Golly needs a rest, because he's just had some bad news. Shall we take him up to bed for a little sleep?"

"Billy, take Mrs Wykes up to your room with Golly, so he can have a rest. I'll go and get Mike."

"Yes, mum," said Billy. "Golly and me will have a rest."

Stanley pulled the brass handle of the front door bell at The Manse. Rosemary opened it as usual with Buster bouncing around behind her.

"Mr Wykes," she said. "Are you alright? You look as if you've seen a ghost."

"I have, kind-of," said Stanley. "I'm afraid I'm the bringer of bad news. Is Vicky in?"

"I think she's in the vegetable garden," said Rosemary. "Come through and I'll get her."

Rosemary put Stanley in the parlour and went to get Vicky, who came running in. "What's happened?" she said.

"It's Billy's dad," said Stanley. "He's been killed. My wife is up at the Thomas's right now, telling him."

"Shall I go up there?" said Vicky. "He knows me well. Of course he's in Lawrence's class now, but he still talks to me every day in the playground."

"The new term opens in a few days," said Stanley. "We spoke of starting the new year with optimism, but it's hard to be positive with this kind of news. I hate to think what else 1941 will bring."

"I've got to talk to Golly," said Billy. "It's private."

"OK," said Molly, and she left the room, shutting the door. She remained on the landing however, and listened.

Billy's voice was muffled, but she could just about hear him. "Golly, Billy's had bad news. Bad, bad news. Billy's dad's died. You remember 'im, don't you, Golly, 'e came 'ere at Christmas last year. Didn't come this year. Might not 'ave died if 'e'd bin 'ere. But 'e wasn't, 'e was at 'ome, Silver-bloody-town-bloody-docks. Oh Golly. What'll we do, Mum? Mum!" Suddenly he started shouting, "Mum! Mum!"

Mrs Thomas ran up the stairs. "I've told Mike. He's in the kitchen." She rushed into the bedroom.

Molly heard a huge wail as she closed the door. She wasn't sure if it was Billy or Mrs Thomas – probably it was both of them. Downstairs she found Mike sitting in the kitchen. "Billy will have to be my brother for ever more," he said simply. "I'll have to share my dad with him."

"That will be very nice," said Molly. "I think Billy will like that."

The officers welcomed in the new year with the home-made hooch in battered tin mugs. "1941," said Bader. "Who'd have thought we'd still be here?"

"Not for long," said Neave. "You'll see: I'll be first back to London."

"You keep telling us," said the Major, "but when will it happen?"

"As soon as the snow melts, Grey, I'll be out of here."

"Do you have a plan?" asked Reid.

"Kind of," said Neave evasively. "It's forming in my head."

"Well, whatever it is, I wish you luck," said the Major. "You'll need it. We drink to the New Year, the end of the war, and freedom. I'm beginning to quite like this strange hooch." He sipped it some more. "Mind you, there's a bottle of sloe gin, hidden in the back of the pantry for when I get home. My wife and I made it a few years ago. We said we'd save it for a special occasion – I reckon when I get home will be pretty special – we'll crack it open then."

"You assume she's not drowned her sorrows in it whilst you've been away?" said Bader.

"She's not the sort to drown sorrows," laughed the Major, "you don't know my wife! She'll be organising everything there is to organise in the town."

Vicky felt she should go and talk to Billy, although she had little idea of what to say. She knocked on the Thomas's front door.

"Why, Miss Jones, how nice of you to call," said Mrs Thomas. "You know that Mrs Wykes was here earlier?"

"Yes, Mr Wykes came to see me at The Manse. How is Billy?"

"He seems to be OK now. He was quiet at first, then had a big howl, and is now being very normal. I think it helps that he'd not seen his dad for a year, and he's made a good life here for himself."

"Shall I talk to him?" said Vicky.

"It would be good for him to know that you know, if you see what I mean, and that you'll be available to talk to; but how he'll react right now is anyone's guess."

Mike and Billy were in the garden, where they played on a tiny lawn whilst Mr Thomas worked on a large vegetable patch. Mr Thomas waved to Vicky from his digging, and stopped to watch the boys. "Miss Jones!" shouted Billy.

"Hello, Billy," said Vicky diffidently, "How are you?"

"I'm OK, Miss Jones. You know my dad died. That's because of the war. I'm gonna 'ave to stay with Miss Thomas for ever an' ever now, and Mister Thomas'll 'ave to be me dad."

"I'm sorry, Billy, about your dad, I mean."

"Yeah – 'e would have liked it 'ere, although I dunno if 'e knew 'ow to do diggin' like Mister Thomas."

Billy paused, and Vicky was unsure what to say. Suddenly Billy turned to her.

"Here Miss Jones, I don't need this no more. You look after it," and he fished inside his shirt and pulled out the key he wore on a string round his neck.

"OK, Billy," said Vicky, "if that's what you'd like me to do."

"What will happen to him now?" asked Marjorie during lunch. "Presumably there are some relations somewhere."

"Not that we know of," said Vicky.

"Poor little thing," said Rosemary. "I suppose this bloody war will make a lot of kids into orphans."

"British orphans and German orphans," said Vicky.

"We're certainly giving as good as we're getting," said Marjorie. "As far as we can tell from the BBC, the bombing raids over Germany are hitting them hard."

"The paper says that our boys are aiming for industrial targets, not like the Nazi vandals who aim for civilians," said Rosemary.

The boys had welcomed the New Year in, at Aldershot Barracks, but Henry was not there for long. With his smashed left wrist healing slowly, he realised that his hand would never function properly again. He talked to his superior officer, telling him how frustrated he felt unable to fulfil his role in the army.

"It may be that we've something equally important, may be more important, for you," said his superior. "We've been asked to keep an eye out for young chaps to go to Whitehall and work alongside the civil servants. You know, a lot of those older men in Whitehall need people like you to work with them in planning strategy. As far as I understand it, the P M and the Cabinet Office draw up broad-based plans and expect their staffs to put them into operation. Some young army blood in their midst could not only ensure the plans are realistic, but probably make them more efficient. We don't want to come out of this war regretting military blunders caused by civil servants' ineptitude."

Within a few days, Henry found himself in an office overlooking Horse Guards Parade.

"My father's twice taken part in the trooping of the colour," he told his new colleagues, "and it's one of my ambitions when this war is over. Standing here, and imagining the pageantry of it all, is a reminder why we fight on, and keep fighting on."

In the move to Whitehall, he had been required to sign the official secrets act; and thus his message to his mother was very short. "Transferred to Whitehall," he wrote, "with lots of the big-wigs, but can't tell more!"

Bobby did not remain at Aldershot for much longer either, finding himself posted to rural Dorset. Just like his brother, his letter to his mother was brief: "Posted to Dorset, but this operation is very exciting and will make sure we win the war. Can't tell you more!"

In fact, Bobby was now a squadron leader in the 4th Armoured Battalion Grenadier Guards, and became heavily involved in the development of Churchill tanks. His men were undergoing rigorous training for driving and operating the tanks, careering around the wild Dorset heath land.

News of successes in obliterating the German factories was arriving with Henry, and filtering through to Bobby. Both boys, quite independently, began to wonder if there would be an invasion of France, and when it would come; and both in their separate roles, realised that they were being prepared for such an invasion. Henry, however, in his new responsibility, was privately aware that in 1941, the country was not capable of, nor ready for, an invasion of France.

"Where's Neave?" said Reid. "Haven't seen him since dawn."

"Went to the latrines, ages ago," said the Major. "No sign of him since"

The men spent the day speculating about their missing compatriot. Had he attempted some kind of one-man escape, as he'd so often boasted, or were the Nazi warders simply keeping him elsewhere in the castle? Towards evening, there was a great clanging of the castle bell, a sound the men had not heard before.

"What the hell?" said the Major.

"Prisoner escaped," said Bader. "They rang a bell like that in my last place. I bet it's Neave. How's he bloody done it?"

The bell ceased its frantic tolling, and several loud shots were heard.

"Hope they haven't got him, or shot him," said the Major.

"He shouldn't have tried to go solo," said Reid. "It's going to be tough enough with us working together, but a solo attempt? I don't think so."

At that the commandant burst into the British officers' mess, accompanied by several of his military personnel.

Laughing, he said, "Good try, but so silly. You friend Neave thought in disguise that he could walk out." The German group burst into renewed laughter. "As it dark got, our spotlights saw a funny little man crossing the courtyard. Is that Charlie Chaplin, we said to ourselves, but no it was little Neave. He thought we'd be fooled by a Polish uniform made to look German, and a funny bright green hat. Shoot over his head, I said, don't kill him, he's so funny."

The British contingent stood solemnly reflecting on their companion's attempt to break out. They knew that many military and civilian personnel went in and out of the castle every day, and clearly Airey Neave had tried to use that simple route.

"We thank Lieutenant Neave for such amusement, and we hope he will be as amused by a month on bread and water in solitary. Oh, and gentlemen, please do not consider such actions in the future. My men may not fire over your heads if you do. Heil Hitler!" The Germans turned on their heels and left.

"Actually, is it quite funny," said Bader, "but thank goodness they fired over his head."

"Knowing him, he'll use his time in solitary, planning his next adventure," said Reid. "I'll bet you anything, that by the time he gets back to us, he'll have his next plan in his head."

"Well," said Marjorie, "1941 is here. It's hard to believe that we've been at war for more than a year."

"Sixteen months," said Vicky. "Sixteen months since I came to Chippy. Mrs M told me that in the Great War, they'd talked about it being over by Christmas, and in the end it dragged on for four whole years. We've now had two Christmases – I wonder how many more there will be?"

"It can't go on for four years, can it?" said Rosemary. "The rationing is getting tighter, and anyone without a garden must be really struggling."

"Hitler thought the Blitz would crush the British Spirit," said Marjorie, "but he's no idea how strong we can be, and will go on being. Churchill understands and encourages us. He told us it would be tough after Dunkirk, and it has been, but he told us that we would be steadfast, and we have been."

"Dunkirk," said Rosemary. "Gosh, nearly a year ago, when the boys came home, Henry injured."

"Dunkirk," said Marjorie. "Nearly a year since the Major was caught. I thought he'd be home for Christmas, even if the war wasn't finished. It is very strange not knowing what's happening. For all we know, he's marching along somewhere in France, heading for home."

"Or still in Colditz Castle," said Vicky. "Remember what the boys said about it: Hitler's most inescapable prison?"

"That won't stop him," said Marjorie. "He's made of tough stuff, and I daresay so are the other officers in there with him. Why, as we sit here talking, they may be making a break for freedom. I know the Major. He'll not be idling away the time."

"Anyone for a game of chess?" said the Major. "I didn't have much enthusiasm for it when I was at school, and we never played at Sandhurst; but it passes the time."

"And it's a game of strategy and scheming," said another. "Keeps our mind active, and you never know, an escape plan may come into our thoughts whilst we play."

"I suppose we'll get better if we practise," said the Major.

"Just as we'll get better at escaping, if we practice," laughed the others.

Stanley had tried to start the new school term on a note of optimism, but he was aware that they were into the third year since evacuation, and with the cloud of Billy's dad's death hanging over them, it was hard to summon up any positive feelings.

Vicky was adamant that singing would be the salvation of the two schools at this gloomy time, and she persuaded Lizzie to rehearse the piano part for "A Nightingale Sang in Berkeley Square."

Once again they were surprised to find that many of the children knew most of the words, and soon Vera Lynn's song was resounding in the school gymnasium. The children sang the poignant words with as much gusto as all the songs they knew. Since discovering Lawrence's clear tenor voice, Vicky had encouraged him to sing with them.

> *That certain night,*
> *The night we met,*
> *There was magic abroad in the air.*
> *There were angels dining at the Ritz,*
> *And a nightingale sang in Berkeley square.*
>
> *I may be right, I may be wrong,*
> *But I'm perfectly willing to swear,*
> *That when you turned and smiled at me,*
> *A nightingale sang in Berkeley square.*

The children always giggled at the word "swear" as if it was rather rude to sing such a word in a song.

> *The moon that lingered over London town,*
> *Poor puzzled moon he wore a frown,*
> *How could he know we two were so in love,*
> *The whole damned world seemed upside down?*

Vicky worried about the children learning a love song, but the tune was entrancing, and they sang with gusto. They would sing on, getting louder and louder, and then

Vicky would get them to sing more gently for the line about the dawn coming up:

The dawn came stealing up,
All gold and blue,
To interrupt our rendezvous.
I still remember how you smiled and said,
Was that a dream or was it true?

Our homeward step was just as light
As the dancing feet of Astaire
And like an echo far away
And a nightingale sang in Berkeley square
And a nightingale sang in Berkeley square
That night in Berkeley square.

The two headteachers, sitting together in their cramped office, would stop and listen. "I love it when she gets them to sing quietly for the rising sun," said Edward. "There's a new song I'm going to get Lizzie to learn, called London Pride. It's by Noel Coward and it's a bit of a tearful one, but it will sound wonderful when the children sing it."

"I know it. It's much harder than the Vera Lynn songs," said Stanley, "although the words are very relevant for our East End children. Vicky will have to teach it in sections; I don't expect the children will know it like they know the Vera Lynn numbers."

"And you're going to have to explain some of it to our rural kids," smiled Edward. "Coster barrows? Cockney sparrows? Or even Park Lane and the Ritz? I suppose Vicky will know all about that. Is she a 'Cockney Sparrow'?"

"You mean, is she a true Cockney? Yes, I believe she is, although she doesn't use rhyming slang, not at school anyway."

Vicky was delighted when they asked her to tackle London Pride, and Lizzie once more battled with the piano part. They decided to break the song into three sections, with the middle of the song being sung by Lawrence, to make it easier for the children to learn.

London Pride has been handed down to us.
London Pride is a flower that's free.
London Pride means our own dear town to us,
And our pride it forever will be.
Woa, Liza, see the coster barrows, vegetable marrows,
And the fruit piled high.
Woa, Liza, little London sparrows,
Covent Garden Market where the costers cry.
Cockney feet mark the beat of history.
Every street pins a memory down.
Nothing ever can quite replace the grace of London
    Town.

Lawrence would then sing the middle section:

There's a little city flower every spring unfailing
Growing in the crevices by some London railing,
Though it has a Latin name, in town and country-
    side
We in England call it London Pride.

London Pride has been handed down to us.
London Pride is a flower that's free.
London Pride means our own dear town to us,
And our pride it forever will be.
Hey, lady, when the day is dawning,
See the policeman yawning on his lonely beat.
Gay lady, Mayfair in the morning,
Hear your footsteps echo in the empty street.
Early rain and the pavement's glistening.
All Park Lane in a shimmering gown.
Nothing ever could break or harm
The charm of London Town.

The children then took up the refrain:

In our city darkened now, street and square and
*   crescent,*
We can feel our living past in our shadowed present,
Ghosts beside our starlit Thames who lived and
*   loved and died*
Keep throughout the ages London Pride.
London Pride has been handed down to us.
London Pride is a flower that's free.
London Pride means our own dear town to us,
And our pride it forever will be.
Grey city stubbornly implanted,
Taken so for granted for a thousand years.
Stay, city, smokily enchanted,
Cradle of our memories and hopes and fears.

At this point Lizzie slowed the tempo and the children's voices became louder and somehow harder as Vicky encouraged them to really "belt it out!"

Every Blitz your resistance toughening,
From the Ritz to the Anchor and Crown,
Nothing ever could override the pride of London
Town.

"Crikey," said Edward, listen from his office, "she's really going for it with this song. I never expected our children to sing with such emotion." He looked at Stanley, who brushed away a tear from his eye.

Molly came into the room. "Did you hear that?" she said. "I'm beginning to think we've the makings of a really good concert. If Vicky and Lawrence keep working with the children this term, we could stage a concert at the Town Hall at Easter. What do you think? We should do it for the Spitfire fund."

"In all my years as a teacher and headteacher, I've never heard singing quite like it," said Edward. "Of course it helps to have such a big choir; on our own we could never make a sound like that, but with two schools together, it's magnificent."

"I'll talk to Vicky, and you'll have to persuade Lizzie," said Stanley.

"Me dad liked a good sing-song," said Billy. "He'd've liked these songs." He and Mike had been singing at home again, and amazed Mr and Mrs Thomas that they knew so many words. They could even sing Lawrence's part in London Pride. "Mum," said Billy, "I should start calling Mr Thomas 'dad' now shouldn't I?"

"He's never going to be your real dad, Billy, and you mustn't forget your real dad. But yes, you can call Mr Thomas 'dad' now."

"He's 'dad two'," said Billy. "An' you're me mum, and Mike's me brother. An' I dunno why, but now and again Golly an' me have a little cry. That's for me dad I s'pose."

Mrs Thomas made an appointment with Mr Harding and Mr Wykes.

"Now Billy's dad is gone," she started, "We're thinking, Mr Thomas and I, that we shall adopt Billy. We don't know anything about the procedure, but he's been with us for more than a year, he's become part of our family, and he's calling us mum and dad. As far as I know, there's nowhere for him to go back to in Silvertown at the end of the war, so he best stay here."

"That's a lovely proposition, Mrs Thomas," said Stanley. "I'll see if I can find out what procedure you have to go through, but no-one will have a better solution. Billy is a very lucky boy to have you and your husband."

"One more thing, Mr Wykes. I'd like to take Billy out of Silvertown School, and enrol him in St Mary's, if that's alright with you."

"Let's wait until the summer," said Stanley. "He's in Mr Powell's class, isn't he? Leave him there this year, and we'll move him into St Mary's next September."

At the same time, Molly received an unexpected invitation which she could not resist. The local Chipping Norton Girl Guides had been led by a very enthusiastic young woman, but she had joined the WRENs, and the troupe of guides had not met for several months. Molly had been a Girl Guide herself, and assisted with a guide troupe in Silvertown. She was more than willing to get involved. "After all," she said to Stanley, "it seems we're going to be here for much longer than we expected, and we're becoming part of this little town. I wouldn't take the responsibility if I thought we'd be leaving soon, but it doesn't look likely. I would like to have a more important part to play in the town."

With help, Molly got messages to as many of the guides as she could, and asked them to come and meet her in the church hall. The rather tumble-down building, overlooking the churchyard, almost at the front gate of The Manse, was little used and damp, and Molly's immediate reaction was that the guides' first project would be to refurbish the old building.

Several girls arrived, some in tight uniforms which they had grown out of, and others without uniform. Many of them knew who Molly was, because they had younger brothers and sisters at St Mary's School, and they were very pleased that their group was re-forming.

Molly was honest with them. "We'll have to work out what to do together," she said. "I was a guide, and I helped with the troupe in Silvertown, but I've never led a group. You'll have to help me. We'll start by writing to the Chief Scout, although I've no idea who it is, or where we write to!"

As Easter approached, rehearsals for the concert intensified at the school. Lawrence and Vicky were relishing the enthusiasm they were developing with the children; and despite her growing prowess, Lizzie was becoming increasingly nervous of her pivotal role as an accompanist.

Stanley and Edward were particularly pleased that every child from the two schools would be taking part. "Our school choir is our school," said Stanley to anyone who asked, and Edward was very satisfied that the two schools had integrated together so well.

No-one was sure who first invented the title "Singing for Spitfires", whether it was Stanley, or Vicky, or Lawrence, but soon everyone had adopted the phrase. The children were asked to design posters which would be displayed in shop windows in the town.

For the Christmas concert, they had managed to fit all the children onto the stage, and in front of it, at the Town Hall. There would be a similar arrangement for Singing for Spitfires. A few days before the concert, the schools had walked in a long crocodile to the Town Hall, and with a rather worried Lizzie at the piano, they had a very noisy rehearsal.

Vicky didn't know what to wear for the concert. "My stuff's all a bit tired and old," she said. "I've nothing smart enough to conduct a concert like this. The Christmas one was rather impromptu, but this is more formal."

"You are right," said Marjorie, "I've not seen you wearing anything remotely suitable. Rosemary, what have you got that will be appropriate for Victoria?"

"I've a blue velvet dress I've never worn. It's very suitable for 'Singing for Spitfires', as it's Air Force Blue. Besides, it's very tight on me, and I think it would be a good fit for Vicky. It would be nice to pin some silk flowers on to it."

"Very good," said Marjorie, "and what will your colleague wear?"

"Lawrence?" said Vicky. "He wears a suit for work; it's a bit worn out, like most of our things are, but we are all making do and mending."

"He's a similar size to the Major," said Marjorie. "The Major's dinner suit is hanging in the wardrobe. I think I will offer to lend it to your man. If he's to stand on the stage and sing a Noel Coward song, he must look the part."

"That's very generous of you," said Vicky. "Shall I ask him to come and try it on?"

The following evening, Marjorie had put the Major's dinner suit, as well as a formal shirt and bow tie, on the bed in Henry's room. Lawrence dressed in the unfamiliar clothing, and came down the stairs to be inspected. Everything fitted very well, but the tie was untied.

"I'm sorry," he said, "but I've never tied a bow tie. I don't know what to do."

"You East Enders!" exclaimed Marjorie, "No breeding. Every well-brought-up young woman knows how to tie her husband's bow. Come here."

To Lawrence's surprise, she stood behind him to tie his tie. Taller than him, it was easy for her, and the others were incredulous that she did it so quickly and efficiently. With a small laugh, Marjorie said, "I suppose I'll have to come to the concert to tie it for you then!"

Vicky stood back to admire Lawrence. The effect of the dinner suit, and bow tie, was remarkable, and she was aware that all the young mothers in the audience would be charmed by him.

Stanley received a parcel at the school. It was obviously a shoe box wrapped in brown paper and string, and he carried it into the office and sat down. Opening it carefully to conserve both the brown paper and the string, he found a letter from Eric. Before lifting the lid, he read the letter.

"Dear Mr Wykes,

"I hope this letter finds you well. You will remember the sad news of the death of Sean McCann, Billy's dad.

It appears that he was crushed by falling masonry when a group of men were trying to retrieve sacks of rice from a damaged warehouse. Mr McCann had few papers on him, but enough to identify him; and his front door key.

"The police asked me to accompany them when they went to visit the house. I was going in my official capacity as ARP warden, but I explained that I also knew the father and son who lived there, and that Billy had been evacuated to Chipping Norton.

"I was saddened to see how impoverished they were. There was little to eat in the pantry, and few clothes in the cupboard. It's a very tiny house, and Billy and his dad slept in one room. There was an old bureau in the living room, and the police looked through the contents of a box in the drawer. There were a few photos: some of a young woman who I guess was Billy's mum; some papers; and surprisingly a large old pocket watch in a leather pouch. With instructions from the police, I collected all the papers which were of significance, including Billy's birth certificate, and his parents' marriage certificate, together with the photos and the pocket watch, packed them back into the shoebox, and have sent them to you.

"This is Billy's now. It's sad: all his worldly possessions fit into a shoe box.

"Best wishes, Eric."

Stanley opened the box with trepidation. Lying on top of a bundle of papers was a small white corsage of silk flowers with tiny seed pearls, wrapped carefully in fragile tissue paper. Lifting up the flowers, Stanley saw a photograph. It was Sean McCann, much younger, with a beautiful young woman by his side. It was their wedding photograph; and pinned to the young woman's dress was the white corsage he was holding. He placed the flowers back onto top of the photograph and closed the box, and breathed deeply. He knew he had seen something very special.

He went to look for Vicky. "You knew Billy better than most," he said. "What do you know about his mother?"

"Billy has always said she died when he was a baby. I've assumed it means that she died in childbirth. I don't know much more."

"Come into the office. I have something to show you."

Vicky took the precious shoe-box to Mrs Thomas. "I think you'd better be with him when he opens this," she said. They sent Mike away to play, and sat Billy down at the kitchen table.

"This is for you, Billy," said Vicky. "It's very special."

"I know that box," said Billy. "It were me dad's box, weren't it? He never let me see inside."

"Now you dad's gone, it's your box, Billy, and you must keep it safe like your dad did," said Mrs Thomas.

"Shall we open it, Billy?" said Vicky cautiously. Billy nodded, subdued by the importance of the moment.

Taking the lid off, Vicky lifted out the fragile tissue wrapping of the white silk flowers. Mrs Thomas gasped, and Billy said suspiciously, "What's them?"

"I think your mum wore these on her dress when she married your dad," said Vicky. "There's a few photos in the box, and one is your mum and dad's wedding."

"I never seen a photo of me mum," said Billy. "Dad never wanted to talk about her much, I s'pose it made 'im upset. It makes me feel a little bit upset," and a tear trickled out of the corner of Billy's eye.

"We can look at the rest another time," said Vicky.

"No, no, I wanna see, I'm big enough to see it now ain't I?"

CHAPTER THIRTEEN

During the morning of the concert, Vicky and Lawrence had a final sing-through of all the songs, and told the children of the combined schools to be restful during the afternoon, not make themselves dirty during playtime, and to enjoy singing in the Town Hall.

Lots of 'Singing for Spitfires' posters, designed and coloured by the older children, had been displayed around the town. There was a great air of anticipation.

Vicky sighed. "You know that beautiful silk corsage in Billy's box?" she said to Stanley. "It would look lovely on the dress Rosemary's lending me, but I can't ask him."

Stanley sent Vicky home with Lizzie for the afternoon, holding the fort in Vicky's classroom himself. Lawrence was despatched to the Manse to change into the Major's dinner clothes, and have Marjorie tie his bow tie.

"It's strange to be out of school in the afternoon," said Vicky. "I feel as if I'm playing hookey."

"You've worked hard for this evening," said Lizzie. "You deserve a little break: this evening will be exhausting for us all."

There was a knock at the front door of the Harding's house. "Who's that?" said Lizzie. "Funny time for someone to call; usually there's no-one here in the afternoon."

Her heart sank when she opened the door to the telegram boy. "Oh, no, not today," she said.

"It's for Mr Wykes," said the boy. Lizzie stood and watched him push his bicycle back up the long steep hill of The Leys. She frowned, and put the telegram, in her pocket. It was not the dreaded official Ministry of War type of telegram, but an ordinary private one. "However bad this news is, it can wait until after the concert," she thought.

As she returned to her cup of tea in the kitchen, Vicky said, "Who was that?"

"Oh nothing," said Lizzie. Vicky looked at her, frowned, but said nothing.

"Heavens," said Lizzie, "the time is whizzing by. We'd better get ready."

Rosemary and Marjorie struggled to hide their excitement as they dressed Lawrence. He was a very handsome man, and looked even better in the Major's dinner suit. Her own sons had never allowed her to fuss around them, and so for Marjorie it was a novelty. The three of them had had a sweet sherry, and were enjoying the tasks more than they should. Brushing up close to him, Marjorie tripped over his foot.

"Oh, I'm sorry," she said. "I didn't mean to hurt you."

"You didn't hurt me," said Lawrence. "In fact you can stand on that foot, and it won't hurt."

"Whatever do you mean?" said Marjorie.

Leaning down slightly, Lawrence tapped on his thigh. "I've got a wooden leg," he said, "and on the end of it is a wooden foot."

Marjorie jumped back. "I'm terribly sorry," she said. "I'd no idea."

"So that's why you're not in the services," said Rosemary. "I knew you limped a little, but I never knew."

"It's not easy," said Lawrence. "I get quite a few people asking me why I'm not in uniform. It's a not a big secret, but I don't wear a badge saying 'wooden leg'. I don't think the children have worked it out, and they're not old enough to question why I've not been called up."

"I've got something for you," said Lizzie.

Vicky had arrived in the Harding's front room wearing Rosemary's blue dress. Lizzie turned and revealed the white silk corsage from Billy's box. Vicky gasped: "How did you...."

Lizzie smiled. "Stanley did it. He explained to Billy that it would be a very special favour for Singing for Spitfires, if he let you have the flowers, just for one day. Apparently Billy didn't think twice, but said it would be a bit like having his mum at the concert."

Vicky took the delicate spray and held it against the blue velvet. "Help me pin it on," she said. "It's just perfect, and a kind of honour to wear it. I saw the photo of Billy's mum. She was very pretty, and for Billy, I'll be her, just for one evening."

"Don't make me cry," said Lizzie. "There's too much to think about."

"Got all your music?" said Vicky briskly.

"Yes, as ready now as I'll ever be. And what about you?"

"I know it all by heart," said Vicky, "and let's hope Lawrence remembers all his words."

Marjorie had fixed a tiny posy of violets in Lawrence's lapel, and she and her sister declared him ready for action.

"It doesn't matter you're not in uniform," said Rosemary, "you're doing your bit teaching those children; and tonight you're singing for Spitfires."

Arm-in-arm the sisters walked one each side of Lawrence up the hill of Church Street. "I'm not sure what the Major would say if he could see me now," said Marjorie.

"Don't worry about the Major," said Rosemary. "Think about what the boys would think."

The children stood in line as Molly went from one to the next tidying clothing and brushing erratic hair. Soon the long crocodile was making its way down the hill to the Town Hall. The children would enter by the small door downstairs and climb the narrow staircase behind the stage to find their places. Many of the audience, afraid that they would not get a good view if they did not come early, were standing in a queue on the main steps, under the grand portico, eager to pay their sixpences for the Spitfire fund.

Molly, as usual, came last, holding hands with the slower children, watching ahead that no-one stepped into the road, keeping everyone safe.

Just as the children started to file into their places, Robert Evans opened the main doors, and announced that he "Wanted no half-crowns, unless you don't want any change. Please have your sixpences at the ready!"

To his surprise, however, he received quite a few half crowns, with the muttered remark, "It's OK, I don't want the change."

Suddenly a car drew up, and a brilliantly dressed Grenadier officer jumped out, carrying his bearskin. Robert looked him up and down, for a moment unsure who he was. "Mr Bobby, or is it Mr Henry?" he said. "I didn't know you were coming."

"No-one knows, Mr Evans, top secret; and it's Henry, by the way. Is mother here?"

"Not yet, Henry, but I'm sure she'll arrive any minute now."

Henry turned on the top step and surveyed the crowd.

"Good God, there she is, and she's got some young man on her arm."

Laughing at seeing her son, Marjorie dropped Lawrence's arm, leaving him to Rosemary, and despite herself, ran up the Town Hall steps to greet her son.

"In full uniform," she said. "How did you manage that?"

"Pulled a few strings, all hush-hush of course. Whitehall can manage without me for one evening, although I can't stop, have to go back tonight." Looking up, it was his turn to gasp. "My God, what's this coming? Who are they?" Turning, the queue saw the little contingent of Italian prisoners of war, marching smartly towards the Town Hall. Unlike the Christmas concert, the Italians were greeted warmly by some of the people in the queue. Meeting them outside the Co-op was the mayor, who escorted them to their small symbolic cage at the back of the hall.

"Very interesting," was all that Henry had to say.

Gradually the children filed in and sat in their places, and Lawrence took his seat at the side of the stage. Treading carefully amongst the children, Edward Harding stood before the throng. The hall went quiet.

"Welcome to Singing for Spitfires," he said. "This evening we celebrate our two schools, brought together in the worst of circumstances, but singing together as only children can. Mr Evans will make an announcement later regarding how much we have raised for the Spitfire fund. Many people have worked hard, not least the children, to prepare for this evening. However, the true hero, whose enthusiasm has brought all this together, is Miss Victoria Jones, of the Silvertown staff. Please welcome her to the stage."

Resplendent in the blue velvet, Vicky walked forward in front of the children and gave a little bow. Turning to the singers, she caught Billy's eye, and gently stroked the silk flowers. Billy gave her a grin and 'thumb's up'.

There was a buzz in the audience. "Who does she look like?" was the question on everyone's lips, and then the answer came back, "Ava Gardner, with her luxurious hair." And then the next whisper, "But she's smiling, she doesn't have Ava Gardner's sultry look."

"Yes," thought Rosemary, "wearing my dress, after all these months, I see it now. She's our own Ava Gardner."

Vicky turned to Lizzie and nodded. Lizzie gave a long roll on the piano, to herald the National Anthem, and all the children struggled to their feet. The audience stood, and with the massed voices of children and their parents, the singing of God Save the King could be heard in Long Compton.

Edward Harding looked at the women dominating the room:

Stanley's quiet lovable wife Molly, dependable, reliable and warm-hearted, without whose quiet support, encouraging the children and keeping them safe, the concert wouldn't be happening; Molly whose peaceful work as a volunteer, supporting her husband, his staff and the children, was usually unacknowledged, usually taken for granted, sitting out of public sight at the side of the stage, ensuring all ran smoothly.

Vicky, the effervescent East End teacher he had got to know in the last year, brimming over with enthusiasm, able to bring the two schools together in joyous celebration of everything British; using singing to enrich everyone's lives; standing proud in the centre of attention, with four hundred happy children, and probably as many parents, all basking in the warmth of her energy.

Marjorie, the town's severe matriarch, maintaining the very standards that the war was being fought for, respected and feared; soldiering on despite having a husband in a prisoner-of-war camp, one son injured, and the other somewhere in the world in some theatre of war; Marjorie sitting proudly, with ram-rod straight back, in the front row of the audience, with her Guardsman son in his striking dress uniform beside her.

Lizzie, his own wife, frowning slightly as she played her heart out ensuring the best possible performances from the children; Lizzie who had been given a new lease of life playing the piano, and who despite her nerves, was doing a remarkable job.

Vicky smoothed down the blue velvet of her borrowed dress and the audience noisily returned to their seats. Some of the children started to sit down, but she signalled for them to remain standing. With a smile and a nod at Lizzie, she mouthed the opening lines of Rule Britannia to remind the children of their first song. Lizzie played the introduction, and the children took a communal deep breath. They sang the tricky first verse quietly:

> *When Britain first, at heaven's command, arose*
> *from out the azure main,*
> *Arose, arose from out the azure main!*

This was the charter, the charter of the land,
And Guardian Angels sang this strain:

Vicky grinned, and gave her signal for the children to sing much louder.

Rule, Britannia! Britannia, rule the waves!
Britons never, never, never shall be slaves.

Although the words were hard, the children had worked hard with Vicky and Lawrence to master them, and they sang sweetly and clearly. Many of the audience did not know the second and third verses of the song, and several clapped spontaneously at the 'native oak' ending of the third verse.

For the third and final chorus, Vicky turned to the audience to indicate that they should join in, and they did with fervour. The singing melted into applause as the chorus finished, and Vicky smiled. She looked down at Marjorie, seated close by in the front row, and Marjorie smiled and nodded a small acknowledgement of the success of the song.

Lizzie breathed a sigh of relief. She had played faultlessly through the first and hardest of the accompaniments, and with her nerves finally conquered, she knew she was set fair for the rest of the concert.

Stanley touched the unopened telegram in his pocket. Lizzie had given it to him when she got to the Town

Hall, and had told him she'd not opened it. Amidst all this frenzied intensity created by the emotional singing, what dreadful news was sitting heavily in his pocket? As the children launched into the next song, Stanley walked quietly to the narrow staircase at the back of the stage, and went halfway down. He sat on the stairs and opened the envelope.

Regret to inform that direct incendiary bomb has destroyed Silvertown School – stop – full details to follow – stop – Eric

Stanley gasped. He could hardly be surprised: this was news he'd expected at any time, but when it came it was shocking. He looked up the stairs to the hall full of passion and joy. He couldn't tell them now that their school was gone, they had no-where to go back to. From the wings of the stage Molly saw her husband had slipped away down the stairs. Instinctively, she followed, and found him sitting glumly, holding the telegram. He handed it to her.

Vicky continued to propel the concert forward. The time came for Lawrence's first solo. Smoothing down the Major's jacket, he stepped gingerly forward on the front edge of the stage. Several of the younger mothers in the audience fluttered their eyelids: they hadn't realised that their children's modest teacher was so handsome.

"I give you a toast, ladies and gentlemen," sang Lawrence, and the children prepared to burst in with the familiar chorus.

"There'll always be an England," said Stanley, "but what will be left of it when all this is over?"

"We'll be left, and the children will be left. Listen to that sound upstairs – that's what will be left. The bricks and mortar may be destroyed, but the spirit of Silvertown lives on. Put the telegram in your pocket, and say nothing this evening." Molly put her arm around her husband. "Come back up and enjoy our children."

There was one hilarious moment when a group of the older girls gave a little dance and mime to the song "We're going to hang out the washing on the Siefried Line". With headscarves hastily tied on by Molly in the wings, the girls came on to the stage miming pegging their washing.

The patriotic and emotional songs chosen by Vicky and Lawrence continued to enrapture the audience, and there were many tears at the end of the concert. To finish the evening, Vicky once more led the entire chorus of children and audience in a noisy performance of God Save the King. The Mayor looked to his Italian prisoners and saw them singing the British National Anthem, as emotional as the rest of the audience.

Vicky stood to one side to show that the standing ovation was for the children, not her, but everyone knew that it was her charisma and charm which had ensured the extraordinary success of the concert.

"I'm so sorry you have to go," said Marjorie to Henry. "Are you sure you can't just stay for one night?"

"No, mother, I'm quite sure. You know you can't ask me what I'm doing at the moment, and of course, I can't tell you, not even give a hint. The car is waiting, and I'll be gone very soon. Have you heard from Father or Bobby?"

"One or two letters via the Red Cross from Colditz," said Marjorie. "The Major's quite safe, but the letters are obviously censored, and contain nothing about escaping. I live in hope of seeing him any day now.

"You must hope, mother," said Henry, "but what little I've heard seems to suggest that Colditz is close-guarded, and no-one's likely to get out. He may be there until the end of the war. Anything from Bobby?"

"Not for a very long time. I just cling to the hope that no news is good news, but I've no idea where in the world he is, nor what dangers he's facing."

Just as they were getting to the car, Vicky caught up with them.

"Bobby," she said, grabbing him, "thank you so much for coming."

"I'm Henry," laughed the handsome soldier. "We don't know where Bobby is."

Henry noticed that Vicky was blushing, and he stored that moment of information away for some future reflection. "Well done, Miss Jones. It was a triumph. Tootle-pip Mother!" and before they could blink he was in the car and roaring away.

Marjorie turned to Vicky. "Yes, well done Miss Jones. Rosemary's dress looked very good on you. Your young singer Mr Powell, in the Major's suit, reminded me of the Major when I first saw him, when we were both young."

"I think you should keep the dress," said Rosemary. "It's very tight on me, and I've never worn it. The colour suits you."

Vicky was about to return to the Town Hall to assist with matching the tired children to their over-excited parents, when an older man in trilby and raincoat caught her arm. "Miss Jones, may I have a word?" Vicky turned. "I'm from the Banbury Guardian. I must say I was surprised to be sent to cover a little local school concert in Chipping Norton, but I'll admit, it was really quite something. I'd like to check a few things with you, if I may."

Vicky asked the reporter to join her in the Town Hall where they could sit and talk. At first the reporter was full of praise for her, for the children, and for the whole event, but then he turned unexpectedly serious. "That young chap who sang the solos, quite a good voice and very handsome: but why isn't he in uniform? I think many of the readers of my newspaper will want to know."

Vicky hesitated, and looked around. She saw Lawrence in conversation with two of the parents, and called him over. The reporter was forthright. "Well sung young man, you have a good voice." Lawrence smiled, but the smile vanished quickly as the reporter went on, "but not in uniform young man?"

Lawrence leaned close to the reporter. "When I was ten years old, I was excellent at roller skating. One day my skate got caught in the tram lines just outside the school I went to. I couldn't get my foot out of the way, and the tram couldn't stop in time. I don't think the army needs one-legged soldiers, do you?" and he turned and walked away.

It was getting late when the last child and its parents had left the Town Hall. The Mayor had congratulated all concerned, and seen the small contingent of Italian prisoners saunter off to their make-shift huts. Stanley asked Vicky if she'd like him to walk down the hill to The Manse with her, but she said she'd be alright. The Hardings and the Wykes went on their way; Lawrence headed down New Street to his lodgings, and the care-taker started to lock up. Vicky walked slowly across the silent marketplace, and looked up at the stars.

"Who'd have thought it?" she whispered to herself. "Little me, orphan Annie from Plaistow, in a posh frock, in the middle of all that." She sat upon a bench, and looked up. There was a full moon, and the blue of her dress glowed in the moonlight. "Well, you Spitfires," she thought, "you won the Battle of Britain; now let's see you win this war." She smiled, "although I'm not sure about going home. Perhaps this funny little town is my home now. Who knows what the future holds?"

She walked slowly down the hill. A fox darted across Church Street ahead of her. "No-one else up this late?" she asked the fox. "Funny, isn't it? All those people, all those children and their mums and dads, and all that noise; and yet in the end we're all alone and silent. The star of the show walks home alone. It must be the same the world over. Perhaps at this moment, some ordinary German school teacher is walking home alone after her school has sung its heart out. And they're trying to kill us, and we're trying to kill them. When will this nonsense be over?"

"Cocoa?" said Edward. "A bit of a cliché, but it seems right after such a wonderful evening."

"We may need something stronger," said Stanley. "I've had a telegram."

"I'd forgotten all about it," gasped Lizzie. "It came this afternoon, when Vicky was here."

Stanley pulled it out from his pocket. "At least it's not about anyone dying," he said, "but still very upsetting."

Molly smiled at her husband. "It was so hard for you to stay cheerful during the concert," she said, "but you did, for the children."

"So did you," said Stanley.

"Tell us, what's in the telegram?" said Edward.

"Here," said Stanley. "Read it for yourself."

Edward took the telegram, and Lizzie leaned over him. They read it together, and gulped.

"I'm so sorry," said Edward. "I don't know what to say."

"I've been thinking about it ever since I read it," said Stanley. "I must tell the staff and the children tomorrow. You can be sure it won't be long before someone in Silvertown gets a message to one of the children: I'd like them to hear it from me, rather than buzz round like a rumour."

Vicky and the rest of the Silvertown staff assumed that getting a message about a short staff meeting before school the next day was to congratulate them on the success of the concert the previous evening: and that was exactly how Stanley started the meeting. "However," he continued, "during the day I received a telegram from our colleague Eric, who you know is an ARP warden for Silvertown. It's not good news." He pulled the crumpled telegram from his pocket, and read it.

There was a moment of silence, and then hesitantly Lawrence spoke, "You mean whilst we were having a joyous time yesterday, our school was burning?"

"By the time we got to the concert, the school building was gone," said Stanley simply.

"But not our school," said Molly quickly. "We are all here, and safe. Silvertown School lives on."

"But what will happen to us?" said Vicky. "We can't stay here indefinitely. This bloody war will finish one day, and perhaps we'll want to go home. What will we go home to?"

"I don't know," said Stanley, wearily. "I just don't know."

CHAPTER FOURTEEN

"Colditz Olympics!" announced the Polish soldier, standing at the door of the British quarters.

"What?" said the Major.

"We challenge you to some sports. We race better than you British, and we can jump higher. We challenge you!"

"That's some challenge," said the Major.

A committee was formed with representatives from all the nations: Belgium, The Netherlands, France, Poland and Great Britain. The Poles took most of the responsibility for the organisation, as they were by far the largest contingent in Colditz. Sports were chosen for the international competition: football, volleyball, boxing and chess. Douglas Bader said, "I shall be your secret weapon. I'm not going to be much help with football or volleyball, and I've no interest in boxing; but I'm an ace when it comes to chess. How do you think I spent all those hours in hospital?"

"They want footballs," said Marjorie, looking up from the Major's latest letter from the Castle. "Do you think it's some kind of code, or do they really want footballs?"

"We have some at school, but they're a constant problem. You have to have a bladder like a tough balloon, and pump it up inside the leather. I think we could buy one or two in Banbury or Oxford, and send them flat," said Vicky.

"And include a pump," said Rosemary.

"They all went to good schools," said Marjorie. "I'm sure they'll know how to pump up a ball, even if they're more used to rugby balls."

"We'll make a parcel, and put a few little luxuries in with the footballs," said Rosemary .

"I can go to Oxford on Saturday," said Marjorie. "Victoria, would you like to come with me?"

Vicky smiled. Marjorie had never offered to take her shopping before, but ever since the Spitfire concert, Marjorie had been easier with her lodger.

"I'd like that very much," said Vicky. "Do we go by bus?"

"No, we'll investigate the trains. Rosemary can hold the fort here with Buster."

Saturday morning saw Marjorie and Vicky waiting for a train, hoping that one was actually going to arrive at the time they'd been given. Happily, a train arrived from Banbury just as scheduled, and they were settled into a rather tired Third Class compartment. "We may not be so lucky getting back," said Marjorie. "We shall have to stay at the Randolph if we're stranded."

As they rattled towards the city, Vicky reflected, "Oxford's escaped the bombing, hasn't it? I wonder why?"

"Very strange," agreed Marjorie, "especially as Hitler must know there's lots of military senior staff billeted here."

"Perhaps he doesn't want to spoil the lovely city," said Vicky.

"Don't be fanciful," said Marjorie, severely. "Never give that monster credit for any feelings or compassion. I believe he'd murder his own mother if it gained him anything."

Walking from the station to Boswell's, Vicky said, "You know I've never been here before. I qualified as a teacher at Queen Mary's, Mile End. We called it the 'People's Palace' because it trained ordinary people like me, from humble backgrounds. It's a very grand building, but nothing like this."

"That's Balliol College," said Marjorie. "If we can do the shopping quickly, I'll take you down Broad Street, and you can see the Sheldonian and the Bodleian."

"Are they colleges as well?" said Vicky.

"Good gracious, no, the Sheldonian Theatre is where they confer the degrees; and the Bodleian Library is one of the oldest in the world. Now, here's Boswell's: let's go and get these balls, and see what else we might buy for the men in Colditz."

Vicky was taken aback by Marjorie's shopping technique. She expected the entire store to stop to attend to her; she asked to see every variety of football available, although there was little choice; and she even lingered over some lacrosse sticks, until Vicky pointed out how hard it would be to post them to an enemy prisoner-of-war castle.

Once the choice was made, Marjorie then sent for the manager, and told him that the balls and other items were selected to be sent to Colditz Castle where the Major and several other senior officers were being held. "Therefore, of course," she concluded, "you will be very willing to donate these items to the armed forces, won't you?"

Vicky was secretly wondering why the army didn't already have plenty of footballs, but she said nothing.

Boswell's manager, caught off guard, gulped and agreed, and soon the deflated balls were wrapped in a parcel, and handed to Vicky to carry.

Back on the street, Marjorie announced, "That was most satisfactory. Now we have time for a little lunch, but first I'll show you Broad Street."

As they turned right out of Boswell's, Vicky saw a familiar figure ahead. The man was in civilian clothes, but walked with the posture of a soldier. "There's Henry!" she exclaimed.

"Don't be silly," said Marjorie, "He's in London. Although I must say it's suspiciously like him."

Vicky ran ahead, and called his name. Stopping, the man turned. It was indeed, Henry. "I thought it was you, Henry," said Vicky. "Assuming, that is, you're not Bobby."

After the initial shock, Henry smiled. "Little Victoria," he said, "and Mother. This is unexpected."

"It certainly is," said Marjorie. "I thought you were in London."

Henry smiled enigmatically. "Look, we can't talk in the street. I'm on my way for lunch at Brasenose. You can come with me. My meeting isn't until mid-afternoon. Let me take your parcel, little Victoria, and we'll cut through by the Radcliffe."

Vicky felt she was in an alien country as they walked though narrow lanes, past extraordinary buildings, all untouched by the war, and finally arrived at Brasenose. As they walked, Henry asked all about his Aunt

Rosemary, and Buster the dog, but revealed nothing about himself or the business that had brought him to Oxford.

Crossing the Brasenose quadrangle, they came to a modest door, with an enormous sundial upon the wall above it. A soldier stood guard at the door, and upon Henry's approach he snapped to attention and saluted. "At ease," murmured Henry, and they stepped into the darkness of the building. A short passage led to another Tudor door, and the dining room. Henry spoke to an elderly man who was stationed at the door, and they were led to a small table in one corner.

Vicky looked around. Several soldiers, in a variety of uniforms, were seated at the long refectory tables, and there was a very hushed murmur of conversation.

"It's as if everyone is whispering state secrets," said Vicky, in a suitably quiet voice.

Henry smiled. "You may well be correct," he said. "That's why we're at a separate table, so we can whisper our state secrets."

"I don't think I know any secrets," said Vicky.

"And I know you'll not reveal a thing to us," said Marjorie, "despite me being your own mother."

"The walls have ears, and careless talk costs lives," said Henry.

Vicky looked around as if he was being literal. "These walls are old enough to have ears," she said.

The men having lunch were all young and fit, in considerable contrast to the team of elderly men, in short white coats, waiting on them. Vicky was struck by the peaceful air, not only of the dining room, but by the whole college, and its grandiose surroundings.

"It's as if there's no war on," she said, "and yet there are soldiers everywhere. It's very spooky."

"This is all part of the war effort," said Henry.

At last, Marjorie's curiosity got the better of her. "So tell me, what are you doing here, and how is this part of the war effort?"

"Mother, I'm based in Whitehall, as you know; but most of the time my duties bring me to Oxfordshire. One day, when the war is over, you may find out more; but for now that's it: I'll say no more. I may even have taken a risk bringing you here, especially as in peace time women are not allowed to enter Brasenose. Now let us enjoy lunch and talk of other things. I've not seen you since that flying visit to your concert Victoria. How is everything?"

With conversation about the concert, the fire which had destroyed Silvertown School, and the parcel of footballs, lunch passed without any further talk of Henry's role in the war. Vicky noticed that Henry used only his right hand when eating, his left remaining in his lap.

"Is your arm healed?" she asked. "You don't need to wear the sling any more?"

"I think it's as good as it's going to get," said Henry. "I've got no grip: it's nerve damage apparently. They tell me it might come back gradually, but I'm not so sure."

Back at the station, they waited to see if any trains would be running, and although very late, a tank engine eventually arrived with two elderly carriages. "All stops to Banbury," shouted the Station Master, so they boarded.

"What an extraordinary day," said Vicky. "Just visiting Oxford was interesting enough, but then we met Henry and saw inside a college."

"Especially seeing inside Brasenose," said Marjorie. "When I was at Somerville, it was strictly off-limits. In fact women weren't allowed into any of the men's colleges. I was at Somerville for three years, but never set foot in any of them. I daresay after the war, they'll go back to the old ways, and be a men-only college. It's probably for the best to maintain the old traditions."

"Queen Mary's was men and women," said Vicky. "It's hard to imagine it any other way."

"I can't help thinking that the request for footballs was some kind of code," said Marjorie. "I hope they're not expecting something different after all this effort."

The Colditz Olympics was a great success, even though the games were somewhat one-sided with the big contingent of Poles fielding a large team. The British did well in the football, but were upset that no other country team was prepared to play rugby, at which they felt they would excel. The French were unexpectedly good at volleyball, but it was in chess, with their unexpected master, Douglas Bader, that the British team won hands down.

The Major surprised everyone, including himself, by entering the boxing championship, and winning through to the final, where he was knocked out by a very large Polish officer. The Major had been a reluctant boxer at his school, Radley, when he had been given the choice of boxing or football, which he loathed. "I'd rather bash someone in the face, than run around a muddy field chasing a wretched leather ball," was his comment at the time; and many years later, in Colditz, the basic schoolboy skills of boxing had returned to him. With his advancing age, he could bring tactics into the sport, and thus did well.

After the sports, and awards of cardboard medals, the Major wrote home:

"To all at The Manse,

"The footballs you sent have been put to excellent use. They are far superior to the poor quality German balls the lads have been using for football practise. They were used for the knockout competition in our Colditz Olympics. There was much enthusiasm for the football games, although for the life of me, I still can't see the merit in the sorry game. Some of the chaps get

very worked up, but I think they are the officers from working-class backgrounds who know no better.

"I was pleased with my own performance in the boxing tournament. The old skills I learned with such reluctance at Radley came back to me, and I boxed through to the final. I have a silver medal, made of a toffee wrapper and cardboard, which I wear with pride."

"Boxing!" exclaimed Rosemary. "I'd no idea the Major could box."

"Nor had I," said Marjorie. "Whenever it was mentioned, he just called it a 'barbaric sport', but it appears that he's quite good at it."

"We all have hidden talents," said Vicky, "although that's quite a surprising one."

"One of our group, the air-ace Bader, turned out to be a chess-ace as well, and won every one of his matches, and thus the British team's only gold medal.

"Life here continues to be dreary, and the standard of food has gone rapidly down-hill. Staging events like our Olympics keeps us sane, and is very good for morale, but we long for freedom and the end of the war. We are lucky that the Red Cross gets parcels through to us, and we appreciate you continuing to send them. At least it shows you haven't forgotten us.

"We get heavily censored German news, which consists mainly of propaganda messages about how well the war is going for them.

"I look forward to hearing all your news. The post is censored, of course, but your everyday gossip won't be deleted. I'm sure everyday life in Chipping Norton must be more exciting that daily life here. Chin up, Marjie!"

Whilst the inmates at Colditz were staging their own Olympic Games, the people in Chipping Norton were coming to grips with clothing rationing.

"We must manage with what we've got," said Rosemary.

"Thank goodness I've always bought good quality," said Marjorie. "Good quality is everything in clothing. Why, I still have several skirts and blouses from my Somerville days, when my mother kitted me out in the very best."

"It's make do and mend, for me," said Vicky. "I couldn't bring everything, and what I left behind's long gone. It's funny isn't it? Somehow we weren't surprised by rationing food, and petrol of course, but I didn't expect a shortage of clothing."

"There's not been much in the shops for a while," said Rosemary.

"We saw that at Boswells," said Marjorie. "With the factories all devoted to the war effort, and nothing coming from other countries, we should not be surprised."

"If going without a new blouse means an airman getting a parachute, I don't think we can complain," said Rosemary.

"We should have another jumble sale," said Vicky. "You never know what might turn up."

Mr Thomas was at work on the farm, when the postman delivered the letter to his wife. With the boys at school, she was on her own, and could not decide whether to open it or not. From its official stamps, she had a strong suspicion what the envelope contained, and with shaking hands, she placed it in the centre of the kitchen table. She continued to prepare vegetables and peel potatoes, glancing every now and again, as if she hoped that the letter would disappear.

The boys came in from school, demanded a snack, and were given a large scrubbed carrot each. "Don't go far," said Mrs Thomas. "Your dad will be home soon."

She picked up the ominous envelope, and shakily put it down again. She'd known it would come sooner or later, but that didn't help her jangling nerves. Mr Thomas had seen the boys at the top of a tree on his way home, and had called them down. With Mike, the lightest, on his back, and Billy trotting beside, they made a noisy entrance to the kitchen.

"I'm starving, mother," he said.

"So are we," said Billy.

"Come in and wash up: supper's ready."

The four sat down, and Mrs Thomas put the big bowl of potatoes on the table. Just as he was reaching for the spoon, Mr Thomas spotted the letter.

"What's that?"

"It's what you think it is:" said Mrs Thomas, "your call-up papers."

Fumbling with his big farmer's hands, Mr Thomas opened the envelope, and pulled out the official documents. His wife and the boys held their breath as he read the contents.

"Next week," he stammered.

Mrs Thomas took the document from him. "Bovington Garrison," she read. "Where's that?"

"Dorset, I think," said her husband. "Somewhere down near Poole, or Weymouth. Look there's a train pass here, for me to go there. I have to go to a station called 'Wool': that's a funny name for a place. There's a lot more here for me to read."

"These potatoes are getting cold," said Mrs Thomas. "Put the call-up papers to one side, and we'll go through them together later."

With the warm summer evening, the boys wanted to play outside, and Mr and Mrs Thomas were grateful to have the kitchen to themselves for an hour. They discovered that Mr Thomas had been selected for training as a tank driver, which was why he was to go directly to Bovington, and not the usual squaddies' first camp at Caterick. At some stage, which he could not remember, he'd been asked about the skills he could offer to the army, and he'd said he was a tractor driver. It seemed this was sufficient to propel him into a tank corps.

The letter contained basic information about what to take, and said he'd be met at Wool Station the following week.

"So, this is it," he told his wife. "I suppose I'm lucky to have been able to stay at home so far in this terrible war. It's nearly two years since it started: surely it can't go on much longer?"

"With the Nazis in France, there's no knowing," said his wife. "We'll miss you."

"The farm will miss me – the men that are left are all much older than I am; and the boys will miss me. Billy's lost one dad already; let's hope he doesn't lose another."

"Don't talk like that," said Mrs Thomas. "I've got to believe you'll be back soon; and with these two growing lads, I'll be busy enough whilst I'm waiting for you."

Marjorie had written a long letter to the Major, and told him at length about the Singing for Spitfires concert. Vicky would have been surprised at how Marjorie admitted to her husband that she'd misjudged her at first. *"Despite her obvious working-class background, she seems quite a personable young woman, and she certainly had a way with the children at the concert. I feel sorry for her born in such difficult circumstances, and I am beginning to admire the way she's risen above her disadvantages.*

"I wonder what the future holds for her, and all the evacuated teachers and children. The Silvertown school building has been destroyed by a fire bomb, and many of their homes, including Victoria's, have been bombed. There does not appear to be much to go home to at the end of the war."

Marjorie was unsure what might be censored from her letters to the Major; was writing about bombed homes and burnt schools permissible? She finished her letter with some very harmless comment about clothing rationing, and Rosemary's remarkable skills to 'make do and mend', again hoping that referring to rationing would not be cut out of her letter.

Once more, she and Rosemary put together a box of preserves for the Major and the inmates at Colditz, wrapped as usual in hay from their own garden.

"I don't know how long we can keep doing this," she remarked to Rosemary. "With such a shortage of sugar, it's hard to make jam; and yet we can't send the fresh fruit, we have to preserve it."

"We may even run out of cardboard boxes and string," said Rosemary. "We have to be economical with everything. I have a cardigan I never wear, so I propose unravelling it, washing the wool and then knitting something which would be useful, perhaps to send to the Major."

"Thankfully, everything is growing well in the garden," said Marjorie. "Not long now, and we'll start harvesting the fruit. We must involve Victoria – she has come on a long way since she first arrived, and couldn't tell one end of a carrot from another. It's monotonous living on vegetables, but we are so lucky we have a big productive garden. It must be dreadful trying to feed a family in the city, coping with bomb damage, and dependent on the limited rations and even more limited fresh food not on the ration."

Rosemary suddenly had a thought. "I wonder how that nice ARP-warden-teacher, Eric, is? You remember he took home a big sack of vegetables when he came at Christmas. Apparently he saw the fire at the school, and wrote to Mr Wykes about it. Once the fruit is ripe, and we've plenty to pick, we should see if he'd like to come for a kind of fruit-picking holiday, and take another big sack back to London."

Billy was feeling especially proud of himself as he rushed into the kitchen. "Mum, mum, you know when dad went off to the war, you said you didn't know how you'd ever get the garden digged?"

"Dug, Billy, not digged."

"Yes, mum, well look out there now. It's being digged!"

Mrs Thomas opened the back door and was taken aback to see two young men digging the vegetable garden. There was a big patch where the new potatoes had recently been picked, and which needed digging.

"Who are they, Billy?" said Mrs Thomas, ominously.

"The Eye-ties, mum, I went and got them to come and do the digging. It's OK, they got permission. They're allowed to do things like gardening, as long as they go back to their hut at tea time."

"I'm not sure about this, Billy. I'll go and have a word with them."

Billy and Mike watched as Mrs Thomas went to talk to the Italians. To their relief, she came back smiling. "Well done Billy," she said. "It seems to be OK, although I'm not too sure we understood one another. They don't speak much English, but they said 'God save the King'. We'd better keep an eye on them at the end of the day. It would be very embarrassing if they ran away."

"They won't, mum," said Billy. "They want to stay here, even after the war finishes. They like it here and say it's peaceful."

"That's as perverse as you could be," said Mrs Thomas. "They're prisoners in an enemy country during this ghastly war, and they say it's peaceful."

"They don't want to go back to Eye-tie-land, 'cos they'd have to go and fight again," said Billy. "Does that mean they're cowards, mum?"

"I don't know. Perhaps there'd be no war if everyone thought that."

Airey Neave decided to spend a lot of time assisting in the prison laundry. Although a mass break-out from a prisoner of war camp seemed exciting, he realised that the best way to escape would be alone or perhaps with one other companion. That way, less attention would be drawn to the plan, and success was more likely.

He always remembered his childhood hero, Mr Toad, who had escaped from prison disguised as a washer-woman, and he remained convinced that there were so many people coming and going at the castle, that walking out in disguise was possible.

In order to get hold of a Nazi uniform, he regularly helped in the laundry, and very gradually he became sufficiently familiar to the daily laundry staff that they became much less diligent about keeping an eye on him. He had noticed that the Dutch soldiers' uniforms were more similar to the Nazi uniforms, and so his costume, based on a Dutch tunic, started to take shape. Nightly he slept on the collection of clothes he was accumulating, hidden under his thin mattress.

The ritual of sitting together after supper and listening to the BBC was becoming tedious. "Once we said 'over by Christmas'," said Vicky. "Now it feels as though this war is going on forever."

"Getting ready for another Christmas at school?" asked Rosemary.

"Yes," said Vicky, "although we've been learning carols for about three weeks, since mid-November I suppose. It will be our third Christmas in Chipping Norton, and our third concert at the Town Hall. Turn the radio off, Marjorie, the news is dull, and confusing. Will we never win against this terrible man and his evil armies?"

"We'll not be beaten," said Marjorie, "but the news is so disparate, from different places and different fighters. It seems to be spreading all over the world, even more than the last war."

"Stop and listen for a moment," said Rosemary suddenly. "Don't turn it off! Something's happening, something big, listen."

They paused in their conversation and were startled to hear the voice of the President of the United States, Franklin Roosevelt. *"Yesterday, December 7th, 1941, a date which will live in infamy, the United States of American was suddenly and deliberately attacked by naval and air forces of the empire of Japan."*

Marjorie gasped. "The United States, and Japan? What does this mean?" They continued to listen to the

President's voice. In solemn and tragic tones he concluded: *"With confidence in our armed forces, with the unbounding determination of our people, we will gain the inevitable triumph, so help us God. I ask that the Congress declare that since the unprovoked and dastardly attack by Japan on Sunday 7th December, 1941, a state of war has existed between the United States and the Japanese Empire."*

They heard the applause of the members of the Congress, as the commentary resumed in London.

"I think this is good news for us," said Vicky. "If the United States is in the war, it must help us."

"The attack in Pearl Harbour must have been dreadful, with huge loss of life, for the President to make that decision so quickly," said Rosemary.

"Churchill will feel some sense of relief," said Marjorie. "We'll lose thet feeling that we are alone in this war. I wonder if the Major and the other officers in Colditz will get the news? I hope that the first they know will not be the arrival of American officers into the castle."

Whilst the men knew that the news they were given by their captors was heavily censored in favour of the Nazi war effort, they also had a tiny radio receiver, smuggled to them in a food parcel, which they could listen to at night. Despite the dreadful reception, they could keep abreast of the news from the BBC, and thus they heard the news about the terrible bombing of Pearl Harbour, and the entrance of The United States into the war.

"We must put some American songs into our Christmas concert," said Vicky, "although I'm not sure if I know any."

"It's tempting to put some Boogie-Woogie into our show," said one of the officers, "although that might give the goons a message that we know about the US coming into the war, and they'll come and hunt for the radio."

"When do you think you'll be ready for this show?" said Neave. "In time for Christmas?"

"No, we'll not be ready. We must try to get some more costumes together, and we need the goons to let us have some time down in the theatre."

"Middle of January?" said Neave. "I'll see if I can help with costumes by borrowing stuff from the laundry."

"What's 'Boogie-woogie'?" said Billy. "We're doing it at school."

"Boogie-woogie at school!" laughed Mrs Thomas. "What will that Miss Jones think of next?

"It's because the Yanks are in the war," said Billy. "We're singing Boogie-woogie in the Christmas concert."

Mrs Thomas turned and watched as Billy and Mike started singing, "Pardon me Miss, is that the Chattanoonga Choo-choo?" but they could not remember anymore and dissolved into giggles. "We've got to learn the whole song by the end of the week. Mr Powell sang it to us this morning: it's very funny and we all laughed, and I think Miss Harding can't really play it on the piano."

"She's Mrs Harding, and she does very well with all you ragamuffins. You're very lucky to have her, and the others, doing all this lovely singing with you. I hope you're getting some other work done as well."

The boys sat at the kitchen table. "Mum," said Mike, "read dad's letter again."

Mrs Thomas went to the clock on the mantel shelf and from behind it pulled out the precious letter from her husband. She sat with the boys, and read.

"It's very hard work here, and no time for resting. We are a squad of men, all farmers, all tractor drivers, and we're training to drive tanks. I'm not allowed to say much in a letter, but I can tell you that our tanks are called 'Crusaders' and they have big powerful Rolls Royce engines. It was very scary at first, but now me and my mates are really enjoying learning to handle them. They are very, very noisy. We have a lot of land in Dorset to practise driving, and we go out in all

weathers. You might be able to get a picture of a Crusader in a comic book or in the newspaper. We'll stay in Dorset until we're good at driving, and then who knows where we will go.

"By the way, there's an unexpected link to Chipping Norton here, as my squadron leader is Captain Anderson-Grey. On the very first day, when we lined up as very raw recruits, he came and spoke to each of us. When I said I was from Chipping Norton, he laughed. "Then you'll know my mother," he said, "Mrs Anderson-Grey, down at The Manse." I think he's younger than me, very young to be a captain, but he's very fair, and very strict. I expect he gets that from his mum!

"Rolls Royce!" exclaimed Mike for the umpteenth time. "Dad's driving a Roller!"

"I don't think it looks much like a Rolls Royce," said Mrs Thomas. "We'll try to look for a picture of a Crusader tank in Timothy White's."

The Italians continued to help in local vegetable gardens but with Christmas approaching, and dark evenings, they were retreating to their huts earlier and earlier. The two who had been working in Mr Thomas's garden were often gone before Billy and Mike got home from school.

"The Italians were here again today," said Mrs Thomas. "With two of them, the garden has never looked so good. Do you know if they will be invited to the school Christmas Concert this year?"

"I 'spec so," said Billy.

"I was thinking," said Mrs Thomas. "Without Mike's dad, and without your dad, Billy, it will be funny to have Christmas with just us. Would you like me to invite them to come here for their Christmas dinner?"

"Not 'arf," said Billy. "They're really nice, even if they are Eye-ties."

"I'll only invite them if you call them by the proper word, Billy. They are Italians."

"Yea, I know, but everyone calls 'em Eye-ties."

"You're what they call incorrigible, Billy McCann, and no mistake."

"What's that mum?"

"You'll find out soon enough," laughed his mother. "And anyway, if they come to Christmas Dinner, they'll be eating vegetables they've grown themselves in our garden."

Once more, Vicky took to the stage to conduct the children in a rousing concert. This time, Christmas carols were interspersed with patriotic songs, and the newest song in the children's repertoire, 'Chattanooga-choo-choo'. Lawrence sang the whole song, all the way through, and then the children repeated it, complete with suitable actions. The audience were delighted.

It seemed that 'Singing for Spitfires' was becoming a tradition for Chipping Norton; and many people noticed that the evacuated children and their teachers had become a permanent fixture in the town. "We'll miss them when they go," was an oft-repeated sentiment.

In January, the British concert party in Colditz Castle was also a great success. The other nationalities imprisoned made an enthusiastic audience. Several of their guards joined them, and seemed to equally have a good time, fuelled in their case, by plenty of good German beer. It was only afterwards, back in their dormitory, that the British contingent discovered that Airey Neave was missing.

The guards, who had enjoyed the concert party, and had a few too many beers to drink, did not notice his absence until the next morning. In his well-prepared fake Nazi uniform, Neave had changed his clothes in a small space under the stage during the concert party, smiling to himself at the proximity of the guards in the audience, unaware of his plan; and had slipped away through a trap door into the deserted laundry.

From there, he had brushed himself down, adjusted his cap, and marched smartly across the courtyard, and out of the castle. By the following morning, when the alarm was raised, he was far away.

CHAPTER FIFTEEN

Through the winter of 1941, and into 1942, Molly worked hard to re-establish the Chipping Norton Girl Guide troupe. Meeting regularly in the dusty church hall overlooking the graveyard, the girls cleaned the hall, and worked on refurbishing their own uniforms. It seemed to Molly that 'make do and mend' was becoming the motto of the guides.

The girls followed the development of the war. Molly was pleased that they not only took a great interest in the various campaigns, but also talked endlessly about ways to help the servicemen at the front. Knowing that many soldiers, sailors and airmen were incarcerated in German prisoner of war camps, they collected all kinds of gifts for the Red Cross to send to the men.

The guides understood that many of the prison camps were in very inhospitable parts of Europe, and that the men were often cold. Molly had to admit that she was not very good at knitting, but several of the girls could knit well, and mainly using wool from old garments, unravelled and washed, they made lots of mittens and socks to be sent to the men. Molly, in turn, found that she enjoyed working with the teenagers, and realised that she was becoming more and more involved in the life of the small town.

As the spring of 1942 turned into summer, many of the younger children were forgetting their old lives in Silvertown, and it seemed completely normal for the two schools to be working together.

"This is our life now," said Stanley to Molly. "It will be very strange to go back to Silvertown."

"You know," said Mrs Thomas to Billy, "it's as if you've been here all your life."

"It was very strange at first," admitted Marjorie to Vicky, "but we seem to have grown used to one another."

"And I even know about growing vegetables," smiled Vicky. "I've grown accustomed to this place, and we are so lucky that it's peaceful, despite the war. Our priority is to support the troops, but we're not in danger ourselves."

"When the war came, I was fearful that I'd not live to see retirement," said Edward to Lizzie. "It was like everything was in danger."

"For many, they are in terrible danger," said Lizzie, "overseas, all around the world, and especially in our cities. We are so lucky that our war in the Cotswolds is quiet and tranquil."

The noise startled everyone in the town. It was in the early hours of Friday 21st August, 1942. The town was used to the sound of low-flying aircraft. They'd identified British bombers departing for Germany, heavy-laden with their lethal delivery; and German bombers bringing equally terrible loads to the cities of the Midlands. They also knew the sound of lighter higher-pitched Luftwaffe bombers returning from their deadly missions.

This time, the noise was different.

"Christ, what was that?" Vicky sat bolt upright in bed. The explosion had woken the whole town, and the continued rumbling and crackling alarmed everyone, as many smaller explosions continued. Buster started howling, echoed by all the other dogs in the town. Vicky grabbed Bobby's big dressing gown, and push her feet into shoes. As she came out onto the landing, Rosemary and Marjorie were also rushing out.

"What going on?" said Rosemary.

"Whatever it is, it's damned close," said Marjorie, heading down the stairs.

As they stumbled out of the front door, a fearsome sight met their eyes, and they quickly understood what had happened. A plane had crashed into a house close to them on Church Street,

"It's John Brigg's," said Marjorie. "Yew Dell's on fire. I'll telephone."

As she returned to the house, the others stood at the front gate of the Manse. The sky was illuminated by the flames, and they could feel the heat from where they stood.

"Don't go nearer, there could be more explosions," said Vicky. "What if the plane had bombs on board?"

"Something's exploding, but it's not bombs. Something smaller – perhaps bullets," said Rosemary.

Marjorie joined them, "Brigade's on the way, but didn't need the phone call, they heard it from the station."

Billy and Mike were woken by the noise, and despite it being two o'clock in the morning, Billy was out of bed in a flash. Standing in the front garden, he could see the glow of the flames and the pall of smoke in the sky. All down the street neighbours were coming out to watch.

"That's down by the church," said Mike, "where Miss Jones lives."

"Miss Jones!" exclaimed Billy. "We must see if she's OK!"

And he was off, running down the hill in his pyjamas and slippers, with Mrs Thomas yelling after him, "Billy, come back, Billy! Mike, you stay exactly where you are."

Lizzie had grabbed her husband when the noise had woken them. "This is what we've been dreading," she said. "The war's come to Chipping Norton."

Standing on the lawn with the Wykes, the two headteachers and their wives stood feeling helpless. "What can we do?" said Lizzie.

Molly was decisive: "It looks like it could be the church, or it could be the Manse. We must go and see if we can help. I'm getting dressed."

Running down Church Street, Billy could see that the fire brigade were already trying to put out the fire. Robert Evans, a raincoat over his pyjamas and his ARP helmet jammed on his head, was stopping people just by the almshouses. "The police say there could be unexploded bombs. No-one is to go any nearer."

"What are them bangs like fireworks?" said Billy.

"Bullets apparently," said Robert. "Why are you here on your own? It's the middle of the night!"

"I weren't gonna miss this," said Billy, the flames reflecting in his startled eyes.

Hurrying down Diston's Lane, Stanley and Edward and their wives caught up with Lawrence. "What's going on?" said Stanley.

"Big fire in Church Street," said Lawrence. "You know I sleep in that room over the arch? Well I was woken by the explosion, and then the room was flooded with light from the flames."

Crossing the churchyard, and turning into Church Street, they saw Vicky, Marjorie and Rosemary standing at the front gate of the Manse.

"I hate feeling so useless," said Molly. "Isn't there anything we can do to help?"

Just as she spoke, they were astonished to see the kitchen windows of Yew Dell flung open, and John Brigg and his wife jumped out onto the street, directly beneath the burning aeroplane, and came running down the street towards them.

"Is there anyone else in the house?" shouted Vicky.

"No, just us, and the cat," said Mr Brigg. "We were asleep when all hell let loose. As far as I can tell in the chaos, the house isn't really on fire: it's the plane that's crashed onto the roof that's burning, and there seem to be lots of small explosions."

"We think that might be bullets," said Vicky.

Breathlessly, Mrs Thomas came running down the hill towards the fire. "Billy," she said as she caught him, "don't you ever do that again. You are a naughty boy."

She stopped and looked down the hill. The burning plane on top of the house was an extraordinary sight, and secretly she understood why Billy had wanted to see it: she was excited by it herself. "I left Mike in bed on his own; we must go home now."

"Let's stop for a bit," said Billy. "It's frilling, innit?"

"You must move back up," came the severe voice of Robert Evans, who had appeared with a policemen by his side. "Back up to the top of the hill. It's not safe here; there could be further explosions."

"There wasn't an air-raid siren," said Mrs Thomas.

"No," said Robert. "No messages, nothing. This came right out of the blue."

"Look," said Billy, "there's another fire, over there on that old castle hill. You can see it through the trees."

As Molly and Marjorie took Mr and Mrs Brigg into the Manse, Rosemary looked up. "Oh no," she said, "there's another fire over on Castle Mound. They'll never get a fire engine over there, but I'll phone the brigade."

She let the telephone ring for a long time, but there was no answer. Clearly everyone from the fire station was attending the drama in Church Street.

Back out in the street, she saw Edward and Stanley at the front door of Number Eight. The elderly lady who lived alone there was just emerging, obviously very shaken and alarmed. Rosemary ran across. "Bring her into the Manse," she said.

At that moment, a policeman came running from the churchyard. "We are evacuating the whole street, and even the old ladies in the almshouses. Those uphill of the fire are being taken to the Salvation Army; those down the hill, into the Church Hall. It's not safe to try and go up the hill past the fire."

"No," said Rosemary. "The Church Hall is very bleak; bring everyone into the Manse."

As dawn broke, and the firemen finally extinguished the fire, an acrid smell filled the air. It being the school holiday, nothing would stop Billy, Mike and several of the children from going down Church Street to see the wreckage. The fire brigade were still there and curls of blue smoke rose lazily from the smouldering wreckage. Surprisingly, Yew Dell was less damaged than might be expected, although it was obviously in a terrible mess: what had not been damaged by the impact had been ruined by the fire brigade hoses.

"That's a Wellington," said Billy knowledgeably. "I never saw one so close before. It's a funny colour, innit?"

"Kind of black," said Mike, "but different 'cos of the fire."

"It's got one wing missing," said Billy. "Look you can see where it tore off. That must be why it crashed."

From her bedroom window, Vicky could see the burning wreckage on Castle Mound. As predicted, the fire brigade had not been able to get near, and since there were no trees close by, they had decided to let that fire burn itself out. Looking further afield, Vicky could see another fire burning in the direction of Over Norton.

Coming down stairs, she was startled to see how many neighbours were sitting and snoozing in all kinds of positions. The old lady from Number Eight was asleep on the couch; Mr and Mrs Brigg, from Yew Dell were sitting at the kitchen table; and several other neighbours were in the parlour and dining room. Rosemary was already up and had two giant kettles on the hob. Molly was helping her, having collected the kettles from the Church Hall.

"We can give everyone a cup of tea," said Rosemary, "and we've enough milk, but hardly any sugar."

Robert Evans smiled as he pulled the brass handle of the bell. It seem a lifetime ago that he'd come to ask Marjorie to take evacuees. How much the town had changed in those years. Marjorie sailed though the assembled neighbours to open the door. "Mr Evans," she exclaimed. "Are you here as a bank manager or as an A R P Warden?"

"As your A R P Warden, actually," said Robert, "and with good news. The police and fire brigade tell me the fire is out and the wreckage safe. Thank you for taking in all these refugees, Mrs Anderson-Grey, but they can go home now."

Sleepily, but with much relief, the neighbours went out into the early morning air. The sun was rising, and it would be yet another lovely day. How incongruous to have the ugly great scar of the burnt plane in the midst of this chocolate-box scene.

"Mr Evans," said Vicky, "there's another fire, looks like Over Norton way."

"Yes," said Robert, "the brigade went there directly once they were satisfied they could leave the fire here. It's another plane, crashed in a field, and set many trees alight."

"Anyone hurt?" said Vicky.

"Not on the ground, but there were two young men in the plane – both killed."

"What about here? How many in the Wellington?"

"It had a crew of six."

"And?"

"All dead. We think one or two tried to bale out, and the rest died in the fire. You saw the blaze on Castle

Mound? That was the wing of the bomber; ripped off by the impact."

"Let's go and see the other fire," said Billy, "the one on the Castle."

Running across the churchyard and over the stile at the bottom, Billy and Mike clambered through the trees and undergrowth towards the Castle. Chipping Norton had once had a small castle, but it had been built of wood, and not lasted the test of time. Nothing was left of the castle except the hill upon which it stood.

As they ran towards the hill, Mike shrieked, "Look, a boot, an airman's boot." He went to pick it up.

"Don't touch it," shouted Billy. "There's a foot inside."

"Yuk," said Mike.

"It's worse than 'yuk'," said Billy. "It's really bad. And there's a bloke lying over there, in the bushes."

"Is he asleep?" said Mike.

"I don't think so," said Billy. "I think we need a policeman. I'll stand guard here, you go and get a copper."

Mike ran off. As soon as he was gone, Billy regretted sending him, as he felt very scared standing alone near the airman, who he realised was dead.

"Oh Gawd," he said, loudly. "Hey, mate, you OK?"

The body did not respond. Billy sat down, stood up again, took a step towards the body, stepped back, and was in a state of considerable anxiety. Although it was only a few minutes, it seemed an age to Billy, when Mike came running back closely followed by a panting policeman.

"There he is," shouted Mike.

"You wait here," said the policeman. "I'll take a look."

They watched as the policeman pulled apart the bushes to look at the body. Turning back to the boys, he said, "Yes, you're right. It is an airman, and he's dead: must have come from the plane that crashed. Poor bugger, don't look very old."

"What'll we do now?" said Billy.

"I'd better stay here," said the policeman. "You go and get help. Go to that big house called the Manse and ask them to telephone the police station."

"I know that 'ouse," said Billy. "My teacher, Miss Jones, lives there."

"Good," said the policeman. "Tell her P C Webb sent you. Get them to explain that you found a body."

Billy and Mike went crashing down the hill, through the trees and across the churchyard. Within a few minutes they were swinging on the brass handle which sent the bell into a frenzy. The dog started barking, and the door opened.

"Whatever do you think you're doing?" said Marjorie fiercely.

"There's a dead body on the Castle 'ill," said Billy. "There's a copper over there wants 'elp and says to phone the cop shop quick."

Vicky appeared behind Marjorie in the hall. "Billy McCann, if this is a joke, you're in big trouble."

"No, Miss, it's not a joke, cross me 'eart and 'ope to die, but it's a n'airman, fell out of that bomber, and 'e's dead in the bushes."

Marjorie turned to the telephone, which was immediately beside the front door, and Vicky came out to the boys, who were getting their breath back, but had both turned pale.

"'Ere Miss," said Billy. "I don't feel very well," whereupon he fainted.

Mike said, "I think I need to sit down too," and sat on the front door step.

Rosemary had come to see what was going on. "He's fainted," said Vicky. "I'll carry him into the kitchen. You bring Mike."

Vicky dumped Billy on a chair in the kitchen, with his head between his knees, and a bucket close by in case he was sick. Rosemary trailed in with Mike who was distinctly green, and sat him on another chair. Mrs Wheeler, the cleaning lady and kitchen helper, who had come to see what was happening at the Manse, filled tin mugs with water from the tap.

Billy sat up, took the mug of water and drained it. "Bloody 'ell," he said. "What 'appened?"

"You fainted, Billy."

"Where am I?"

"In Mrs Anderson-Grey's kitchen."

Billy looked around, and shook his head. "I fink I'd better go 'ome," he said, started to stand up, and promptly sat down again.

"In a minute," said Vicky. "I'll walk home with you, but you'd better just sit still for a bit."

Billy looked round the kitchen. "Cor," he said, "wait till I tell 'em at school. What a story. I shall write it down and call the story 'The Unknown Pilot'. I wonder if there's a reward for finding 'im?"

Over the weekend, the police stationed a man in Church Street to prevent anyone from approaching the wreckage. Four badly burnt bodies were recovered from the debris; another body was found in a field near the town cemetery; and with the body that Billy and Mike had discovered, the crew of the Wellington had been accounted for. A mangled and burned wing of the bomber was found on the far side of Castle Mound, presumably sliced off of the fuselage by the other plane.

The assumption was that the two aircraft had collided. The smaller plane, an Oxford Airspeed trainer, had crashed into a copse near Over Norton, with the loss of two young lives.

John Brigg and his wife went to stay with his brother in Kingham, whilst their cottage on Church Street was repaired. After the plane wreck was removed, everyone was surprised that the cottage was not as damaged as expected, and eventually the couple were able to move back in.

The wreckage was displayed in the market place for some time, with a sign remembering the deaths of the eight young men, and encouraging the townsfolk to dig deep for the Spitfire Fund.

School resumed in September. Billy was now in one of the Saint Mary's classes, officially leaving Silvertown School, whilst Mrs Thomas was dealing with the papers for his adoption. Billy, of course, made a great deal out of his 'Unknown Pilot' story, but did not admit to anyone that he'd fainted. "And if you tell," he said to Mike, "I'll say you're lying."

The war dragged on. Marjorie was frustrated by the lack of news. The letters from her husband did little more than tell her he was still alive; clearly he could not write much without the Nazi censor refusing to pass it on, or indeed putting himself at risk. On the rare occasions she went to Oxford, she watched out for Henry as if he might regularly walk down the High, but she didn't see him again; and she had only the briefest of notes from Bobby, who was still in Dorset.

One autumn morning, there was a ring at the front door bell. Rosemary opened the door to find a smartly dressed young soldier, who saluted her.

"Mrs Anderson-Grey?" said the soldier.

"No," said Rosemary, "I'm her sister. Please wait a moment, I'll fetch her."

In the parlour, she said, "There's a soldier to see you Marjorie. I don't know who he is, but he's some kind of senior officer, very handsome."

Marjorie went to the door. "I'm Marjorie Anderson-Grey," she said. "Can I help you?"

The soldier saluted again. "Airey Neave, Ma'am. Very pleased to meet you Mrs Anderson-Grey."

Marjorie hesitated for a moment, then realised to whom she was talking. "From Colditz," she gasped, and repeated, "from Colditz?"

"Can I come in?" said Neave.

"Of course, of course," said Marjorie, flustered and excited, "Is the Major with you?"

"No, he's still in the castle, Ma'am. As far as I know, I'm the only one who's escaped."

"Are the others trying to escape?"

"All British serviceman are trying to escape, Ma'am, and that includes your husband. Unfortunately, Colditz is particularly hard to escape from. That's why your husband is there, because he's escaped twice before from other camps."

"You must stay for lunch," said Marjorie. "Rosemary, can you ask Mrs Wheeler to lay for three in the dining room?"

Over lunch, Airey Neave explained how he'd created a Nazi uniform, and walked out of the castle in the twilight. He'd had just one other man with him, a Dutch officer who spoke good German, and they'd used their apparent Nazi army rank to travel by train to Leipzig. They'd walked through snow and over mountain passes to get into Switzerland, where they had ditched their uniforms and stolen non-descript clothes from washing lines. They'd made it into France, walking mainly at night, stealing food as they went. Finally they'd walked over the Pyrenees into Spain where they'd contacted a safe house in Barcelona. With assistance they had eventually been taken to Gibraltar.

When Marjorie apologised for the rather mediocre lunch, Airey was quick to tell her that the fare in the castle was very poor, and the Manse lunch was very acceptable indeed. "We all went to good schools, and I can tell you that the food at Colditz was very much like the food at Eton!" He told her that parcels and letters had been arriving, although it appeared to take a very long time for them to be delivered.

He told them that the prisoners never stopped thinking about escaping. They'd considered being sewn into a mattress, crawling through the sewers and tying bed sheets to form a rope to climb down the outside wall of the castle. They'd even considered trying to build a glider, but dismissed this as impractical.

He'd said that whilst one or two more might escape, it was unlikely that there would ever be a big break-out, and that most of the internees would be there until the end of the war. He was sorry that that probably included the Major.

"I feel very sorry for all the officers imprisoned in the castle," said Rosemary.

"Oh, you needn't," said Airey, "it's really very similar to being at a public school, just an awfully long time waiting for furlough."

After lunch they walked in the garden, and Airey was amused to realise that the jam he'd enjoyed in the prison had come from the raspberry canes he was admiring. He said the British officers in Colditz had always shared the contents of their letters and that he'd like to meet Miss Jones. They had all liked the story of the 'Singing for Spitfires' concerts, but that Flight Lieutenant Bader had thought only having one leg was a poor excuse for not being in the services.

"I'm sorry I missed him," said Vicky that evening. She had returned from school long after Airey Neave's train had departed. Marjorie was in an uncharacteristic depression.

"It's bad enough to think that this war will go on and on," she said, "but it's very demoralising to know that the Major will remain in the prison for as long as it takes. It may be years before we see him."

"At least he's safe," said Rosemary.

"It's ironic, isn't it?" said Marjorie. "I know he's safe because he's in a German prison, but knowing him as I do, he will be very frustrated that he's not contributing to the war effort."

For many of the children from Silvertown, their memories of their school, and to some extent the memories of their homes, were fading. Some of the children had been very young when they were brought to Chipping Norton, and after such a long time in the Cotswold town, it was becoming their home. Vicky and Lawrence watched them in the school playground.

"You know, it's getting very hard to remember which are the Chippy kids and which are our's," said Lawrence.

"Many of them are very settled here," said Vicky.

"And we don't know what there will be for them to go home to, if they ever go home," said Lawrence. "The school buildings are gone, and I don't suppose they'll rebuild for some time; and who knows how many homes are gone."

"Eric's coming to visit soon," said Vicky. "He'll bring us up to date. We've not seen him since the incendiary hit the school."

"I didn't know you kept the link to him," said Lawrence.

"I don't," said Vicky, "but Rosemary, Marjorie's sister, has exchanged many letters. She rushes to the front door to get the post when it's delivered. I think she's becoming very friendly with our Eric, and she certainly doesn't want her sister to know how often she gets a letter."

Lawrence laughed: "A wartime romance? That's nice."

Rosemary tried to introduce the news casually at breakfast. "Oh, by the way, Eric's coming to stay for a few days next week. He can have leave from his ARP duties.

I hope it's alright that I invited him to come to the Manse."

"Is that the young man who came for Christmas?" said Marjorie. "I thought he was very personable, and he was very grateful to get away from the London bombing. Has he nowhere else to go?"

"I don't know," said Rosemary, "but he wrote to me and asked if he could come here, and I said 'yes'. It will be nice to have a fresh face in the Manse. He can tell us about the war in London. He said that he would try to telephone to tell us which train he'll be on, so I can go and meet him at the station."

"I'm sure he'll remember how to walk to us from the station," said Marjorie. "It's not very far."

Rosemary blushed. "I just thought it would be nice to meet him," she said.

Vicky smiled.

Mrs Thomas had another letter from her husband.

"It's great fun here driving these great monsters, and I'm in line for a promotion. Of course we all know that one day it won't be fun at all, when we have to use our tanks to fight. There's talk amongst the men of going to France, but the officers say we shouldn't have such conversations.

"I hope the boys are still doing well, and working hard at school. I expect they're growing up quickly now. I miss them very much, and I miss you too, my dear wife.

"We're sure to get moved on from here soon. I don't know if I will be allowed to tell you where we are, but I will write if I can."

"It's the not knowing that's hard," said Mrs Thomas to the boys.

"I bet it's bleedin' wonderful driving a dirty great tank," said Billy, and he and Mike drove imaginary tanks around the kitchen and out into the garden, roaring and spitting as they made up the noises they thought tanks would make.

"Yes, it's the not knowing....." said Mrs Thomas, thinking she was talking to no-one.

The Italian gardener, standing in the doorway, smiled. "I know," he said, nodding.

"Stanley, I need to talk privately to you about something," said Edward.

"You make it sound sinister," said Stanley.

"No, it's not, but I'd like to talk. I shall be sixty-five shortly, and I'm thinking about retirement. It's a little odd, coming as it does in a time of war. The thing is this: your school in London has gone, hasn't it?"

Stanley nodded.

"How would you feel if I recommend to the governors that you take over my job?"

"And make Chipping Norton my home for the future?" said Stanley.

"Yes," said Edward. "Molly is getting more involved with the town, with her interest in the guides, and you seem to have settled very well into the life here."

"It's a lot to think about, and I must talk to Molly. It seems a few of the children will be staying here when the war ends; and those that go back to Silvertown will be dispersed amongst other schools, at least for the time being. There have been so many ironies with this war: how strange that it should bring the possibility of such a complete change in our lives. I'm very pleased that you've confided in me, and flattered that you would recommend me for your job. Let me talk to my wife."

"You may be too late: I think Lizzie will have spilled the beans."

"I'll support you," said Molly later. Lizzie had told her about Edward's suggestion, and Molly was delighted at the prospect of remaining in the Cotswolds after the war. She hoped that her husband would be as keen.

"Very well," said Stanley. "I will tell Edward that I'm very pleased to fill his shoes, and hope that the school governors feel the same."

"We will have to find a home of our own in the town," said Molly. "If we are to remain here, we cannot lodge with the Hardings indefinitely."

"There's a house for sale in Church Street, down the bottom of the hill, opposite the Manse. Vicky told me that the old lady who lived alone there, had died. You remember we saw her when the Wellington crashed into Yew Dell. Her house was the tall one just down the hill from there. We could think about that, but I haven't got the job yet. We must not count our chickens."

The Vicar was also the Chairman of the school governors, and it was he who was pleased to bring the good news to Stanley. "I was fearful that we would have a problem if Mr Harding retired before the end of the war, and we could not fill his position. We are very pleased to offer you the post of headteacher of Saint Mary's Primary School."

Molly and Stanley went to look at the house at the bottom of Church Street. It was very old-fashioned. The old lady had been a widow for some time, and lived alone, using only two or three of the rooms. They decided with a great deal of work, they could make the old house into a good home, "and maybe, even start a family," said Molly.

There was an untidy garden sloping down to the bottom of Diston's Lane, behind the church hall where Molly's Girl Guides met, and she was soon imagining an extension with a modern kitchen overlooking a lawn, flower beds and a vegetable patch. They realised that although they could dream, no elaborate plans would come to fruition until the end of the war.

By the end of 1943, the Wykes had moved into Number Eight, Church Street. On their moving day, Vicky had arrived with a bunch of flowers, cut from the Manse garden.

"Not only the headmaster of Chipping Norton School, but also a neighbour," she said. "So much has happened since that fateful day when we were evacuated here. This place seems like home, doesn't it?"

"When a full-time post becomes available at Saint Mary's," said Stanley, "will you apply for it?"

Vicky didn't hesitate. "Most definitely! I've nothing to go back to Silvertown for."

"You used to say you were dedicated to the kids of the East End," said Molly.

"And now I'm dedicated to all these rural kids," smiled Vicky, "and of course many of the kids won't be going back to the smoke, like Billy McCann. You know, we had many deprived children from poor homes in Silvertown; but I think there are just as many needy children here in rural deprivation."

The concerts had also become part of Chipping Norton life. Each Christmas, the combined schools would stage a carol concert; and sometime in the early summer, they'd be back at the Town Hall with their annual concert of patriotic songs. Although the programme was much the same every year, with Vera Lynn's songs predominant, everyone, parents, teachers and children loved the extremes of emotion and excitement created by the music-making.

'Singing for Spitfires' became a central plank of the town's Spitfire appeal, and the Mayor's fund was boosted every Christmas and summer by the receipts from the Town Hall. Almost every small town in the nation had its name inscribed on a real Spitfire, and there was great excitement when the town's name was added to that list, and announced on the BBC. Although most of the donations were small, by 1944 the town had raised over five thousand pounds.

CHAPTER SIXTEEN

The others had just gone up to bed leaving Rosemary listening to the wireless. Suddenly she called them down. "Come quickly, drop what you're doing, this is important," she called to the others, "it's Richard Dimbleby."

"What's going on?" said Vicky. "It's the middle of the night."

"Listen," said Rosemary urgently, "the first aircraft with parachutists are taking off to invade Europe."

They heard the voice of Richard Dimbleby.

"The sky is now full of the noise of these paratroop planes as they circle the aerodrome before they take their course."

The three women could hear the roar of the planes. "At last," murmured Marjorie. "It's started."

"Aboard them are some of the toughest and finest and bravest men that we have in Britain, and they go out today to face their greatest trial."

There was a crescendo of aircraft noise, and Dimbleby's voice was drowned out.

"It will be hard to sleep tonight," said Rosemary. "We must pray to God that the men have success."

"It's hard to imagine what it must be like for them," said Vicky. "Imagine parachuting into enemy countryside."

"It's what they've been trained to do," said Marjorie. "I know from what the Major's told me in the past: the training is hard and thorough, which it needs to be; although you can be sure, nothing prepares them for the real thing."

"I wonder if they will know in Colditz what's going on?" said Vicky.

"Airey Neave said they have a secret wireless set at the castle. If the Nazis haven't found it, they'll be listening."

All around the town, all around the nation, few had a good night's sleep. The tension and excitement of the invasion gripped everyone, and everyone was tuned into the BBC at breakfast-time. Richard Dimbleby's messages about the beginning of the invasion were repeated, and listeners were told to stand by for an important announcement at midday.

"I've been tossing and turning all night," admitted Marjorie. "I keep thinking about Bobby. I bet his tanks are involved in the invasion. It can't just be airborne troops, they'll be taking ground troops by ship."

"Listen to this," said Mrs Thomas to the boys. She had turned the wireless on during breakfast. "The invasion has started. I bet your dad's in all that. Perhaps he'll be driving his tank across France."

"I don't want to go to school," said Billy. "He said stand by for something at midday. That's twelve o'clock, innit? Let us stay at 'ome mum."

"No, it's Tuesday, so it's a school day. Perhaps Mr Wykes will put the wireless on at school."

"The children will all know about this," said Molly. "Their parents will all be listening, and told their kids."

"We'll put the BBC on at noon," said Stanley. "The older ones will expect it and they will understand what they're hearing. They should witness this historic moment."

"I wonder if the kids will come to school," said Vicky. "It will be funny if I get there and they've all stayed at home to listen to the news."

Suddenly the telephone rang. "That's odd, so early in the morning," said Marjorie. "I wonder who it is."

Hurrying down the hall, Rosemary picked it up. "Bobby!" she shrieked. "Where are you?"

"Can't tell you, but just a very quick message for mother."

"I'm here," said Marjorie, "How are you? What's happening?"

"Listen: this is all I can say. Things are taking off. Get a message to that Mrs Thomas, you know the one who adopted that Silvertown kid. Tell her, her husband's with me, and things are taking off."

"Bobby!" shouted Vicky, "Take care." The line went dead. "I'll be able to tell Billy at school," she said, "that's if he comes to school."

Henry looked around the room at his team of young women. All were listening intently to their headsets, jotting down notes and nodding; but something had changed. They were all smiling as they'd never done before. He looked out of the window. The grass at Bletchley Park seemed to be greener than before, almost glowing with the news of D-Day.

Bobby had been waiting impatiently in Poole. His tank brigade had been loaded and ready in the harbour; line after line of tanks; line after line of ships. He looked across his forces, at the strange collection of modified Churchills he commanded. Close by, a tank had 'The Chippy Winner' chalked on its side, and he knew the driver was Sergeant Thomas, from his home town. He gave a 'thumbs up' to Sergeant Thomas, who waved back.

Using a crude megaphone, Bobby read the Order of the Day.

Stanley brought all of the children into the assembly hall, and told them that they must be very quiet. The school's wireless was hardly suitable for a large room and so many listeners, but it was the best they could do. Vicky and all the teachers sat with the children, holding their breath.

At the Manse, Marjorie and Rosemary had invited Molly to come across the road and share their salad lunch in the parlour. They tuned in to the BBC.

At home, Edward and Lizzie listened; Mrs Thomas brought Luigi, her Italian gardener into the kitchen. Robert Evans, at the bank, allowed the radio to be turned on in the banking hall, and asked his staff to stop work. Collectively, the nation's heart was thumping.

In the early hours of the morning, at high tide, Bobby's convoy had inched through the narrow channels of Poole Harbour, and sailed through thankfully quiet waters towards the rendezvous point, nick-named 'Piccadilly Circus'. The full moon illuminated the sea, and from all directions the tank crews could make out huge numbers of craft, most of them sailing out of Portsmouth. They turned south and headed across the Channel. Whilst it had seemed fairly calm close to shore, the sea was choppy, and many of the soldiers were sick.

Under cover of early morning darkness, the tank landing craft chugged towards 'Sword' beach. With the swell and rough seas, the ship's commanders edged as close as they could to the beach, then gave the order to disembark. The tanks rolled one by one into the surf, some struggling to gain a hold on the sand, and with engines roaring, fought towards dry land.

As Bobby looked around, he saw the countless other craft disgorging tanks onto the shore. Never had such an invasion of so many been staged, and his heart thumped with a combination of pride and fear.

In his tank, Sergeant Thomas fought with the controls. Despite all the hours of training at Bovington, the chaotic splashing into the water and the wrangling of the caterpillars to find solid ground taxed his skills to the limit. Water crashed into the tank, and the crew clung on for their lives, ready to take to the sea if the tank filled with water.

Sergeant Thomas battled on at the controls, but felt that his formidable machine was sinking. His crew leapt into the sea, and suddenly he found the freezing water rising up and over him. The tank sank rapidly, taking Sergeant Thomas to a watery grave inside it.

Bobby's tank ploughed on, and at last the tracks were grinding on sand. Slowly the behemoth struggled out of the water, through the last of the surf and onto the beach. The trials were not over, indeed had hardly begun, and fierce fire from the Nazi defenders rained down upon them.

The tanks were pitifully exposed as dawn broke over Sword Beach, as their caterpillar tracks ground onwards. Bobby was thankful to see solid ground ahead, as the tanks cleared the sand at last. Looking around, he knew he did not have his full compliment, but it seemed most had made it to the coastal fields.

At noon on Tuesday 6th June, 1944, John Snagge read the bulletin:

"D-Day has come. Early this morning, the Allies began the assault on the north-western face of Hitler's European Fortress.

"Under the command of General Eisenhower, Allied Naval Forces, supported by strong Air Forces, began landing Allied Armies this morning on the northern coast of France."

Mrs Thomas shuddered. The news was exciting, but she'd had the message from her husband's senior officer, and she knew he was involved. Was he in his tank, about to land in France? Would he survive? Luigi hugged her.

"The Allied Commander-in-Chief, General Eisenhower, has issued an Order of the Day addressed to each individual of the Allied Expeditionary Forces. In it he said:

"Your task will not be an easy one. Your enemy is well trained, well equipped and battle-hardened. He will fight savagely. But this is the year 1944. The tide has turned. The free men of the world are marching together to victory. I have full confidence in your courage, devotion to duty and skill in battle. We will accept nothing less than full victory. Good luck, and let us all beseech the Blessing of Almighty God upon this great and noble undertaking."

Marjorie and Rosemary, spoke together, "Amen."

John Snagge continued, *"His Majesty the King will broadcast to his people at home and overseas at nine o'clock tonight."*

The children could not resist, and broke into a buzz of conversation. Billy was proud to tell everyone near him that, "My dad's in the landing!" Vicky looked around the room. How many fathers were involved? It was just chance that they'd had the message that Sergeant Thomas was there: there must be more.

Stanley found that he was quite emotional as he turned off the wireless, and faced his school. "Thousands of brave men are risking their lives for us, for each and every one of us. We must pray for their success. You are young, but you have a part to play, not only in saying heartfelt prayers, but also giving comfort to those at home, especially those of you with your father or brother called to the fighting and your mother anxious and worried."

Bobby's squadron made swift progress across the fields, and crashed though gates and hedges to gain the tracks and roads of the farmland. There was less resistance than expected, and a strange lack of the local population. The people living in the area had received the messages to evacuate, and had done so. After a while, they stopped to re-group.

A farmhouse stood nearby, and intermittent gun fire was coming from it. Bobby's driver held the controls firmly as the turret swung, and a single shell hurtled towards the farmhouse. The building erupted, and a small group of very frightened German soldiers came running out, coughing and choking in the smoke and dust.

Climbing nervously out of his battered tank, Bobby raised his gun. The Nazi soldiers looked around, dropped their own weapons and with hands in the air, walked towards the group of tanks. They were surrendering, and would be added to the growing number of prisoners taken during that first momentous morning.

Bobby looked back at the masses of foot soldiers marching up the beach. His job was to go before them to clear any Nazi fire-power, and enable the soldiers to advance safely. He turned and gave the order to move forward, and the tank guns blazed at each and every building in their path, blasting out of existence any cover for further Nazi snipers or bigger guns.

After school, Billy and Mike ran home as fast as they could.

"We heard it in school," they told Mrs Thomas breathlessly. "Mr Wykes brought the wireless into the hall, and we all listened."

"D'you think me dad's in France?" said Mike.

"I expect so," said his mother.

"We all said some prayers with Mr Wykes," said Billy. "They said the King will talk on the wireless this evening. Can we stay up and listen to him?

"I suppose so," said Mrs Thomas. "I've invited Luigi to come and listen. I hope you don't mind."

"No," said Billy, "he's nice even if he is an Eye-tie. He used to be the enemy, but he wants us to win the war. He wants to stay here after the war's over."

"I'm proud to have a son involved in this momentous event," said Marjorie, "but it's worrying."

"Of course it is," said Vicky, "but you know he's well-trained and brave. It's a time of anguish for us all, but this is the moment we have been waiting for."

"After all these years of preparation, we are finally pushing back against Hitler and the Nazis, but all over our nation, there are mothers and grandmothers, wives and sisters and daughters, desperate for their men," said Rosemary.

"We must be ready in the parlour for the King's Speech," said Vicky.

The nation listened to their King:

"Four years ago, our Nation and Empire stood alone against an overwhelming enemy with our backs to the wall. Now a supreme test has to be faced. The challenge is not to fight to survive, but to fight to win the final victory for the good cause. We and our Allies are sure that our fight is against evil.

"Let us pray that the Lord will give strength unto his people: the Lord will give us the blessing of peace."

"Amen, and amen again," said Marjorie.

The King's speech was followed immediately by the nine o'clock news read by Joseph MacLeod.

"All still goes well on the coast of Normandy. Mr Churchill reported that in some places we've driven

several miles into France. Our great airborn landings –
the biggest in history – have been carried out with little
loss. About four thousand ships, with thousands of
smaller craft crossed the channel this morning.

"An observer who saw the first assault forces land
had already watched the naval guns pound their targets
out of existence. It was, he said, a magnificent sight.
Wave upon wave of troops were soon surging up the
beaches. Transport lorries, guns, equipment of all sorts
was trundling ashore."

Vicky turned to Marjorie and Rosemary. "It really
looks as if the tide has turned. Can we, dare we, hope
that the end of this bloody war is in sight?"

"How much can we believe Mr Churchill?" said
Marjorie. "He says that there has been very little loss.
I'm not so sure: such a great undertaking will come with
a cost. If our boys achieve this invasion, we shall all be
eternally grateful; but it will not be without some loss of
life. I'll find no rest or peace until I hear from Bobby."

Luigi stood up. "Thank you," he said. "I must go back
to the camp before it gets dark. We have a curfew. We
pray for the end of the war; and we pray for Mr
Thomas. I'll come back tomorrow to see if you have any
news."

Mrs Thomas held the kitchen door open. "You have
become a good friend, Luigi," she said. "Thank you for

your prayers." The Italian slipped away into the gathering dusk of the summer night. The perfume from a jasmine bush wafted into the kitchen.

"I wonder if we'll get a message from your dad?" said Mrs Thomas wistfully, smelling the jasmine. "It seems so peaceful here, and yet there must be so much chaos and fighting on the French beaches. He's a brave man, your dad; they are all brave men; but they must be scared."

"I bet he's in France driving his tank. I bet he likes driving his tank, even if it is scary. How will we find out what's going on?" said Billy.

"We'll listen to the BBC," said Mrs Thomas. "There'll be news every morning before you go to school, and every evening when you get home. Now it's late, and you must go to school tomorrow, so off to bed."

Frank Phillips was reading the eight o'clock news the following day, Wednesday, when the telephone rang at the Manse. Marjorie ran down the hall to answer it.

"Bobby!" she said.

"No, it's Henry," said her son. "Now listen carefully, and don't ask any questions. I cannot tell you where I am, nor how I know this information, but I can let you know that Bobby is safe and in France."

"Praise be!" exclaimed Marjorie "And..."

Before she could say anything, Henry interrupted. "No questions. Just be grateful that I got that much news." The line went dead.

"How does he know?" said Rosemary as her sister returned to the kitchen.

"I don't know, and I can't ask. We must just be thankful for knowing he's alive."

At lunch time, Marjorie was surprised by Vicky phoning her. "Can you come to school this afternoon?" she said. "We will be celebrating our troops' successes so far in France. I think you will enjoy it."

That afternoon, Vicky and Lawrence brought the whole school together again in the school hall. To their surprise Mr and Mrs Harding were there, Molly had joined them, and Marjorie and Rosemary were seated on small child-sized chairs. Stanley Wykes was smiling.

"We have heard good news from France. You will all know that our troops achieved a successful invasion, and I am sure you will all be following their progress. We pray that they will soon enter Paris. After that we hope they will hasten to Berlin, and that we will see the end of this terrible war.

"Remembering always that there is much to do, and many difficulties ahead, we shall have a celebration of the success so far; and we shall celebrate in the way we know best, by singing. Mrs Harding, welcome back to school. It's lovely to see you and Mr Harding back with us."

Lizzie smiled from behind the piano, and played the introduction. Vicky signalled to the children to stand up, and Lawrence once more sang the familiar verse of their favourite song:

"I give you a toast, ladies and gentlemen."

At the chorus, every voice rang out:

"There'll always be an England."

CHAPTER SEVENTEEN

Billy McCann rang the door bell at Number Eight. "Come in, it's open," called Molly.

Billy walked into the front room where the old lady was waiting for him.

"My, you look good in your best suit," said Molly. "Very smart: I'm not used to seeing you without your butcher's apron."

"Feels a bit funny to be all dressed up like this. I'm usually up at the allotment on a Sunday. I hardly ever wear this suit; I've had it for years. Got it at the Co-op. Ready to go?"

Molly smoothed down the skirt of her best dress. She'd considered wearing her old Girl Guide uniform, as it seemed appropriate to be in some kind of uniform; but her old kit was far too tatty and battered for such an important occasion. As they stepped down in to the street, the bells of St Mary's church were ringing. A small crowd was gathering outside Red Robe House.

Bobby and Vicky Anderson-Grey opened the front door of the Manse at the same time. They blinked in the morning sunshine: facing east, the front of the Manse was always brightly illuminated by the rising sun.

"Fifty years," said Vicky. "Where have they gone?"

"I was down in Dorset when you had this plane crash," said Bobby.

"And I was here: in bed asleep. The noise was extraordinary, but I suppose nothing like you suffered on D-Day."

"I don't talk about D-Day," said Bobby. "It's such a long time ago. It feels strange, really, to have been there and taken part in what is now part of history."

"There's Billy McCann, with Molly. He was still at school when the planes crashed: now's he's nearing retirement."

Seeing Vicky and Bobby, Billy said, "Molly, can you wait here for a moment. I want to go and talk to Miss Jones." Molly smiled at the remembrance of Vicky's name before she married.

"Miss Jones," called Billy, "Brigadier Anderson-Grey! Good morning. What a lovely day."

"Billy," said Vicky, "I've not been Miss Jones for forty years."

"I know," grinned Billy, "but you'll always be Miss Jones for me. I've got something for you." Carefully, he pulled a little paper bag from his pocket. "You see, I've never forgot. It's just a lend, for today, like last time."

Vicky opened the bag. Inside was the spray of silk flowers with the tiny pearl decorations. She'd not seen it for fifty years.

"Billy," she said, "I'm quite overwhelmed."

Billy looked at Bobby. "Miss Jones wore it at the first Singing for Spitfires concert. I was only a nipper then. It would be nice if she wore it again today."

"What's the significance of it?" said Bobby.

"Long story," said Vicky. "I'll tell you later."

"Me mum wore it when she married Luigi," said Billy.

"I remember," said Vicky. "Is she coming today?"

"Mike's pushing her down in her wheelchair," said Billy. "You know she's ninety-one? Luigi's never let on how old he is, but we think he's about the same age as mum. He's slowed down a lot, which why I took over the allotment."

Molly had walked over to Vicky. "Is that what I think it is?" she asked.

"Yes," said Billy. "The same little flowers me first mum wore for her wedding to me first dad; and me second mum wore to me third dad; and what Miss Jones wore at Singing for Spitfires."

Molly's eyebrows shot up. "I'm glad we've got that sorted out," she laughed.

Billy looked at Molly. "And another thing: I've still got me grandad's gold watch. Look – here it is," and he showed them the old pocket watch which had been in the shoe box all those years ago.

"Vicky!" came a shrill call from the lane.

"Rosie!" replied Vicky, "look what Billy's brought for me."

Closely followed by Eric, Rosemary admired the little keepsake. "How lovely," she said. "Let me help you pin it on." With the silk flowers secured in place, Rosemary looked around.

"Bobby," she said. "Not in uniform?"

"I considered it," said Bobby, "but Auntie Rosie, it would upstage all the ladies, and anyway, I'm retired and I'm not supposed to wear it in public."

"Pity," said Rosemary. "It would have been fine to see your bearskin again, and that lovely red jacket."

"I've not worn the full fig since the last time I did the Queen's Birthday Parade," said Bobby. "You remember, the time Henry and I were both there together, when the television made such a fuss about twins being on parade."

"The Trooping the Colour," said Vicky. "I was there, an officer's wife. And you were jealous because the BBC interviewed Henry," she laughed.

"Talking of him, there he is," said Rosemary, "smart as ever."

"My brother must be the only person wearing a bowler hat in Chipping Norton," said Bobby. The group started to walk slowly up the hill, and the two brothers saluted one another smartly.

"There's me mum," said Billy. "She's not been out much lately, so it's good to see her in the sunshine. There's Luigi – he's looking old, too. He was a very strong man when I was a kid."

"Is this the actual fiftieth anniversary today?" asked Eric. "I was in Silvertown at the time, but Rosie's told me all about it."

"No, not the exact date," said Vicky. "We tried to get it on the actual day: it was the 21st August."

"And today's the 20th September," said Molly. "So we're a month late."

"The plaque was late coming from the foundry," explained Vicky.

A man in a smart R A F uniform approached them. "Brigadier Anderson-Grey?" he enquired, saluting Bobby.

Bobby saluted back. "I am, and this is my wife, Victoria; and my brother Henry."

"I'm Wing Commander Dale," said the R A F man. "As this is technically an R A F memorial, it's fallen to me to unveil it, although I wasn't expecting a Brigadier to be present."

"I'm a civilian now," smiled Bobby, "so my rank is irrelevant. Do you know who all these people are?"

"I understand that some of the witnesses of the crash are here," said the Wing Commander, "but I do not know who they are."

Bobby smiled again. "My wife was asleep in the Manse, over there, on that fateful night. My Aunt Rosemary was also living at the Manse at the time. My mother, who passed away a few years ago, was with them."

"And your father, the Major?"

"He was in Colditz," laughed Bobby, "stuck there for most of the war. I wish my brigade had been there to liberate the castle, but the Yanks got there first. I'd have loved to see my father's face if I'd been first through the gateway."

"And this lady?" asked the Wing Commander, turning to Molly.

"I'm Molly Wykes," said Molly. "I was evacuated with Silvertown School, because my husband was the headmaster. We were also in bed at the time of the plane crash, but we came over as quickly as we could, because it looked like it could have been the Manse on fire."

"Didn't you go back to London after the war?" said the Wing Commander.

"No, because my husband became the headmaster of the local school, Saint Mary's. We became very involved in the life of the town."

"And Mr Wykes became Mayor of the town," said Billy, "which meant Miss Wykes was the Mayoress."

"My husband and I were Mayor and Mayoress of Chipping Norton when her Majesty the Queen and Prince Philip visited the town. That was the highlight of our time as Mayor and Mayoress. It is strange, isn't it? Thanks to the war, and the evacuation, my husband and I came to make this lovely town our home, and we had our family here. Silvertown seems a very long way away, and a very long time ago."

"As soon as the boys from the Air Cadets get here, we'll be ready," said the Wing Commander.

"Not quite," said Vicky. "The mayor's not here yet, nor the vicar."

As if on cue, the Mayor and Mayoress, in full civic splendour, turned the corner from Spring Street and came hurrying down the hill, with a rather dishevelled town clerk in hot pursuit.

"There's the chain gang," laughed Molly.

From the opposite direction, from the church yard, came the Rural Dean and the verger accompanied by a small contingent of Air Cadets, including one bugler. The slightly breathless mayor stepped up to the microphone. He pulled a postcard out of his pocket and read:

"Good morning Brigadier and Mrs Anderson-Grey, Wing Commander Dale, ladies and gentlemen, and especially guests who were witness to the tragic events of Monday 21st August 1942. I am very honoured to be present at this very special occasion. Some of you will know that my own grandfather was Mayor of Chipping Norton at the time of the crash. Thanks to a prolonged campaign by the local historical society, we have at last a permanent memorial to the eight young men who lost their lives on that dark summer night. Following today's ceremony, there will be a small reception in the Town Hall, where I am sure we will be very interested to hear some of the stories from the witnesses. There is a modest exhibition of photographs assembled by the Historical Society."

"I found one of the bodies," whispered Billy to Molly.

"I know," whispered Molly, "the whole school knew: you couldn't stop talking about it!"

The Mayor continued, "I am pleased to invite Wing Commander Dale to unveil the memorial."

The Wing Commander stepped up to the microphone. "Brigadier and Mrs Anderson-Grey, The Worshipful the Mayor of Chipping Norton and Mrs Hannant, Rural Dean and your good lady wife, special guests...."

"It was always like this on the chain gang," whispered Molly to Billy. "Some time the list of titles was longer than the speech, especially if all the local mayors were got together."

The Wing Commander continued, "I am pleased to honour the memory of eight young men who gave their lives in their support of the war effort." He pulled the cord and the Union Jack fluttered away from the wall to be caught expertly by Billy. The young air cadet bugler put his bugle to his lips, and played the Last Post. Everyone stood very still. As the notes rang out across the valley, everyone of the crowd was reading the words on the memorial.

In memory of the air crews who died here or nearby after a night flying accident,

21st August 1942.

Private A W Stillwell

Sergeant E Downs

Sergeant M Haynes

Sergeant F Gillard

Private A M Henderson

Sergeant J M Rankin

Sergeant P O'Brien

Sergeant N F Boxwell

Per Ardua ad Astra